About the Author

Daniel Kelly grew up with a love of history and stories in the village of Creeslough along the north coast of Donegal before qualifying as a chef from Tourism College, Killybegs, and moving to Dublin.

The Fall of the Phoenix

Daniel Kelly

The Fall of the Phoenix

Olympia Publishers
London

www.olympiapublishers.com
OLYMPIA PAPERBACK EDITION

A CIP catalogue record for this title is
available from the British Library.

ISBN: 978-1-78830-195-4

First Published in 2018

Olympia Publishers
60 Cannon Street
London
EC4N 6NP

Printed in Great Britain

Prologue

Under the warm morning sun one man stood alone in a circle, surrounded by enemies bent on destroying his city. His circle of twenty, his personal bodyguard, unmoving; facing outwards with heavy shields, spears in hand and sheathed swords, they seemed a fairly flimsy barrier around the ring.

Resplendent in the heavy bronze armour of a prince of his city, Hector looked out across the sea of faces, all of whom wanted him dead. He didn't fear them, however; he knew that none dared approach, though unafraid of him: any of them would die happy if they were the one to take his life, knowing that their name would live down through the ages. A trumpet blasted further down the beach, and at this he did feel fear; it echoed in his head as his own death toll, because this was the day he would die. The man who held his enemies at bay was approaching.

Achilles, his childhood friend, his training companion, had claimed the right to his life that very morning as revenge for the death of his little brother: a right Hector could not deny. Watching the approach of the black-armoured Myrmidons leading Achilles on his chariot, Hector recalled every training bout he had ever fought against Achilles, and vainly tried to remember some slip, some weakness shown.

Achilles was a legend come to life; he never made the same mistake twice, and remembered every trick. At fourteen, he had bested his tutors. In any other generation, Hector would have been considered a great warrior, and, in truth, he was; but he knew that here and now he was sorely outmatched; not for the first time, he wondered if Achilles really was the demigod his followers claimed.

A pathway opened up through the watching Greeks, as the Myrmidons made their way to the circle where Hector waited with the priests of Hades and Aries, closing quickly behind when Achilles passed through. Everyone wanted to be as close as possible to see him die. Looking back, he saw the walls of Troy packed with his own soldiers, unable to do anything but watch. Further back still, on the palace walls, his father stood beside Hector's wife and mother: an old man now after ten years of war, much changed from the man Hector remembered. He felt rather than saw Achilles arrive, as silence descended around him and he turned to face his fate.

The Myrmidons spread out quickly around the circular trench that they had dug the previous morning; Achilles, inches taller than those around him, stepped down from his chariot clad in armour as dark as night. Sun-darkened skin from his time on the beach of Troy, blond hair just touching his shoulders, he carried confidence as other men carried their shields; today, however, his expression could have cut rocks. This was not the face of the boy Hector remembered; it was harder and colder than that he knew, even with reddened eyes from a night spent weeping for his brother. When those eyes turned to Hector, their rawness seemed to radiate the burning hatred therein.

Hector tried to convince himself that the sweat running down his back was just from standing in the midday sun in full armour, but a little voice in his mind gave it the lie, screaming "Run!" over and over in the back of his mind. As Achilles crossed the trench, surrounded by Greeks, even that slim chance was taken away; a burning torch was tossed into the trench to send flames leaping into the air all the way around the circle where they would do battle.

Seconds passed, which felt like hours, before the priests tossed a sword through the flames to each of them, landing a few feet away in the sand and sending up a small cloud of dust as they fell. Hector knelt and lifted a handful of sand, rubbing it between his hands to dry the sweat and give him some grip on the hilt of the sword before he picked up both sword and shield, keeping his eyes on Achilles. Stabbing his sword into the ground, he forced his legs forward towards Achilles, unarmed; just a few paces across the sand, but a great distance.

"Achilles," he pleaded, "I didn't know who he was. He was in your armour, he moved like you; I thought it was you."

Achilles, who had been taking a few practice swings to stretch his muscles, suddenly swung a huge underarm sweep which hit the dead centre of Hector's shield, sending shivers up his arm.

"And you thought the great Hector could beat *Achilles*?" he roared.

"No, I expected to die." Hector dodged another overhead swing as he danced back to pick up his own sword. "And even then, I fought in defence; it was a freak accident when he moved forward into my sword. Achilles, we trained together, grew to men as brothers, fought together: even if it had been you, I didn't want your blood on my sword," said Hector, bringing up his weapon to block another overhead blow from Achilles, "nor did I want mine on yours. I was fighting for my life too."

"He was my *brother*! He came to train with me, under my protection, and you killed him."

Achilles' teeth bared in a rictus snarl as he swept past Hector, deflecting Hector's shield with his own to sweep his sword behind. Dancing back saved Hector from taking a blow to the upper thigh, but he was being pushed further back towards the fire pit surrounding the battle. It was time to do something before he ended up pushed into that pit; he couldn't keep on defending. Rolling left, he came up with a swing at Achilles' groin that made the bigger man dance back with a half-smile, half-snarl.

"That's better," said Achilles. "At least give them a show before you die."

He swung the edge of his shield, achieving a glancing blow off Hector's helmet which he wasn't fast enough to evade; Hector dropped and rolled away again, giving his head a chance to recover, as Achilles' sword struck the ground where he had been standing a second before. The thought occurred to him that Achilles didn't usually miss, a painful memory from training with him, but before he had time to consider the matter he was lashing out at Achilles' exposed leg as he came out of the roll. Achilles had anticipated him, lifting his foot just enough for Hector's sword to pass underneath it, and was now striking like a viper towards the joint between his breastplate and helmet.

Hector twisted frantically to one side and felt the blade miss by a hair's breadth, scraping along his armour and scratching his shoulder. He lifted his own sword for an underhand blow at Achilles' stomach which made Achilles move back again and dance away himself.

When he had a few feet between them, he glanced at his shoulder to see what injury he had sustained - just a scratch - and moved forward again to strike at Achilles. Time seemed to slow as they moved through the forms which they had been taught together as children, never thinking that they might use them against each other. A slow, beautiful, deadly dance ensued as they came together in a clash of bronze and a flurry of blows, until Hector lost track of time. He felt the scratch burn on his shoulder; another, a deeper wound on his upper thigh, dripped blood down his leg. The burning grew worse, becoming hard to bear.

Glancing at his leg to see whether the cut was worse than he'd judged it, he thought: *it shouldn't burn like this*. The distraction nearly cost him another wound to the arm, as Achilles came at him again. He had fought Achilles in training many times, and had always thought himself faster than this. His muscles felt as if he were moving through jelly, and it was all he could do to hold off the onslaught as he took blow after blow on his sword while watching for the razor-sharp edge which he knew Achilles had filed on the base of his shield. That little surprise had cost many of his opponents their lives.

Again and again he tried to bring his sword to bear, but, every time, Achilles seemed to be there before him; and what had started out as an offensive slash to buy him a few precious seconds in order to get his bearings turned into a desperate attempt to bring his sword back to defend himself.

His shoulder began to ache where he had taken the nick, and his leg burned with every step, Achilles adding more scrapes to his upper arm, as, yet again, he was too slow. It struck him that Achilles might be punishing him for the death of his brother by bleeding him into the death of a thousand needles. Soon he would be losing small amounts of blood from a dozen minor scratches. If he didn't manage to do something soon -

The thought turned to panic as his legs went out from under him. Rolling away, to avoid a spearing thrust from Achilles which stabbed hard into the ground where his shoulder had just been, he swung back his shield hard, hearing a crack as it crashed down on Achilles' sandalled foot. He swung his sword around as he scrambled back to his feet. Across the sand, Achilles had limped back a few steps and was testing his foot.

He came forward again and his sword hit Hector's shield with the force of a wave crashing against rocks. Hector felt his world spinning and dropped to one knee, attempting to swing his sword under his shield, but his strength seemed finally to be failing him. As his grip slipped on the handle of his sword, he watched the weapon spin towards Achilles' legs and carve a small line above his ankle before spinning on. It was enough to turn Achilles' killing blow into a glancing thump off Hector's shield; a light enough blow, but Hector felt the world darken around him.

Achilles jumped back at the cut to his leg and Hector attempted to regain his feet, pushing himself up from his knee; his strength gave out as his grip loosened and his head fell towards the sand. He couldn't believe what was happening, not yet, not yet! But he lay face down in the sand and watched sandalled feet shuffle unsteadily towards him while the world seemed to fade, dimming. *It couldn't be night already*, he thought blearily, but as the feet stopped in front of him he knew he was gone. The world went black.

Chapter One

Bleary eyes opened slowly to darkness. There was a noise, but what was it? Something far away, but it was hard to make himself care. He looked up at rough wooden beams covered with thatch, turning his head towards the wall; the bare whitewashed walls were just starting to brighten as light flooded around the rag hung over the window to act as a curtain.

That noise came again, ringing in his head like the remains of cheap wine, and suddenly his eyes shot open as the last remnants of sleep were driven away by that familiar noise. Jumping from his cot in the corner of his small room, Diomedes pulled back the curtain to see that it was already full day. Strapping on his armour took only seconds; his greaves took slightly longer to lace up. Fastening his sword belt and picking up his sparkling bronze shield and crested helmet, he turned to open the coarse plank door.

Outside, the narrow dirt street was already buzzing with soldiers hurrying along, some still struggling into their armour. Civilians were setting up shops and going about their lives, as they had for the ten long years since the Greeks first set up their siege, though they still looked decidedly uncomfortable hearing the alarm and seeing all the soldiers rushing by.

Making his way through the crowds, Diomedes rounded the corner heading on to the main paved road to the wall. Suddenly the breath was pulled out of his lungs and pressure built around his throat as he was lifted backwards off the ground and sent flying through the air; he slid to a stop on his lightly-armoured backside on the hard-packed dirt path he was just leaving. Looking up, he saw the scowling, heavily-lined face of Pedasus. Fringed with what survived of his long white hair, it was the face of a career soldier made captain after thirty years of service; his expression said that he knew that he'd got the promotion because everyone above him had died.

"Uncle, what the hell did you do that for?" shouted Diomedes, climbing back to his feet.

"I have told you before, Diomedes: put up that armour. When you're old enough, you can wear your father's armour, but for now you will carry out your duties as my shield-bearer," growled Pedasus.

"It's my armour now, the only thing my father left me," Diomedes said sullenly, wet tears glistening in his eyes. "I'm ready to take my father's place in the phalanx."

"No, my boy, and I say that as a phalanx file leader," replied Pedasus. "As your uncle, I remind you that when your father lay dying I promised him I would look after you, and see you trained before you joined the phalanx."

Putting a hand on Diomedes' shoulder, which was still only chest-high to him, Pedasus went on. "At the minute you're not big and strong enough for the phalanx; you would get yourself killed, and the men around you too, by being a weak spot in the line. Come, let's get you changed and pick up the weapon more suited to your place in this battle. Where is that bow you won? It would be more use from the wall, anyway."

"What about the alarm call?" said Diomedes, still trying to turn towards the wall, but Pedasus had a grip on the neck of his breastplate that nearly pulled it over his head, and was guiding his feet back down the lane towards the small house he shared with his mother.

"Some fool on alarm duty panicked; it's just Achilles, riding up and down in front of the walls, calling for Hector. I was doing the rounds of the towers this morning when he showed up. I stopped the alarm and came back for you; this is something you'll want to see."

Curiosity, overtaking annoyance at his uncle's intervention, hurried Diomedes' feet into his house and he pestered Pedasus all the way over what he was bringing him to see. With weary patience the same reply kept coming back. "Hurry up and get ready, and you'll see for yourself."

Diomedes took off the armour, scowling all the while; he slipped it loosely over his head without even having to undo the straps, which were already tightened as far as they would go, and replaced it on the wooden stand in the corner of his small room. Clad in his blue-trimmed white tunic, he turned to the door, where once again Pedasus grimly blocked his path.

"Your bow," he said, nodding to the corner where stood his unstrung, double recurve horn bow. A rarity, this bow had been won in an archery competition and presented by Diomedes' greatest hero, Hector himself. Brought from far Asia, its engravings were inlaid in gold and silver leaf.

Tying a quiver of arrows around his waist, Diomedes picked up his bow and was finally let out of the door. Pedasus led them through the streets to the wall, soldiers and civilians parting before him, due to a combination of his rank and the scowl which tugged at a jagged, puckering scar running right up his jaw, splitting his ear in two where a spear had struck under his helmet.

Diomedes trailed at his heels like a hound, also scowling, but his frown was directed at Pedasus' back. He still wouldn't say where they were going or what they would see. His uncle had been like this ever since his father had died in battle three years ago.

Now, he had been a real man. Adrestus and Hector had killed gloriously on that day. They had broken away from the phalanx as Ajax and his Locrians were fleeing. People still talked about it, about the dance of death they had weaved through the Locrians as they fled the battle. They called it beautiful to watch. Diomedes wished that he had been old enough to be there that day, to watch his father dance; but he had still been tied to his mother's apron strings, too young even to be allowed to watch from the walls.

Achilles and his Myrmidons had come up behind the Locrians then; taken by surprise in the open, facing an enemy phalanx, the pair had never had a chance. His father died a hero, while bloody Pedasus, the coward, hid behind his shield in the phalanx. He'd screamed at the rest of the phalanx to hold their position when they'd wanted to rescue his father and Hector. Hector survived only after being knocked unconscious by the phalanx eventually passing over him; they'd held the Myrmidons long enough for Hector and the body of Adrestus to be retrieved, before backing away from the battle once again.

The wall came into sight again, still lined with soldiers, but Pedasus had been right; there was no battle. Most of the people he could see on the wall looked bored, in fact. Making their way to the tower, Pedasus led them up the stairs to the towers and bridge over the main gate.

Looking out over the field, nothing made sense to Diomedes. Achilles was nowhere to be seen. His Myrmidons, however, were a few hundred feet out, digging holes. The rest of the Greeks seemed to be making their way up from the beach; none were armoured, though they still wore belted swords over their tunics. It looked as if they were going for an afternoon picnic rather than making ready to attack the greatest city in the world.

"What are they doing?" Diomedes asked.

"Preparing. Waiting," replied Pedasus sadly. "Today they'll probably hurt Troy more than they have in ten years." Pointing down to the Myrmidons, he said, "See down there? They're digging a pit around the duelling grounds. Achilles has challenged Hector to a duel."

Diomedes was confused by his uncle's remarks. "But Hector will win," he said confidently. "Hector has never lost a battle. He's the greatest warrior in the world!"

"Hector has never lost a battle where he led the army, that's true enough," said Pedasus, "but neither has he won every one; in some battles, both sides walk away on an equal footing. This isn't a battle, Diomedes, it's a duel, and Achilles is a warrior without equal. Our best chance to beat Achilles was in a phalanx, where his true skill couldn't be brought to bear. In one-to-one combat, Diomedes, I don't think he can be beaten; and only one man can leave that circle alive."

"You're wrong," shouted Diomedes. "Nobody can beat Hector. Nobody!"

Dropping the bow and quiver, Diomedes ran for the stairs with tears running down his cheeks, silently watched by soldiers and his uncle who wished fervently that the boy were right. He ran till his lungs burned and his legs ached, and kept on going. Finally curling in a ball in one of the many alleys throughout Troy, he hid behind some pallets and cried.

***

Pedasus looked out over the sands in front of Troy, dreaming of what the boy saw. He stood there watching, as the fire pit slowly took shape, and began to estimate how long Hector had left.

Looking up at the slowly-rising sun, already half-way to its noonday peak, he concluded that by noon it would be ready. He turned to look at the city rising behind him: his city, for which he had spent his whole life fighting.

The famous golden roofs of the city were gone. They had actually been bronze, but when the warriors returned from a distant battle, and caught sight of their beloved city, the roofs shone in the reflected sun, the inner city glowed and the bronze took on a golden hue. All were now covered in thatch and wood, the bronze sold to pay for mercenaries over ten years of war or used to make weapons as the old were lost or damaged; even the single roof on the highest tower in the palace which had actually been gold and given birth to the legend was now a dull brown.

Shaking his head slowly at how far they had fallen, he picked up Diomedes' bow and quiver and started out for the tower stairs to find the boy. The other soldiers on duty on the wall seemed to snap out of their own daydream as he stepped past, and he was followed by the noise of soldiers slapping fist to chest in formal military salute, which he barely heard.

He hated trying to look after the boy. He couldn't look at his face without seeing his brother, which led inevitably to the memory of his brother dying in his arms, the Greek spear broken off but still in his side. They had been too slow to get back into the phalanx, or the phalanx had been too slow in reaching him; either way, Pedasus had failed him. While he was alive, therefore, he would keep his last words to his dying brother. He would train Diomedes. He would keep him alive.

After a long hour spent looking for Diomedes in the blazing sun, asking after him, even recruiting a few army friends to help in the search, he was ready to quit. He was considering breaking Diomedes' bow over his knee and leaving the shattered remains on the street outside his house for him to find when he got home.

Then one of his friends came jogging back up an alleyway to tell him that he had heard of a boy matching his description running down an alleyway to drop behind a large wooden pallet, sobbing.

Pedasus thanked his friends for their help and sent them back to watch from the gate. No boy of that age, a couple of years shy of joining a phalanx, wanted the seasoned veterans to see him cry.

"Keep me a good spot on the wall, Heraclitus," he called after his friend's departing back. "I'm holding you responsible if I don't get to see," he jested.

Walking down the alley to which he had been directed, Pedasus soon heard the laboured breathing of someone weeping. He spoke to Diomedes from behind the pallet.

"I was trying to prepare you for what to expect, Diomedes, nothing more. I wanted you ready to be the man I know you to be. I couldn't have you falling apart on top of the wall, holding my shield, with all the men around."

He wasn't sure at first if the boy even heard him. He didn't feel comfortable around children, never having had the chance to get used to them, as his own wife and child had died during the birth. With as many civilians as possible having been evacuated from the city ten years ago, before the siege began, he'd been left with little chance to try again. All he had to draw on were faint memories of his own father raising him. A tough man, his father; he remembered being scared to let him see anything gentler than the soldier he expected each of his boys to grow into.

The boy's snuffling seemed to quieten, and he heard cloth moving, and sandals scuffing the dirt street. "One day, Diomedes, if this war lasts that long, you will have to lead sons of this city into battle. Even if this war ends, there will always be another battle, and your bloodline is that of a leader. Men will not follow you because they like you, lad. They have to fear and respect you in equal measures, both for your ability and in the knowledge that you will take them away from a battle, won or lost, with as few casualties as possible; that you will give them a chance to survive the day."

"Me, lead men? You won't even let me into the phalanx, uncle, so how can I gain the experience to lead?" Diomedes stood looking up at Pedasus with red-rimmed eyes, challenging him.

"Leaders don't learn by dying in their first battle, boy. I have trained you in sword and bow and paid for the best classes in both, but you *are not* big or strong enough for the phalanx yet, and don't talk to me about taking your father's place. Your father was two years older than you are now before he was allowed to take *his* father's place. Now hold your tongue, boy, and do as I tell you."

Pedasus put a hand on Diomedes' shoulder and looked him in the eye. "Watch every battle you can. Understand how leaders decide when to engage and when to pull away, and learn the use of shield carriers to harry the enemy's flank; use your bow for that at every chance you get. That is why you carry my shield, boy, and why you watch from the walls when other phalanxes engage. That is how you live to be a leader."

Straightening up, Pedasus turned back on to the street. "Here's your bow, though I'm not sure you still deserve it after leaving it on the battlements. Now run back to my barracks; I want my helmet and shield polished and ready for me in front of the gates before Hector marches out. That gives you one hour, boy, and I want them to sparkle. I won't allow you to embarrass me during Hector's honour guard."

With that he started walking back up the street, listening for Diomedes behind him. Silence for three strides, then four and five; just as he was about to turn around and give Diomedes a tongue-lashing, he heard sprinting sandals as Diomedes passed him at full tilt, heading for the garrison barracks. Shaking his head, Pedasus realised that his throat was very dry, and decided he needed a drink. The situation being what it was, that was likely to be a rough brew made from what was left of the wheat after the edible husks had been removed. Sometimes he thought the lack of wine was the worst thing about this bloody siege.

***

Hector's honour guard, Diomedes thought sluggishly; one hour. Suddenly he sprang into action. He had to be there on time. If everything wasn't right, his uncle would send him home again; he had done it before. If Pedasus was right about today then he, Diomedes, must be there holding his uncle's shield; he had to meet Hector.

Sprinting past his uncle, he couldn't help glancing at him, with the passing thought that the boring old man had no life outside the army. Diomedes rounded the corner at a sprint, almost knocking over a few people out buying pies from a street vendor.

Shouting what might pass for an apology, he ran on to the sound of their complaints. On the main southern thoroughfare, he took the most direct route, straight down the main street, to the barracks his uncle shared with the other officers.

This barracks was considerably bigger than those shared by the common soldiers, yet it was still a spartan outfit. Large wooden beams around the door towered over him, eight foot high and wide besides, but it still looked small as he hurtled straight into Achenia's solid armoured chest.

The man was heavy now, but he carried it as most men wished they could. Towering over six foot and as wide as Diomedes was tall, or at least it looked that way, the veteran had grey hair in a thick plait, like a belt reaching down to his waist.

Although outranked by the officers, he had been head pole march, civilian commander of all Trojan armies for over ten years, a record for Troy, and a lot of the officers deferred to his opinion. His presence meant a high-level meeting with some officers. His uncle had been strolling through the streets looking for him; that thought floated over the surface of Diomedes' mind, but he had to get ready quickly.

"Where's the fire, Diomedes?" said Achenia, a thick hand pressed to his chest. His ready smile made him popular with the soldiers under him, and Diomedes had always liked the man.

"Pedasus sent me to clean and polish his shield and helmet for Hector's honour guard, Achenia. If I don't have it done on time, he won't let me stay to see Hector fight," explained Diomedes, trying to squeeze past Achenia, but the soldier's big hand was like bronze on his arm, holding him immobile.

"Not just yet, Diomedes; there's a closed meeting inside. The officers are just finishing up. Give them two minutes, and talk to me while you're waiting." The friendly tone was overlaid with tension; he was worried about something, but then everyone was anxious about the duel. Diomedes squirmed in his grip, still attempting to get past. "Stop struggling, lad. I'll explain to Pedasus, but you should still have time to get the armour shining. Now, how's your training going?"

Realising that there was no point in wrestling with him, Diomedes reluctantly gave up.

"Pedasus still won't let me wear my armour and join the phalanx," he pouted. "He made me take it off after the alarm call this morning."

"And he was right to do so." Achenia looked down into his eyes, his expression no longer friendly. "If he hadn't stopped you, I would have. Do you really think I would allow you to endanger an entire phalanx by letting you join one? You're still too small,

Diomedes. Your ability with a bow is beyond question, boy; that's why you won that prize. You must now master the sword. It may save your life if you're ever in a phalanx that breaks. These are necessary things to learn before you join the phalanx, lad; by then, you will have grown a few inches and put on a few pounds, and your arms will be strong from swinging a sword all day, if I remember your uncle's training methods correctly."

"Yes, sir," Diomedes replied sullenly. "It's just that - " His words trailed off as he glimpsed something passing behind the tiny sliver of space between Achenia and the wooden door frame: men in armour which looked black as night in the shadow of the barracks. Breastplate, helmet, even the crest; all were dark as a raven's wing. "Who are they?" he asked curiously.

Glancing back, Achenia looked suddenly uncomfortable. "That's just some of the officers getting ready," he answered quickly.

"But they're in strange armour," Diomedes insisted.

"It's just a trick of the light in there with the doors closed," Achenia said, turning to glance inside. He seemed happy with whatever he saw; Diomedes could just make out the swirl of an old cloak being settled. But Achenia looked at Diomedes again as the hall quietened. "You'd better go inside, now that the meeting is over, and get your uncle's shield ready," he said, standing to the side of the doorway to let Diomedes through. The honour guard! Diomedes had been distracted by the officers. He ran inside to his uncle's room and set to, scrubbing the shield.

***

Passing through the doors from the bright daylight outside to the dark interior of the inn, it took a moment for Pedasus to adjust his eyes to the light. The whitewashed room was still mostly empty at this time of day.

Drinking during the morning was frowned upon in the army, which is why those few like himself who indulged in the habit chose this particular inn in a secluded area of town. Most people associated soldiers with the rougher, rundown taverns near the barracks at the city walls. Here he could disappear from the world for a couple of hours' peace.

A few men sat with their drinks, playing dice along the long wooden tables at the back wall; they looked up as he walked in. He recognised all but one, who seemed to be one of those outlander mercenaries sent by trusted neighbouring cities' states, mercenaries who were all over the city lately.

Pedasus walked to the bar and ordered a drink. It was a rough, clear liquid that burned on the way down, but it numbed his memories, and that was why he came here every morning. After his night shift it helped to block out the dreams about his wife, dreams that plagued him whenever he got to sleep for a few hours, or at least his memory of those dreams.

Today held no such luxury. He sat in a corner by himself and gazed around the room, rolling his cup between his hands. What should he do with Diomedes? The thought swirled around his head. The boy just wouldn't stop pushing. Pedasus must keep his promise to his brother to protect Diomedes till the lad was ready, and then he could finally join his wife.

Half an hour passed like that before he realised he had finished his cup of this new drink. He wanted another, but it was time to go to the gates. Rising, he made his way to the door, then stopped. It was good manners to bring along a drink when watching a duel; the others would appreciate it.

Turning to the greying innkeeper, he asked, "Can you sell me a keg of that swill to take away?" and tossed a few gold coins on the bar.

The innkeeper scowled, muttering about that being the only alcohol available in the city and scooping up the coins. He came back a minute later with the small keg and some change. Tucking it under his arm, Pedasus ducked outside and made his way to the gate, a good fifteen minutes away.

Diomedes was waiting when Pedasus came in sight of the gate, standing proudly beside his shield and helmet, polished until they shone in the reflected sunlight. It was an advantage in battle; if the sun was just right, a well-polished shield or helmet could blind the enemy for a split second, which was often all that made the difference between life and death. Today, though, it was all for show, to grant Hector the honour he deserved.

Crowds had begun to gather for the day's fight, and people were trying unsuccessfully to get a space on the wall from which to watch, or an arrow-slit in the wall to peer through. The soldiers weren't giving up their places on the wall, on the ostensible grounds that, if things went badly out there, they might end up defending the wall as the fight finished with so many Greeks in close proximity. However, everyone knew that the soldiers wanted to see the duel just as much as the civilians did.

Street vendors stood on every corner, jostling for the best places after so many quiet weeks around the city. Today's news had everyone crammed into one place. Even those soldiers on duty to patrol that part of the city wall not in view of the duelling grounds had almost to be physically forced to begin the circuit of the walls, knowing that they would never make it back around the eight-mile perimeter wall before the action was over.

Pedasus had to weave a path through them, occasionally physically moving someone out of his way if they weren't quick enough to recognise his rank. Eventually he reached Diomedes in a small knot of officers and shield-bearers which was like an island of calm in the tumult swirling around them.

He knelt quickly to inspect his shield and helmet before standing to clap Diomedes on the shoulder for a job well done. The boy never slacked or did less than his best, he had to give him that; he just pushed too much. Shaking his head to dispel the thought, he handed the keg to Diomedes. "Bring this to Heraclitus and Achenia. They're on top of the gate tower, keeping a seat for us. Tell them I said that anyone who opens it before I get there will be doing my night duty for the next month! Then come straight back to me." He was already turning to the other officers before Diomedes had left.

Conversation centred around the same mundane topics which the officers usually discussed when they got together: troops, distribution, supplies, enemy formations; anything to keep their minds off what they were there for. Hector had been the hero of this city for the entire ten-year war, but nobody rated his chances today. Nobody rated anyone's chances against Achilles.

Suddenly a trumpet blared in the street, and everybody turned to see a wave of polished bronze making its way down the road, Hector's personal bodyguard and shield-bearer taking up the front. It was likely that few of these would survive the day; every one of them had sworn to follow where Hector led, even to Hades.

Today they would follow him out into that sea of Greeks and work together with Achilles' Myrmidons, forming a solid ring around the duelling grounds to prevent anybody else from interfering in a battle of honour. Pedasus couldn't see many surviving the Greeks when Hector went down, and he couldn't imagine them being allowed to leave unscathed in the unlikely event that Achilles should fall. Maybe if Greeks had honour - but everyone knew they hadn't.

Then came Hector himself, shining like the sun. He wore

armour which made that of Pedasus look cheap and worn, a cloak of scarlet flaring behind it, with the phoenix of Troy emblazoned on the back in intricate embroidery. Hair as black as night hung down his back, plaited in two intricate braids to pad out his helmet, and swaying in the light breeze. He was mounted on a blond stallion which might itself have been cast from gold.

Turning to pick up his helmet, Pedasus found that Diomedes had already returned, and was holding it out to him. He granted the boy a small smile before sliding the helmet on to his head, hiding his features, and pushed Diomedes in front of him with his shield into the corridor of officers through which Hector would pass; all the shield-bearers were at the front, holding the shields at waist-height and slightly tilted out at the bottom.

Every man among them stood straight and stared directly forward, each one precise and every uniform identical, with the exception of Diomedes; he held his bow in his off hand with a quiver of arrows at his waist, but since the bow had been a gift from Hector himself, that could only be taken as an honour.

The crowd packing the open square around the towering gates seemed to part like summer drapes to the breeze that was Hector and his entourage, who barely slowed as they moved into the crowded area. Onlookers leaned back on each other in their haste to back out of the way of the oncoming cavalry. Cavalry were a rare sight in the city lately, little more than ceremonial.

They kept coming until they were only a few yards short of the honour guard when they pulled up, Hector tugging sharply on his reins and causing his stallion to rear up pawing the air as the warrior punched his spear in the air to cheers from the watching soldiers. Hector was ever a showman.

Behind the 'Y' opening in their helmets, Hector's eyes and those of the bodyguard never moved from the gate. It was as if they were already seeing what lay beyond, a sea of Greek faces waiting to witness Hector die.

As they dismounted from their horses, a group of grooms who had waited among the crowd came forward to take the animals. The bodyguard kept formation around Hector as he moved forward toward the gate. It was as if they couldn't or didn't see anything around them as they walked down the lane formed by the honour guard. Hector stopped suddenly, so abruptly that the bodyguard walked on a step before realising that Hector had stopped. Turning his head, the warrior looked Diomedes in the eye.

"Do you still practice with this thing, or do you leave it in the corner and just look at it?" he asked.

Diomedes seemed lost for words but eventually managed to stammer, "N-no, sir; I practice with it every day."

"Good. I'm glad to see you take such good care of it, then. Always remember that it may be shiny and valuable, but it's just a tool; it's to be used, not looked at." Raising his eyes, he looked at Pedasus and nodded in respect. "Look after him, Pedasus, and hold this for me; I won't need it out there today." He handed Pedasus his spear, and, with that, they moved down the lane towards the gate.

While they were still approaching the gate, three men were lifting the locking bar out of the slots, while eight more took up ropes attached to the huge gates and began to strain to pull them open.

A loud crash high on the wall caught everyone's attention, then another. Soldiers on the wall were banging their spears against their shields in salute to Hector. As they watched, more and more soldiers took it up until the entire wall echoed with the resounding clash of spears against shields.

Hector stood looking along the wall. Pedasus thought he saw a hint of a smile through his helmet as Hector nodded and raised his shield high in salute before jogging out through the gate, exuding confidence with every stride. The gates slowly slid shut behind him. The soldiers on the wall continued their rhythmic beating after he'd disappeared outside, but the soft thud of the closing gates still left a hollow echo in the square; it sounded like the ominous peal of a funeral bell to the ears of the group of officers whose eyes remained locked on the gates.

As if breaking out of a trance, Pedasus finally looked away, glancing at the back of Diomedes' head, then towards the other officers facing them; and, as if his movement was a signal, the others moved as well. "Better get up to the gate tower," he said, clapping an almost-unsteady hand on Diomedes' shoulder to guide him away, with a quick flick of his head to Priscus and Arimnestos to join him.

They weaved their way through the crowd as quickly as they could, till they reached the side of the gate and went up the stairs. Priscus, who was leading the way, was almost barred entry to the top by Heraclitus until he saw Pedasus and Diomedes as well and let them all up on to the broad open square on top of the gates.

Moving to a few rickety stools set near the edge - nobody would carry a chair up those stairs - Achenia tossed Pedasus one of half a dozen small wooden cups he had ready beside Pedasus' keg, sarcastically asking, "May I open it yet?" After a second's hesitation he tossed Diomedes a cup too, remarking, "I suppose you're old enough to have one on an occasion like this."

"I wish they'd just get on with it," said Pedasus, settling himself carefully on a stool.

"Anyone taking bets?" joked Arimnestos.

"Do you honestly think anyone would bet against Hector, Arimnestos? It would be almost treasonous." Priscus was incredulous, which was probably the effect Arimnestos was looking for; he seemed to enjoy annoying the younger man.

"It isn't treason to accept the truth, Priscus. He is out there facing a man who is widely recognised as the world's best warrior. Hector's a legend, but most people think Achilles is some sort of demigod." Arimnestos seemed to be enjoying the reaction he'd provoked, when another voice broke in on the group.

"It might not be treason, it might even be the truth, but you would make an old man happy if you'd refrain from saying so lightly that his son might well be about to die out there."

Arimnestos was turning his head, looking annoyed at whoever had butted in on his fun with Priscus, when the full import of the words hit him; his head snapped around to stare in wide-eyed horror at the caped and hooded form of Priam looming at the top of the stairs. In a moment he had risen, knocking over a stool in his haste, and bent on one knee, fist pressed to the ground.

Stammering out, "My king, I am very sorry; I meant nothing by it; it was only a joke-" His words trailed off, as the other men fell to their knees around him.

"Peace, man," said Priam. "I've been standing there long enough to know you were teasing Priscus, but I'd still prefer not to hear it."

Priscus raised his head in surprise on realising that the King actually knew his name.

"Arise, arise. Today I am here not as your king, but as a father come to watch his son. Priscus, Pedasus, off your knees. I ask only for your company, to share a stool with you and maybe a cup of your beverage if you can spare it."

"Highness, take mine." Achenia indicated his stool as he went to kneel again, but Priam's hand on his shoulder stopped him.

"I said I'm not here as a king, my friend. Treat me as an equal just for once, with no one watching me," he said, though he slid the cloak from his shoulders and took the proffered stool. As the hood dropped from his head, Diomedes was struck by the resemblance between Priam and Hector; despite his advanced years, he was a large, strong man with a bull neck and a nose which had clearly been broken more than once.

The stories said that this man had created Troy from nothing but the inner city, essentially the place where the palace now stood, fighting the local tribes and binding the villages to him, to create the largest settlement this side of the great green in his youth. Then an agreement with the Hittite King Mursili II had seen the Hittites send builders and planners to help design and build Troy's great outer walls where they now stood.

Priam's part of the agreement had been to send men to the army of Mursili II when needed, and to use Troy to protect the westernmost reaches of his empire. Looking at Priam now, Diomedes believed the stories; he believed in the legend that was this man, and his years on the throne didn't appear to have softened him in the least.

Stepping over to Diomedes, Pedasus plucked the wooden cup from his hands. "Maybe another time, Diomedes, but now I need you to wait on your king. This is a great honour, boy; ensure his cup remains full, and be there if he should require anything." With that, he brought the cup to Priam and poured some of the strong liquor from the keg for him and the others before passing it back to Diomedes to hold.

"My eyes are not what they used to be, so tell me, Pedasus: what's happening out there?" asked Priam, as he accepted the cup.

Pedasus looked a little uncomfortable at being obliged to tell the king what was happening when he was sure how this was going to end. He didn't want to be the one to tell a king who was reported to have a vicious temper that his son had been struck down and killed.

"Ah, Majesty, well, let's see; Hector has just arrived and crossed into the circle. The bodyguard are spreading around the circle; they look a little lost in the middle of all those Greeks," said Pedasus.

"They'll be safe under the white flag; having them there is really a formality," replied Priam. "The Greeks are not in armour, so even if they were to try anything they would lose hundreds against twenty armed and armoured men." Taking a sip, Priam coughed. "That's strong! Where did you get this? It's certainly not wine, but it's not bad compared with what's been going around the city lately."

"It's some barley concoction I purchased in a tavern on the way here," replied Pedasus, taking a drink himself.

"Typical of Achilles to be late; even for revenge he has to make a show," commented Priam, shaking his head and holding out his cup for Diomedes to refill.

"He can't be far off now; there seems to be some commotion further down the beach," said Pedasus, straining to see further. Sure enough, trumpets began to blow. "Yes, here he comes." Priam nodded.

"Majesty, I don't question your wishes, but shouldn't the king be watching this from up there with the queen and Andromache in the royal palace?" Arimnestos asked hesitantly, obviously loth to point out the obvious to Priam but feeling obliged to do so, as no one else seemed to have the courage to say it. With a slight shake of his head, Priam turned to look sadly at Arimnestos as he spoke.

"Arimnestos, I know my responsibilities; don't think I have forgotten them." He hesitated. It was disconcerting to see the king unsure of himself. "Do you know General Glaucus?"

They nodded. Every general on Troy's inner war council was well known, even to the lowest soldier. There could be no question of their authority to give a command. "Well, look at the palace." They did so, and there stood Priam, Hecuba and Andromache on the palace walls, watching – or so it appeared to their eyes.

"Today he has the honour of representing me as king. Don't look at me like that; he bears a resemblance to me and I needed to be here, as close to my son as possible. Hecuba and Andromache understand and agree with me. Have you ever had a son, Arimnestos?" Arimnestos looked down in embarrassment and shook his head. "Then you cannot understand why I am here now until you do," replied Priam, and that was the end of that.

"Achilles is there now," Pedasus said suddenly into the silence that followed. He understood why Priam was here, and looked at him with renewed respect. He really wasn't the king just now; he was a father praying to all the gods to bring his son back to him one last time.

"Good, then things can finally get under way," replied Priam, visibly steeling himself for what was to come. "At least I can see something from here," he laughed grimly.

The Myrmidons whom Achilles had brought as his bodyguard were spreading around the duelling ground, interspersed with Hector's own bodyguard, alternating with them so that there was almost a solid ring of bodyguards to ensure that no one outside the battle could interfere with this matter of honour. Both Hector and Achilles had brought only their shields and armour with them. Two priests brought swords, blessed by the gods of death and the afterlife, from the edge of the pit around the duelling ground. They would shortly be thrown into the ring.

"What in the name of Hades is that?" breathed Priam, as a burning torch was tossed into the pit which the Myrmidons had spent the earlier part of the morning digging around the circle. The ring went up in a whoosh of fire which could be heard all the way back to the walls.

"Looks like they got their hands on some naphtha," said Achenia. "I didn't think Achilles would stoop so low as to offer an open insult like that, as if Hector could get away through all those Greeks, even if he wanted to leave."

"It's not like Achilles; he knows Hector. There has to be some other explanation," said Priam, while Achenia was barely restraining himself from running out there to avenge what he saw as a calculated insult to Hector's honour.

The priests from outside the pit threw the two swords over the fire, and they landed in the middle of the arena. Hector walked over towards one, knelt down, set his shield on the ground and rubbed some of the dry sand between his hands.

The atmosphere was tense now, as Hector stood with sword and shield in hand. Looking relaxed, Achilles strolled over to the other sword and picked it up, taking a few practice swings to stretch his limbs. Even from the wall, Hector looked recognisably apprehensive; then he suddenly turned the sword in his hand and drove it into the ground, before walking to within a few yards of Achilles, where he stopped.

"What is he doing?" Pedasus glanced at Priam, who didn't seem aware he had spoken aloud, a sure sign of how uncomfortable he was.

"They're saying something," Pedasus replied, "but it's too far away to make out." As if to give him the lie, suddenly over the crowd came one screamed word: "ACHILLES!" followed by a roar of approval from the watching Greeks. It seemed to hit Priam like a physical slap to the face, but it wasn't the word that had affected him; as it was screamed Achilles had struck, almost too quickly to see, stabbing the point of his sword straight at

Hector and striking his shield hard. That was followed a second later with a huge overhead swing towards Hector's head, blocked by Hector who raised his shield high. From the corner of his eye Pedasus watched Priam, who seemed to be on a string with Hector, lifting his arm in the same motion as if willing Hector to move faster.

"Pick up your sword, damn it!" he whispered. "Lift your accursed sword."

As if on cue, Hector was forced back toward his own sword, dancing back from Achilles in a defensive twirl which Diomedes remembered from his own lessons. The sword seemed to jump into Hector's hand as it passed over, and then it was in the air just where Hector needed it to block a lunge for his head.

Then Achilles was charging straight into Hector, using his shield as a battering ram against him, driving Hector's own shield up under the blow as Achilles' sword attempted to flick under Hector's upraised shield, but Hector was dancing out of range of the blow. He was out of range, but being pushed constantly back towards the pit and the fire within. He must be feeling the heat from those flames already.

Everyone on the gate tower was now leaning forward on their stools, having temporarily forgotten their drinks. They forgot to worry how to behave in front of their king, caught up in the heat of the moment. Pedasus shook his head in wonder; right now, their king was exactly like every other man there, and did seem to have forgotten his crown. Pedasus regretted his inattention as he took a swig from his cup and half-choked, having forgotten what he was drinking.

Coughing, Pedasus turned his attention back to the fight, and just caught what looked like a very quick attack to Achilles' groin. It was a good move, notoriously hard to avoid without losing your balance, but Achilles hadn't gained his reputation for nothing. He seemed almost to glide out of range of the launch, going into a sidespin which brought his shield around in a circle to strike at Hector's head and seemed to strike his helmet; the impact must have been light, for Hector reacted well, going with the strike down into a roll half around Achilles to give himself more space to manoeuvre, and swinging for Achilles' legs as he came up.

Achilles seemed to see the move coming, because he didn't even hurry, just lifted his foot barely enough for Hector's blade to pass under. As Hector was thrown slightly off balance by his own swing, Achilles struck again, aiming for his neck this time. Pedasus leaned even further forward; Achenia groaned; Arimnestos mumbled an almost inaudible, "No!" and even Priam flinched slightly, in imitation of Hector's own reaction, as Hector pulled to one side.

Hector danced back from the attack, giving himself some space, and looked down at himself. Pedasus couldn't see very well from that distance but he was sure he could see blood running down Hector's arm; however, he still looked steady, and seemed to be checking his shoulder and not his neck, which was a good sign.

Pedasus became aware of his death grip on the wall, his knuckles white, and broke away to swallow what was left in his cup; he shouted for Diomedes to refill it, which the boy rushed to do, then filled everyone else's as they all seemed to have developed very dry throats. When he looked back, Hector had a slight wound on his thigh. "What happened?" called Priam, but nobody seemed to have a definite answer and the wall milled like a kicked anthill as everyone leaned over to see what was happening. Hector was limping now.

The sun moved slowly across the sky as the battle progressed, each man proving why he was considered the best by his own people. Half an hour later, both men were tiring from their exertions and the battle was showing some effect; Hector stumbled with blood coming from several wounds and Achilles limped a little. Suddenly Hector's leg seemed to fall from under him and he hit the ground hard. As he pushed himself up with one arm, Achilles seemed about to deliver the killing blow but Hector dropped to the ground and lay still.

Everyone was now standing on the wall, stunned. Pedasus couldn't understand it; the killing blow should have fallen. Something was wrong. Achilles stood there with his sword raised, looking down at Hector, his arm dropping slowly; he looked back at the sword, down at Hector and then drew his sword down in front of his face. Whatever he was doing had some result, because he shouted something. There was the silence of death up on the wall, but the cheering among the Greeks drowned out whatever Achilles was saying; however, the bodyguards of both men suddenly came to attention.

Pedasus' mind left the battle as something flashed in the corner of his eye and he whipped his head around. Diomedes was standing there, bow in hand, a stunned look on his face. Pedasus reached out and pulled the bow from his grasp as he whispered, "What have you done, boy? What have you done?"

Chapter Two

He watched the head thump down on to the sand, and raised his sword for what would be the killing stroke. Hector shakily raised himself up on his arms, but they seemed to give way below him, and he thumped back down on the ground, eyes slowly closing, as if he hadn't the strength to keep them open.

Confusion and grief were at war inside him. Who to hate, Agamemnon for urging Patroclus on, or Hector for the killing stroke? He knew Agamemnon's tricks well and had grown to adulthood loving Hector like the brother he had lost. Hector was a man of honour.

The crowd around him screamed with excitement, urging Achilles on, and he cautiously moved forward on the balls of his feet; it could be a clever feint, after all. Something seemed wrong, though; it was hard to think through his hate-fuelled rage, but he had fought Hector before in practice, and it had never ended like this.

Hector was a warrior of legendary fame, and killing him would be enough to seal Achilles' place in history. This fight had gone on a long time, much longer than any other duel he had ever fought, but Hector should have been able to keep going for another hour at least. Though the air burned in his own lungs, Achilles knew that, in the heat of battle, he himself could have done so.

Quickly scanning Hector's injuries, Achilles saw that, although there were many minor wounds, there was nothing that would account for his sudden collapse; therefore, his eyes were drawn to his own sword. He looked back at Hector, then back at his raised sword. Bile rose in his stomach at the realisation that the old man had been right. He brought his sword down towards his face and smelt the blade, and his breath caught at the familiar odour of venom.

"Eudoros," he screamed, "shields up, come together!" The words were barely out of his mouth when he heard the shields slam together, Myrmidon alternating with Trojan as if they had trained together all their lives.

"Poison!" he said. "Bring me those priests."

The priests were still at the edge of the pit from whence they had tossed the swords; as they heard the summons called out, they rose from their prayers as one and stepped forward into the fire pit to their deaths, their screams of pain mingling with cheering from the crowd which hadn't quite abated.

Sensing danger had kept Achilles alive many times in battle; it's a skill which a soldier develops. That's the only way he could describe what happened next, as it was too fast to hear: suddenly, without warning, Achilles spun around as fast as he had ever moved, bringing his shield up just as a single arrow buried itself deep in the protective weapon. He could feel the point just poking through the back, scratching his arm.

Looking from whence it had come, he was amazed that someone could have fired that shot from the wall and still have so much power in the arrow as it struck. He swung his sword around, breaking off the shaft of the arrow near the head before the majority of the surrounding Greeks could see, letting them think he was showing off. The crowd didn't seem to notice, being so preoccupied with the fall of Hector.

His Myrmidons, paying much closer attention, broke through the crowd to join the twenty members of his bodyguard;

spaces opened up in the shield wall to let them through. The Trojans looked worried and confused, as the Myrmidons pulled straps out of the sand, which was piled up where it had been removed from the fire pit, to reveal their shields and spears hidden inside. They quickly joined the shield wall, giving a double lair of shields and spears pointing out.

"Eudoros, a bridge," commanded Achilles, and, seconds later, a thick wooden door taken from the ship, which had been hidden with the shields, slammed into place across the fire pit. It was thick enough to hold off the flames for only a short time before it would also start to burn. As quickly as he could Achilles sheathed his sword, kicked Hector's away from his body, just in case, and bent to scoop the limp form of Hector from the ground. One arm under Hector's head and the other under his legs, he was gentle, almost tender as he lifted Hector to his chest and made his way across the bridge to his men. Eudoros was waiting for him.

"My lord, what are you doing?" asked Eudoros.

"He was poisoned, Eudoros. Poisoned! There is no honour in this. It was Agamemnon, it must have been," replied Achilles. "We are bringing him home. Just keep those Greeks off my back."

"As my lord commands," said Eudoros, turning to give orders to his men who began tightening up the protective ring around Achilles. He was a good man, Eudoros, never questioning; he just followed his orders and gave advice when it was needed. Even his missing eye didn't seem to hinder him in the phalanx.

Achilles had moved him to the file soon after the injury, and there had never been a man who had tried to turn in the phalanx since he'd put Eudoros there. It might have had something to do with his constant threats to lance the first man to turn, but once it kept discipline in the ranks, that was all to the good.

More slowly than Achilles would have liked, the ranks formed around him. The Trojans fitted in without missing a beat; from Hector's personal bodyguard, Achilles would have expected no less. Finally, he was surrounded by a wall of shields. Orders went out to keep the spears up; fewer injuries now would leave them less likely to face a riot from the surrounding Greeks. They might be unarmed, but with ten thousand around his hundred - well, it would be challenging to say the least. The rest he had ordered to remain in readiness in his camp, but they would be too far away to help now.

Treating the surrounding crowds like an enemy phalanx, the Myrmidons put their backs to their shields and began pushing a path through the crowd for Achilles. Most of the Greeks moved out of the way when they saw them coming, but in such crowds that they couldn't always get space to move quickly enough, and got pushed along in the wave of people caused by Achilles' ceaseless advance.

Nearly a quarter of a precious hour later, they were pushing out of the crowd. The road opened up, and before them were the huge gates in front of Troy, only a few hundred metres away. The ranks opened up, and marching became a lot easier. Making much better time, they marched straight to the gates.

"Open the gates," Achilles screamed at the soldiers, who were gaping at him, probably wondering why they should open the gates to an enemy force just because one of them carried a dead Trojan. No doubt they were worried about a trap. He could faintly hear argument behind the gate. An unmistakable voice rose above the rest, a voice from his childhood: that of the man who had virtually raised him when he had spent his summers with Hector. This voice was more dear to him than that of his own father.

"You heard the man," bellowed Priam at the top of his lungs

from the main gate tower. "Open the damned gates! Do you think thousands of my brave warriors couldn't conquer a hundred Myrmidons?" Silence for a second, and then, "Move, you cowards! Must I open the gates myself? That's a prince of Troy in his arms!"

Slowly but surely, he could hear the huge locking bar being removed from the gates. Seconds later, the gates split in the centre, and Achilles could see a sliver of light between them. The gates opened enough to admit his ranks only and began to swing shut again immediately they were inside. Instantly, the Trojan guards peeled away from the ranks of Achilles' own men and came forward to gently take Hector's still body. They carried him to a waiting covered wagon, and laid him in the shade of the flat wooden bed of the wagon, covered in straw.

Priam rushed down the stairs to the side of the gate tower with several men, obviously officers who had gathered there to watch with a few younger boys, attendants or shield bearers. Achilles' eyes latched on to a bow he remembered all too well. Priam came straight to Achilles, without any of the obvious fear which most men felt when approaching him. There was a tear in his eyes as he reached Achilles, but he held himself like a king in front of his men.

"I offer you thanks for bringing him back to us," he said in a solid voice for all to hear and embraced Achilles. In a whisper for only Achilles to hear, he added, "How did it ever come to this?"

Achilles had no answer for the man, but hugged him back.

"The old man was right," Achilles said eventually.

Priam merely nodded. Reaching inside his armour, Achilles took out a folded piece of parchment and handed it to Priam with a small leather water bag. "Odysseus, he said that it's slow, and this should help. I found it hard to believe, even of Agamemnon, until now. I'm sorry to have doubted him".

"Thank you," said Priam, in a shakier voice, then turned and marched to the wagon where Hector lay; he climbed in beside his son, and the wagon began its journey back to the palace.

Achilles watched him go with a sudden sense of loss, similar to what he had felt on discovering his brother had died, and the energy seemed to drain out of him. Glancing down at his shield, he remembered the arrow. He looked around the silent crowd of Trojans, and raised his voice as he lifted his shield high, asking, "Who is responsible for this?"

If he had thought it was quiet before, now it was eerily silent. Worried faces turned to look at him. It was as if everyone had just been delivered to the headsman. People looked at one another, then at the ground, but not one could hold his cold hard stare without looking away. Even the hard-bitten soldiers seemed embarrassed that they couldn't. One man slowly took a step forward. Glancing back at a youth behind him, he straightened his back, and took another more purposeful step.

"It was I," came in the solid bass voice of a man used to giving commands. Achilles looked him in the eye, and the man held his gaze, as if challenging him. A flash of light reflected off something, that bow again, and it distracted him for a second as he looked at the boy holding it. His eyes returned to the soldier. "What's your name, officer?" he asked.

"Pedasus, sir. I served with you and Hector in the east," replied the man; and Achilles found himself remembering a good, solid soldier who always held tight with the phalanx. He remembered facing him outside these very gates a few times also. Now they were on opposite sides, and he felt a pang of regret that he might have to kill yet another man he respected. Warriors like himself seemed to be doomed to repeat that process many times during their lives.

"I remember you," Achilles said. "Why would you sully

Hector's honour like that? Do you think him a coward?"

"You talk of sullying Hector's honour?" replied Pedasus heatedly, anger in his eyes. "You light a fire around the man as if he would have tried to run away from the duel, and yet you preach to me?"

"In case you hadn't noticed, that fire also kept the Greeks out, you fool. Don't attempt to question your betters."

He seemed to wilt at that. Of course, it hadn't occurred to them that he would have worried about whether the Greeks might rip Hector's body apart when he fell; but someone had to.

"I don't know why I did it," the man replied, looking down in shame. "I saw Hector fall, and the next thing I knew, the arrow was in the air."

Again Achilles' eyes flicked to that bow, and the boy who held it.

"You know I must challenge you now? I have no wish to see you dead, but you have left me no choice, Pedasus," said Achilles slowly, in a low tone.

Pedasus nodded his head. "I know."

The man had just begun to draw his sword when the boy with the bow stepped forward, shouting, "No, no, it was I! I'm sorry. It was I who shot the arrow."

"Get back and shut up, boy," growled Pedasus, putting a hand in front of the lad.

"No," insisted the boy. "You've always told me to take responsibility for my actions. I won't let you die for something that I did."

"Is this your father, boy?" asked Achilles, again looking at the bow.

"No, he's my uncle," replied the boy.

"Can you even use that weapon?" Achilles indicated the bow.

“Yes. It’s mine. I won it in an archery competition. Hector gave it to me with his own hands.” The boy puffed up proudly with the admission, then remembered what he had done, and deflated again. He was a small boy, about twelve at a guess, and thin; this was an indication of the shortage of food in the city, because of the siege. His cheeks were sunken and his hair dishevelled; he would probably not put on the bulk needed for the phalanx, with the limited rations in Troy.

“Can you use a sword, boy?” asked Achilles.

Pedasus seemed to lose his senses at the question, drawing his sword and running at Achilles. “You can’t kill the boy,” he screamed, though it was more of a plea than anything else. Achilles didn’t even draw his sword, which was still laced with poison.

He pulled back his stomach, away from the wild sweep of Pedasus’ sword, then moved inside the swing to seize Pedasus’ sword arm. Pulling him forward, he brought his elbow down on Pedasus’ face, hearing the man’s nose break under it, and knocked him back; Achilles’ hand followed the elbow to hit him hard across the face. Then, as if it had been in his hands all the time, he brought up his belt knife and stabbed it through Pedasus’ forearm between the two bones; the sword dropped from his hand before Achilles released the arm, and the man dropped to the ground.

It all happened so quickly that it was over before anyone else could react to his sudden attack.

Looking down at Pedasus’ still form, Achilles shook his head sadly then refocused his attention on the boy. “As I was saying, can you use a sword?” he asked again. The boy looked at him, tearing his eyes from the prone form of Pedasus, and nodded dumbly.

Pedasus stirred on the ground and Achilles looked down at

him. "I don't resent your attack on me; I respect you for trying to protect the boy. But how could you think that I go around killing children?" Achilles spat on the ground, showing what he thought of the idea. He had fought in many wars, even alongside Pedasus himself apparently, but had never participated, nor allowed those following him to participate, in the slaughter of innocents. Honour had its own rules.

His attention returned to the boy. "What's your name, boy?"

"Diomedes, sir," was the hesitant reply, as he continued to alternate his eyes between Achilles and Pedasus.

"Leave your bow and quiver here, Diomedes. I won't kill a child, but you do need to make reparation for the honour Hector lost when you attacked me during our duel under a white flag of truce," he said, looking at Eudoros who nodded his agreement, ever the silent mentor. "You are going to work off that debt as my servant boy."

Achilles turned and offered a hand to Pedasus to help him rise. Pedasus looked at it in disgust. "At least this way the boy will live," he said in a low voice.

"And I will make sure he is better fed and trained than is possible here at present," said Achilles quietly.

As if a compromise had been reached, Pedasus took Achilles' hand with his uninjured one, and pulled himself to his feet. Wrapping a dirty piece of cloth around his arm, Pedasus made his way over to Diomedes and spoke in a low urgent voice with the boy. Achilles couldn't make out precisely what they said, but the boy was arguing with his uncle and gesturing towards Achilles and the gate. Eventually, he seemed to deflate further.

Achilles made his way over to the boy, taking him by the arm to lead him away. Pedasus called out, "Your bow will be waiting when you get back, Diomedes."

It finally seemed to strike the boy what was actually

happening. It was probably the first time he would have left the city, given how long the siege had lasted. He was leaving with the man who had just killed his hero, into the midst of several thousand of the enemy. Trying to pull his arm free, he called back to Pedasus, "No, uncle! Don't let them take me; you can't let *him* take me."

"Go, boy. You have a debt to work off. Accept your actions and return to me a man," Pedasus called back, though Achilles could see his wet eyes as the boy was being led away.

"Coward!" Diomedes screamed over and over, becoming hysterical in his fear. Achilles watched Pedasus drop his head; he had seen men broken before, but could not understand how it had just happened to this man. He wasn't even Diomedes' father, but when the boy screamed out his accusation of cowardice, Achilles could see that whatever had held this man together had just snapped.

He took a firm hold on Diomedes' arm, and pulled him through the gates, which were held open for him and his men. Diomedes stopped screaming only when he could no longer see Pedasus for the hundred Myrmidons marching behind Achilles; with the dull thud of those huge gates closing behind them, the last of the boy's strength seemed to seep out of him. After that, he simply followed where Achilles led.

Achilles brought the boy back to his tent. He had scarcely been noticed in the crowds of Greek revellers celebrating the death of Hector, except for the occasional few who stopped Achilles to congratulate him and tried to drag him into their festivities. Diomedes sniffed now and again, but showed no other reaction as he followed. Before going inside, Achilles called to Eudoros. "Have the men disperse. That was good work at the pit," he said. Orders were being called out as he turned to go inside.

As they entered his tent, Achilles realised they were not alone; Agamemnon and his retinue were inside waiting for him. Quickly, he sent Diomedes to a quiet corner. "Keep your mouth shut, regardless of what you hear, boy," he warned.

Agamemnon, relaxing on his plush, cushioned carpet, raised a cup to him as he returned. "Ah, the returning champion," he laughed. "Well fought, Achilles." He laughed, but to Achilles it sounded a little forced. "Another great victory for my army. That will help morale."

"Thank you, Agamemnon," responded Achilles. "Did you call over just to congratulate me, or is there something else on your mind?"

"Straight to the point as always; that's what I like about you, Achilles," the king laughed. Then the smile left his face, and he leant forward on the cushions, staring at Achilles like a hunting eagle spotting a mouse. "Why did you return the body?"

"He was a prince. He is to be buried with all the ceremony which his position deserved." Achilles wasn't intimidated by that stare. He had faced much worse on the battlefield.

"I wanted his armour, Achilles, you knew that; and I wanted to display his body for the army." Agamemnon's grip on his cup was white-knuckled. "You took that from me."

"That was a personal duel, Agamemnon," Achilles almost hissed back. "You may claim it for the army or the war if you wish, but that was a duel over my brother; the armour and the body were mine, to do with as I liked." As he finished speaking, he turned away to pour himself a drink.

"You will learn respect, boy; you will learn that I am your king," said Agamemnon in a low, dangerous voice, and Achilles heard the low rasp of sword being drawn from leather sheath.

Dropping his cup of wine, he continued the move into drawing his sword and dropped to the ground, rolling away from the table and coming up on one knee with his sword at Ajax's throat. Ajax the Locrian was a good warrior who might have some chance against Achilles, but right now his face was full of fear.

"You are right to look afraid, Ajax. You obviously know that this sword – the sword supplied by your priests, Agamemnon - was poisoned." He spoke very slowly and deliberately. "You removed any honour I might have gained from that fight by poisoning the sword, Agamemnon. That is why his body was returned to Troy."

Agamemnon sat back a little, trying to look relaxed. "Put that sword away, Ajax," he ordered. He had once been a huge warrior, feared on the battlefield, but time and easy living had taken its toll on the king. Where solid muscle had once stood out proud he now had quite a girth, and an extra chin or two, hiding under his beard. Achilles might have worried about facing him in his prime, but he was well past that now. "Obviously I would not want to risk the life of my greatest champion in a silly personal duel, lad. I had to give you every possible advantage."

Ajax always followed Agamemnon's orders, his perfect little soldier. Achilles scowled at the man as he put his sword away, and did not lower his own. "How very considerate of you, Agamemnon," Achilles replied, "but the two swords were thrown together by the priests. Wasn't it lucky that I got the right one? If I went back out there for Hector's sword, what are the chances that I'd find that to be poisoned also?" Lifting his cup of wine from the table, with the sword still close to Ajax, Achilles took a long swallow and kept his eyes firmly fixed on Agamemnon.

Looking shocked at the indictment, Agamemnon sputtered in outrage. "Those filthy priests, you can't trust any of them," he shouted. "Odysseus! Odysseus, bring me those priests. I want them hung up by the ankles and flogged."

Odysseus rose from the corner of the tent to fetch the priests. Achilles met his eyes. "Sit down, old man. The priests threw themselves in the fire pit when I called for them after the fight. They didn't die pleasantly," he said. Looking back at Agamemnon, he eventually sheathed his sword. "Convenient, wouldn't you say?"

"Not for me, if it means you are still accusing me of this treachery," said Agamemnon.

He really intended to continue with the charade, knowing that Achilles knew. It was embarrassing to watch. Beginning to unbuckle his armour, Achilles turned his back to Agamemnon and called for hot water to be brought to him. He barely glanced at Agamemnon as he said, "Unless you wish to wash my back, I would appreciate some privacy while I bathe."

It would have been a considerably rude dismissal even to an equal, and Agamemnon considered himself much more than that.

"I am your king, and I will have a more respectful tone from you," thundered Agamemnon. "You do not dismiss me, I dismiss you."

"No, Agamemnon; my father is my king. He swore to you to protect our people and I followed his orders to take the Myrmidons and fight for you, but you are not *my* king."

"A time will come when you kneel before me, Achilles. I would have had you killed for what you've just said if we were not at war with Troy." He had good control over his temper, but Achilles could see that he was trying to be more cunning now that he was no longer the warrior who could solve everything with his war hammer. He relied heavily on Odysseus for advice; the old man was clever.

"Get your men ready, Achilles. We will be attacking the city later this evening, while they are still in shock from Hector's fall today."

"You may be, but my men and I will not," Achilles replied, without looking. He was stripped to his loincloth now, and water was arriving for his wash. "A prince deserves his funeral. My men are standing down today and tomorrow."

"Very well, but you may not be among the first to enter Troy," replied Agamemnon as he swept out of the tent, followed by Ajax and Odysseus.

Achilles laughed as Agamemnon left, murmuring, "I think you'd better stop the army drinking and celebrating; you could be attacking on your own, great king." The curtains swung closed behind Agamemnon, and Odysseus turned to wink slyly at Achilles as he departed. Achilles smiled.

Now they were gone, Achilles had time to deal with the boy, and called him to come over. "So you can control yourself when you have a mind to," he said. The boy still looked terrified. "I thought Agamemnon talking about Hector might have set you off again." Tapping his fingers on the side of his cup, thinking, he looked up again at Diomedes.

"If you had started mouthing off to him, and he had realised where you came from, he would almost certainly have demanded you in exchange for Hector's body. Do you understand that?" he asked. The boy nodded reluctantly. Achilles was beginning to wonder if he'd ever speak again. "There would have been precious little I could do to stop him, but I don't want to give you to him; it's to me you owe the debt, myself and Hector. While you are here, you are to behave as my servant. You will find I am not a harsh master. Now eat and clean yourself."

He gestured to the food at the table and the washing water he'd had brought, as he finished drying himself off. "There should be a few clean tunics in that chest over there, which belonged to my brother." He turned away. "You are about the same size as he was when we first arrived in troy."

"Hector was poisoned?" muttered a small, scared voice.

Glancing over his shoulder, Achilles saw the pain in the boy's eyes. "Aye, lad, he was poisoned," he replied. Pulling on a fresh tunic, Achilles sat down on the bed which Agamemnon had vacated. "I am innocent of that." He shook his head sadly. "Hector was my friend. War put us on opposite sides but he didn't deserve that, any more than Patroclus did."

"But you killed him," Diomedes pleaded.

"I survived," Achilles replied. "Remember, Hector was trying to kill me at the same time. You don't have to hate someone because fate has made them your enemy." That was what life had taught Achilles. He had killed a lot of good men in his lifetime, men he had liked and respected, but, at the time when they had died, they had been the enemy. To look at it in any other way would drive you mad. If you thought of it as killing your friend – ah, Hector -

Looking at the boy, Achilles decided that some good might yet come out of that fight.

Chapter Three

Agamemnon stormed out of the tent. He would show that arrogant fool! He would take Troy and leave Achilles sitting in his tent, lost to history like so many of the dead and forgotten.

"Ready the men, Ajax," he shouted. "We attack!"

"Ah, sir-" Ajax hesitated, and Agamemnon rounded on him, ready to gut him, until Odysseus intervened, putting a restraining arm on Agamemnon's shoulder.

"Peace, Agamemnon. Look around you. The men believe that killing Hector means we can't lose the war now. They've already been drinking for half the day; if we attack now, they won't even be able to climb the ladders. It would be easy for Trojan archers to pick us off," said Odysseus.

Agamemnon took a calming breath before shrugging off Odysseus' hand.

"What would you suggest, then? Should we give them time to overcome their shock and raise another hero in Hector's place? Then we will be back where we started. Meanwhile, that arrogant shit sits in his tent and laughs at me. I should have him killed!" he fumed. He turned to stare at the tent as if he wanted to go back in and do just that.

"Ten years, Odysseus! We have been here for ten years. How much longer?" He seemed to slump under Odysseus' gaze; the strain of holding this army together for so many years at war was showing. Maybe he was ready to listen to Odysseus' plan.

"I don't know that, Agamemnon, but I'm working on an

idea," said Odysseus. "Perhaps it might solve both problems, if I can just work out the remaining details."

"Not another attempt to distract them, Odysseus. That hasn't worked whenever we've used it before. We need to get inside," Agamemnon interrupted.

"Not a distraction, no; something different. It's a big risk, but if it works we will be past their walls," replied Odysseus, watching the interest in Agamemnon's face.

"What's your plan, then?" asked Agamemnon. "Tell me."

Yes, he was ready. He would take the chance Odysseus was offering him; anything to get inside those gates, where they could bring their numbers to bear on the much smaller Trojan army.

"Just give me a few more days to work out the details, Agamemnon, then I can bring you the finished plan and you can have the glory instead of Achilles." Odysseus kept his face perfectly straight as he watched with interest how Agamemnon's eyes lit up. That last had sold it to him. As much as he wanted to take Troy, he wanted more to be able to take credit for it and not have Achilles basking in conquering glory.

"For the present, join your men. Be seen to be one of them," Odysseus said. "Celebrate with them, and they will start to associate the victory with you. It will bind them more tightly to you. Tomorrow you can attack, when they have sobered up."

Agamemnon was nodding his head thoughtfully. "Maybe you're right, Odysseus. I'm just growing so frustrated, sitting here. It feels like we are doing nothing but bleeding men to assault those walls. Get your plan together, and bring it to me." Having made up his mind, he finally seemed to relax. "I like your plan for tonight," he said. "Let's go and find some wine." Wrapping an arm around Odysseus' shoulder, he led him away towards the sounds of festivity.

Hours later, Odysseus finally managed to pull away from Agamemnon, and head for the comfort of his own tent. Already he felt the effect of the wine he'd drunk, and he wasn't looking forward to an assault in the morning. 'Bleeding men,' Agamemnon had said, but it was more like cutting an artery; a sword to the stomach wouldn't bleed as much. As many men as Agamemnon lost throwing them at the wall, he replaced by bringing new recruits from Greece. The latest batch were little more than beardless boys.

The Trojans hadn't lost a third of the number they had, and with those roof gardens they had begun growing inside the city, the chances of the siege's ever actually starving them out were looking slim.

Still, if Agamemnon took his advice with this plan, all that could be over soon; the Greek army would get inside the gates. If it came to fighting in the streets, the superior numbers of the Greek army would count for a great deal, for they had nearly five times the numbers that the Trojans had. Getting inside, that would be the trick. Greeks loved their tricks; the only thing better than beating an enemy was outsmarting him.

He would outsmart them all right; he always had. While Agamemnon was a hammer, smashing all resistance to build his empire, Odysseus was always planning. He had held his own through patience and by outsmarting those who would try to take it from him. Now was not the time for planning, however, not with a head full of wine; any decisions he made now would be questionable, to say the least.

Stumbling down another sand dune, he made his way to where he thought his tent should be, tripping over his own feet in the cool night sand.

"You're going the wrong way, old man."

The voice, calm and sober, carried over the sand, over the

sound of a party that might last all night. With bleary eyes he looked around, scanning the sand and the dunes. Even for someone in his position, being alone on this beach at night could be dangerous; maybe especially for someone in his position. Anyone wanting to hurt Agamemnon might well see him as the brains behind the throne.

"Who's there?" he called, trying to sound more sober than he felt, standing up straighter.

"Your tent is up the beach," came a reply from the darkness. "Walk towards that flickering fire you see up the beach; you should find it there."

Letting out a breath which he didn't know he had been holding, Odysseus looked to the left, halfway up a sand dune, searching for any reflection of the jet-black toughened leather armour he knew would be there, since he'd recognised the voice. He couldn't see what he was looking for, but walked in the direction from which the voice had come.

"What are you doing, out here in the dark alone?" he said. "I thought you were developing wisdom earlier when you asked about the poison on the second blade; you shouldn't try to prove me wrong by leaving yourself open to Agamemnon's henchmen like this." Stumbling up the last few feet, using his hands to help himself up the slope, he fell down on his back beside Achilles.

"Don't worry, old man. There are a hundred of my men, sober, within calling distance from this dune. I had to signal that you were no threat so that you could safely approach me." He took a swig from a wineskin he was holding and offered it to Odysseus. "As for what I am doing here, after today I needed some time alone to think and this is the closest I can come to it." He accepted the wineskin back. "I thought you would still be celebrating with Agamemnon."

"I'm not a young man anymore, Achilles. I can't keep up

with the likes of you or even him, and, by the gods, that man can hold his wine." Sitting up straighter, he looked out over the bay from where they sat, moonlight on the horizon reflected on the calm seas. No wonder the Trojans fought for this place, he thought; it was beautiful. "Is there anything that talking to an old man can help with?"

"I just wonder if I am fated to be remembered for killing everyone I ever respected. You are known for your wisdom. If Troy survives, Priam will be remembered for building one of the greatest cities of the world, Odysseus. Even Agamemnon will be remembered for building an empire." Taking a long drink from the wineskin, he offered it to Odysseus again, but Odysseus declined. "If you're going to sit talking to me, you're going to drink with me," Achilles insisted, pushing the wineskin into the old man's hand. "Me? I'll be remembered for killing my friends."

"War makes butchers of all good men, Achilles. You know this; you have lived through it for long enough."

"But why does it have to be my sword that finished him? Why does fate line me up with them, Odysseus?"

Taking a long drink from the wineskin, Odysseus looked Achilles in the eye and seemed to sober temporarily. "Fate lines you up with lesser men too, Achilles; you just don't remember them, their names or their faces. They are lost to history. Achilles, you are a champion and there is always someone wanting to know which champion is the greatest, so you will end up facing the other heroes and they will often be friends, or your own heroes. How else would you have earned your name?"

Sitting there in silence, Odysseus felt something of Achilles' pain. After a while the question came to him. "Achilles, do you want to do what is right, or are you more concerned about how you are remembered?"

"Can't a man have both?" replied Achilles, but his tone and

face admitted that he didn't believe it likely. "I understand why my father swore his oath to Agamemnon, Odysseus. I don't blame him for it; it was the only way to save our city from being wiped out. I just wish there was some other way."

"I know, son; I was forced to do the same thing myself. Achilles, today you performed a great deed. Your name, your place in history, has been secured for all the ages. No Greek will ever forget the day Achilles slew the greatest of Troy's heroes." Taking another drink from the wineskin, he continued, "They all saw him fall; to them, what you did was right."

"Yes, but you and I know he didn't deserve it, Odysseus. You heard my brother's last words as he lay dying. It was Agamemnon's fault, not Hector's; Agamemnon promised Patroclus my father's throne, knowing Patroclus hated him." There were tears glistening by the moonlight in Achilles' eyes. "You warned me about the poison, and for that, I thank you."

"There is no need for thanks among friends, Achilles." Odysseus looked away over the waves. "I cannot wait to return home. I miss it, and my old bones long to take their ease in front of the fire."

Achilles snorted a laugh with no humour in it. "Don't worry, old man," he said. "With Hector down, Agamemnon will throw everything against those walls. The Trojans should collapse, though there may be one among them who can rise to a defence and hold the walls."

"You know that Agamemnon will not allow you to take your father's place after him, don't you, Achilles? That's why he tried that game with Patroclus, lad. Frankly, I'd be surprised if he let you live to return home." He tapped Achilles on the arm. "He can't risk having someone strong like you on the throne of the Myrmidons. You would argue with him too much; that's why he wanted Patroclus. He was softer, easier to manipulate, and

Agamemnon could have controlled him."

"I don't think too much about getting home, old friend," replied Achilles. "My mother told me before I left that if I went to Troy, I would seal my place in history, but would never return home."

"That's right; your mother has the gift of foresight, doesn't she? I had forgotten," said Odysseus.

"I don't know if that's true, old man; it may be old wives' tales. I think she listens and understands men. I think she knows that if enough people believe something will happen, they will work to see it happen. After that, I think she guesses." Achilles laughed and took another drink from his skin.

"Don't discount the old ways, son; old wives' tales often prove to be true. Old wisdom is passed down through the generations and proven true again and again. The fates have a way of making things so, regardless of what we do."

Achilles laughed again. "Very well, old man; you would know," and this time there was true mirth in his laughter.

"Agamemnon doesn't intend to go home after this, Achilles. We were talking over a few drinks, and it seems he intends to subjugate the Phoenicians before moving against the Egyptians, if he can take Troy. He wants to control the entire Aegean Sea. I'm afraid he has run mad from trying to take Troy." Odysseus watched carefully for Achilles' reaction. "It could be a while before any of us sees our home."

"Didn't you talk to him and tell him that was crazy?" Achilles was incredulous. "The men need a break, Odysseus. They have families, and the army needs rebuilding."

"Regardless of all that, Achilles, if he beats the Trojans here there will be no stopping him, not while he still has an army. The question is, Achilles: are you more concerned about doing what's right or about how you will be remembered?"

"What are you getting at, Odysseus?"

"I have a plan which I intend to put before Agamemnon tomorrow, one which may get us inside the city. If all goes well, it would place enough men inside Troy to hold the gates open for the Greek army. It will be extremely dangerous, but do you still want to be among the first inside the city?"

Screaming and shouting from the direction of the city caught their attention, and moving as one they both sprinted to the top of the sand dune on which they were sitting. Grabbing a Myrmidon by the arm, Achilles shouted, "What's happening out there?"

"It's the Trojans, lord; they seem to have attacked the Greeks in the dark."

Chapter Four

That arrogant whoreson! Who in Hades did he think he was? Killing Hector was one thing, that was a matter of honour after Patroclus had fallen to Hector's sword, but to take the boy while still under the peace of the duel? That was uncalled for. Achilles was just flexing his muscles, trying to prove that he could do as he pleased. And to claim it was for Hector's honour! Yes, the boy had fired the arrow, but he was just a boy.

"I liked the kid," Achenia muttered to himself.

The whole square seemed to have stopped in stunned silence, staring at the gates that had shut behind Achilles' back only moments before. He looked around at the sea of shocked faces, all immobile, until his gaze fell upon Pedasus sitting on the ground. Diomedes' uncle had sunk back down as the boy had been led away. He was the exception; instead of looking at the gate, he was huddled over, his injured arm wrapped in a cloth which had started out white, but now had blood staining its length. In his good arm he held the keg he had brought up to the gate tower, taking an occasional swig out of it while muttering to himself and shaking his head.

Achenia had been there for the death of his brother, and had heard his oath to look after Diomedes, but against Achilles Pedasus was like a child grabbing at his father's legs. He couldn't be blamed for what had just happened, but Achenia knew that that was what he was doing to himself.

"All right, you sons of goats, stop gawking like a group of

old women!" shouted Achenia in his best parade-ground voice. "Get that damn white flag down; I want to see the phoenix flying in one minute. All archers on the walls! I want a double rotation doing circuits of the walls, in case those accursed Greeks try to catch us on the hop."

That snapped most of them out of their shock, and the soldiers started to do as they'd been ordered. All the extra archers piled on to the walkway, along the crenellations.

"Post some sharp reliable lookouts up there, Heraclitus, then get yourself down here," Achenia shouted. "I want to know if it looks like they're going to attack. Arimnestos, Priscus, come here now."

Heraclitus, a tall, lean man in his late thirties, bearded, with long hair thinning on top, raced along the crenellated battlements; he stopped with a few archers to issue orders, before making his way to the stairs. Priscus and Arimnestos were already on their way across the square towards him.

Achenia walked over to where Pedasus was sitting on the ground, holding his arm.

"Pedasus?" he said gently.

It didn't look as if Pedasus had heard him; he kept on muttering to himself.

"Pedasus, are you okay? Can you stand?" he asked quietly. It would be bad for the common soldiers to think that one of their commanding officers might be losing his mind.

"Pedasus!" Achenia slapped Pedasus lightly on the cheek, snapping the man out of whatever trance his mind had been in.

"He took him, Achenia." There was a haunted look in Pedasus' eyes. He didn't seem to be looking at Achenia so much as looking through him. "I tried to stop him. I tried."

"Can you stand? How's your arm?" Achenia tried to lift him to his feet, but Pedasus' legs didn't seem to be supporting him.

Achenia got a waft of his breath and was nearly knocked back by the reek of alcohol. "How much of this have you had, man?" Achenia asked, grabbing the small keg from Pedasus' grasp. Shaking it, he found the keg nearly empty, and tossed it away across the square. "Heraclitus, give me a hand with him, will you?" he called over and Heraclitus helped him lift Pedasus under his other shoulder. "Back to the barracks with him; we'll let him sleep it off." Fortunately the barracks was only a short walk away, but when they left him in his bed he was still mumbling to himself as he lay there.

"Try to get some sleep, Pedasus. The boy will be all right," said Achenia, though he had trouble believing his own words.

Leaving him there, they made their way outside to where Priscus and Arimnestos waited and he called them into the barracks, closing the solid wooden door behind him. They made their way to the meeting room in the back where the officers often met to discuss strategy, rations, deployment and all the other little things that kept the army and the siege going.

"So," Achenia said, as they settled themselves around the table, "what now?"

"What do you mean?" Arimnestos asked wearily.

"I mean exactly what I say, Arimnestos. Hector fell to Achilles' blade, and Pedasus is as good as useless in there; what can we do to salvage something from this situation?" He looked around the table, but few of the men would hold his intense gaze, their eyes dropping to the table as if embarrassed. "The morale of the men has been seriously damaged today. The Greeks think that because our leader is dead our men are disheartened. They're going to press home this advantage; you know it as well as I do."

"And what would you have us do, Achenia?" asked Priscus. "What can we do?"

"Well, for a start, the officers can stop looking like the war has already been lost!" thundered Achenia. "The men take their attitudes from those leading them."

"How dare you speak to us like that, Achenia! We are nobility in Troy, you are but a soldier. Pole march you may be, but still a soldier."

"And in wartime that means I outrank you, boy, which I do right now!"

"Calm down, both of you, or we're going to start doing the Greeks' work for them in here." Heraclitus was ever the voice of reason. Even in the heat of battle, Heraclitus always seemed calm and in control when all about him were frantically fighting for their lives. He seemed to enjoy stress, to thrive on it.

It was just as well he was here, because Achenia could feel his own heat rising as these boys he had considered friends started to condescend to him, though he knew it was just the stress they were under after such a day.

"Let's hear him out, lads; it's obvious Achenia has something in mind," said Heraclitus.

So far Priscus seemed to be taking a back seat, watching the others as he leaned back and started cleaning his nails with his belt knife. He was short for a Trojan, and most people thought his mother had had a little extramarital experience while his father was away; apart from his size and stocky build, this was partly because he didn't act like a noble, enjoying a good brawl after a night's drinking. No one would have dared say it to his face, however.

Achenia looked around the table, and this time the others were heeding him. He took a deep breath. "It sounds as if the Greeks are out there celebrating Hector's death; is that right, Heraclitus?"

Heraclitus nodded.

"So they're all drinking and feasting?"

Again Heraclitus nodded; his face showed that he knew what Achenia was going to say next. "Then what if we hit them tonight, when it's dark and they're not expecting it?"

"That's crazy," spluttered Arimnestos. "Their army outnumbers us by at least ten to one, Achenia. Look, I know you want to hit back at them, but even drunk there are enough of them to swamp us."

"I'm not talking about trying to destroy them, Arimnestos, I'm talking about butchering as many as we can in a short raid; a small victory to raise the men's morale. As soon as we face resistance, we pull back."

"There's something you don't know, Achenia," said Priscus slowly. Achenia leaned forward to listen, but Arimnestos spoke right over Priscus.

"No, Priscus; he could be on to something here. A short, decisive one-sided victory would help morale and hurt the enemy." He looked around the table as he spoke. "You all saw them; they're drinking all evening and not a man out there is wearing more than a belt knife. Heraclitus, could your archers provide cover?"

"Yes," Heraclitus replied, looking interested, "but as soon as those gates open, the Greeks will be on to us and we would have armed men pouring out of their camp before we got twenty paces."

"No," said Achenia, looking deeply into his eyes, trying to install his own sense of belief in Heraclitus. "Here's how we can do it."

An hour later, as the sun slowly began to descend towards the horizon in that slow crawl typical of late summer, the four commanders strode purposefully from the barracks, showing none of the lethargy which had slowed their footsteps when they'd entered. The square in front of the gates was still half-full of soldiers talking in hushed voices, looking decidedly uncertain about what they were doing there. The emergence of their commanders brought more than one of them to attention. Those who didn't notice the officers kept talking and found themselves getting a sharp elbow in the ribs that brought them up short.

The commanders looked around at the gathered soldiers, then exchanged glances between themselves before, one by one, they each nodded to Achenia. Nodding back, he strode forward as a hush fell and a sense of anticipation spread. The only sounds came from a celebration over the wall as the Greeks partied into the evening.

"I want every man armed and armoured within the hour. The first thousand back in this square get to have some fun tonight," he shouted. The soldiers were shocked by the order and looked at one another in hesitation. "Go now!" he called in his parade-ground voice, and suddenly the square was emptying. Men scattered in various directions as they made for their barracks or homes, or wherever they were staying and storing their equipment. Suddenly they had a purpose again, something they had lost as they'd seen Hector carried through those gates.

During the lull as they waited for the men to return, Achenia led the other commanders to the barracks mess hall where the cooks had a stew of tough donkey meat and black bread, standard military food on the current meagre supplies.

"So, you'll have five hundred archers on the wall covering us, Heraclitus?" Achenia had just finishing organising the placement of the soldiers for the night's action while they were eating. "I wish Pedasus was ready for this; it might pull him out of the stupor he's in. I would feel more comfortable having him by my side."

"Yes, he's first rate on the line," Arimnestos replied, "but I'm a little afraid that this has broken him. The man's suffered a lot, what with his wife and kid dying, and then his brother too, last year. This war has been hard on everyone, but I don't think he's been coping too well since. Anyway, he isn't going to be fit tonight, so we must make do with what we have."

"We'd better get back out there and see who we have, then," said Priscus, rising from the table.

"Heraclitus, would you mind taking a run up to the wall and checking on the Greeks? Priscus, Arimnestos, come with me." Achenia stood up as well and they began making their way back out to organise their men.

Twilight had fallen when they emerged to the eager eyes of five thousand waiting soldiers in neatly-dressed ranks. Shields were held at waist height, spears erect in every hand. The three men walked forward as Heraclitus ran to the wall and up the steps to the battlements, taking them two or three at a time. When he'd reached the top, Achenia watched him look out over the wall before walking quickly across to talk to a few of the men whom he'd put on watch earlier. Exchanging a few words, and nodding his head, he moved on to the next.

It wasn't easy to make out what he was doing in the fading light, but Achenia had always had sharp eyes. Heraclitus finished talking with his fourth lookout, and stopped for a minute to watch the Greeks with his own eyes, before turning and making his way back down to where Achenia waited with Priscus and Arimnestos. They were making a show of examining the ranks to kill time until he came back, and had sent seven men home already because their uniforms weren't up to standard. Little things like that might seem silly and petty when they were about to go into action, but it was one of the first things Achenia had learnt in his time in service: distract the men with a trivial worry to keep their minds off what was about to happen; put them off asking any questions, as they all suddenly become very conscious of their own uniforms.

Heraclitus came close and whispered quickly into Achenia's ear. "It's as you thought; they've been drinking and celebrating since they brought him back, and they're still out of armour."

"Perfect," muttered Achenia and stood back a few paces looking over the army. All through the ranks men seemed to be leaning forward, trying to catch a whisper of what was happening. Nervous anticipation was rife.

"Cyrus!" bellowed Achenia. "Which ten commanders were back on the field and formed up first?"

The young commander stepped forward from the ranks. "Archilogos, Demeos, Drussos, Brasides," the names came instantly as he rhymed them off. "Bulos, Vaako, Tenor, Pedotoleus, Kerberos and Castiel, sir," he bellowed.

"The named commanders, step forward," said Achenia and the men moved out of rank towards him. He looked them over. "You're ready to take back some honour from the Greeks?" He walked up to the front, looked over all the men assembled in the huge square and raised his voice and pitch to carry as far as possible. Of course the men at the back wouldn't hear, but those closer would pass on what he said and it would filter through.

"Today the Greeks slew mighty Hector," he said, as the silence of a frosty night fell over the men. The only noise came from the Greeks, like the buzzing of a hornet's nest over the wall. "Today they slew one of the greatest men in all of Troy, thinking that the fall of Hector is the fall of Troy." His head swivelled, looking across the sea of faces.

The feelings of the men were easy to see from where he stood. Sadness, anger, shock, all the emotions he himself was feeling; from more than one, however, he could sense fear. That was what Hector's death was intended to do: to sow fear through all of Troy, fear that they had indeed lost everything in the loss of Hector.

The morale of an army was as important as their arms and weapons, as Achenia had learned while fighting beside Hector and Achilles for the Persian 'king of kings' when they were all young men. He stopped searching the faces and chose one, that of a young soldier, on which to focus his attention as he spoke.

"But today I tell you that Troy is not dead because of the fall of one man, because Troy is much greater than any one man! Troy is the spirit, the embodiment, of all men who want to be free of the yoke of Mycenaean oppression. I tell you today that, as long as one man is left to defend the phoenix, then Troy lives."

A roar accompanied his words, as men thumped spears against their shields in appreciation of his words. But the fear was still visible in many of their faces. After the loss of Hector, they wouldn't believe that the Greeks could be defeated unless he could grant them a victory, and if that didn't happen soon, then despair could break his army before the Greeks made another attempt on the gates.

"They have taken their shot and think us broken," he shouted. "Now is our time to show them that we are not."

He had never enjoyed giving speeches, but someone had to.

Pulling aside the ten officers, Achenia spoke quickly. "Archilogos, Demeos, Drussos, Brasides and Bulos, you're with Arimnestos and Priscus. Arimnestos is in command. The rest of you, get your commands; you're with me. Remember, Heraclitus," he added, turning back to him, "every archer on the wall, but try to stay low and out of sight until you're needed."

He turned back to the rest of the assembled men, and immediately picked out Demetrius.

"Vaako, you're in command here. Form up all the men left with you to hold the gate for us to come back, and have them ready in case anything goes wrong. Arimnestos," he said, gripping his forearm, “I’ll meet you in front of the gate.”

With that they turned away from each other and moved to their commands.

It was impossible to move five hundred men in full armour silently in the dark streets; there was creaking and the light clash of thigh guards against breast plates on armour that in many cases had originally been made for the soldiers’ fathers before they died in the war. It created quite a clamour, even when they were trying to be quiet, but Arimnestos didn’t think that the Greeks could hear anything over the noise they themselves were making, drinking and carousing.

At the north gate, the watch on the walls were surprised to see the men arrive and Arimnestos had to show his seal of command before they would let him near the gate – even he, with five hundred men behind him.

The delay irritated him but he was glad the twenty men on watch at the gate were taking their duties seriously. After all, they would all die if he decided to take his men against them to escape the city, but they would probably make enough noise to alert more guardsmen to hold the smaller gate. Death before dishonour, and all that.

“What’s it like out there?” he asked the gate officer, an older man who would already have been retired and living off his pension on a nice farm if it had been a time of peace.

“Dead on this side, sir. We can hear them in the distance but the party hasn’t moved in this direction. Occasionally someone walks around with a torch to take a piss but that’s about it,” he replied. “What’s it like out front? Are you going to be coming back this way, sir? We can watch for you and try to hold the gate open.”

“No, as soon as my men are out you lock it tightly again unless you hear from me directly, All right?” The man nodded.

"The front – well, the front is like the spring festival of Demeter. It almost makes you wish we could go out there and join in the fun," he chuckled, "but we're going to have a little party of our own instead."

Turning, he called Priscus forward. "Do you want to take the lead? Go out before the men and look around; keep them in order and quiet as they come out. I'll follow."

Priscus nodded and headed out through the gate. Seconds later, he was calling the soldiers to follow.

Arimnestos and the gate guard stood back, to let the soldiers through the gate, and spoke a little of inconsequential things, passing the time it took for five hundred men to pass through. Time seemed to go slowly, as it so often does before a battle, and Arimnestos had to hold his hands to his sides to prevent himself fidgeting irritably while he waited. A commander had to project confidence or his nervousness would leak into the men, and that sort of thing led to silly mistakes. Any mistakes here could see them all killed. The Greeks were over-confident, but that didn't mean they were all fools; they had men like Odysseus and Achilles, after all.

After what was probably only a few minutes, but felt like most of an hour, the last of the soldiers passed through the small gate into the dark night outside. Arimnestos clasped forearms with the gate officer. "Good luck tonight, lord. I'll watch from the gate tower in case you need to return this way," the man said.

"You have my thanks, but pray that isn't necessary. If it is, it means we have failed in our mission." Arimnestos passed through the gate into the dark night beyond, where he could just make out his men shuffling for position in the darkness.

Calling his commanders to him, he explained what they were about to do that night. Even in a night so dark, with no moon, he could make out the serious lines of their disapproving faces.

There was little honour to be had in killing men too drunk to defend themselves. It would be like wiping out a village of women and children.

"This is how it must be," he told them. "Come tomorrow, those same men will be climbing our wall, intent on wiping our city from the earth. Think of your families still inside those walls. Think of your children. Tonight, we give them a slightly better chance."

Grimly they nodded. Knowing that it was necessary did make it any less distasteful.

Keeping as close as possible to the walls of the city, they made their slow way west along the wall towards the front of Troy. The main gate and beach of Troy was just ahead of them, along with a sea of Greeks, as far as the eye could discern.

Looking behind, Arimnestos saw his own wave of men creeping along the walls, rarely even glimpsing the shine of reflected light on their polished bronze armour. He could see the hands of the gods in the night being so dark, with no moon to give away their position. Low clouds concealed even the stars.

They made the corner without their position being discovered and Arimnestos looked around. It looked as if half of Greece was right there in front of their gates, just outside bow range from the walls, but Arimnestos knew that this represented only about ten per cent of all the Greeks who had come to destroy Troy. The rest would be in camp on the beach, or already asleep somewhere in the sand dunes, or, indeed, still on duty. The Greeks had a good system and always had a quarter of their soldiers on duty, but looking out there, he could see only the drunken reverie of celebration, as if they had already taken Troy.

The twang of a bowstring almost directly above brought Arimnestos quickly out of his thoughts; he heard the arrow thump down somewhere out in the darkness to his right. Squinting into the blackness, he could just make out dim whiteness falling over in the distance. Apparently, a Greek had needed to use the latrine and they hadn't seen him until now. Looking up towards the top of the walls he could make out Heraclitus, leaning over the wall to salute him with his bow. Arimnestos released a deep breath.

He turned to his commanders who had moved up close to him, awaiting their orders. They were mostly young men, often too young for the position they held, but having risen through the ranks through a dedication rooted in hatred of the Greeks. Archilogos, only seventeen, had lost his father and two older brothers defending Troy. Demeos was an older veteran, bearing a scar across his repeatedly broken nose which dominated his face. Drussos had just begun in the army at fifteen when this war had started, and was now twenty-five. His family home was outside the city walls; his family had been taken in the arrival of the Greeks, and were now enslaved to Ajax. Brasides and Bulos were Spartans who had turned after Menelaus swore to follow Agamemnon, taking Sparta into his war as a kingdom sworn to him. Menelaus had been made king as a foreigner who happened to have married the old king's daughter, and that was bad enough, as he had no Spartan noble blood; but swearing allegiance to another foreign power was unthinkable and had alienated them. If it had just been troy, they would have understood it for the betrayal by Paris, but Agamemnon had been spending spartan lives all over the Aegean to build his empire long before this. They had been taken in by Priaam and found a new home, and a new loyalty here.

Whispering quietly, Arimnestos began to give his orders.

"When Achenia moves into position over at the south corner we will receive a signal," he murmured, looking at the grim faces. "Then we slaughter everyone we can get our hands on until we meet serious resistance." He looked down, embarrassed at what was coming next, but knowing that it was necessary to the survival of their city. "At the first sign of organised resistance, we fall back into a phalanx twelve deep to face whatever's coming. We retreat the phalanx towards the front gates and make our way inside."

Especially for the Spartans, this would be seen as cowardice, but even the Trojan commanders looked annoyed. Years of training, however, had taught them not to question their commanders while on a mission. The necessity of it was plain to them all, but that couldn't make them like it. Drussos, however, saw the risk to the city while the others just grumbled. He was a smart man and a good commander for his age.

"What happens if we face a full assault before we get back inside? If we leave the city gates open with the Greeks coming down on us, it will put the whole city at risk," he pointed out.

"If they can organise that so quickly we're in a lot of trouble, but the rest of the army are formed up inside to hold the gates and the walls are heavily manned with archers to cover our retreat. Don't allow your men to go too far outside the archers' range. Beyond that, the last rank out will have to hold the enemy while the gates are closed with them outside."

That was a hard pill to swallow. Now for the details.

"Okay, Achenia should be in position by now. I want you to spread out your commands. We form a long, solid line covering as large an area as possible. Priscus, I want you in the centre of that line. I'll be on the far side, to stop our men going outside the range of archery cover from the wall. If anything happens to me and we hit organised resistance, form up into a phalanx on Priscus." That was met with nods from the men staring back at him. "I want two shield bearers from you, Bulos: men whom you would trust to watch my back. The enemy aren't armoured, but enough of them still have swords, and they're all carrying knives, so no heroics. Kill quickly, and move on till we meet Achenia in the middle. Okay, men, go to your commands."

In seconds, they had disappeared, becoming almost wraiths in the dark, swallowed by shadow. No reflection of their polished armour was in evidence as they moved along the shadow of the great wall. The occasional scuff of sandal on rock was the only real proof that this wasn't imaginary.

Faster than he had imagined, four figures moved up alongside himself and Priscus. He thought he recognised two of them, but was only sure of one, so it was he Arimnestos spoke to.

"Xenos, you're our shield-bearers?" he asked.

Moving gently to avoid noise, Xenos slapped his hand to his heart in a quiet salute. "We have that honour, my lord," he replied. Arimnestos nodded. The soldiers were beginning to move forward.

"Remember, form a line, tight ranks, kill and move on. Make sure they're finished off. Now line up and wait for the signal."

Arimnestos nodded to Priscus and started moving out wide in front of the walls, staying well outside the light cast from the Greek fires. Moving slowly, he kept looking back to check the distance from the wall, observing his men to make sure everyone was in position. All the parts were in place, now they just had to wait for the signal.

As with every battle he had ever been in, time seemed to slow as he waited for the signal to begin. Too much time to think; every breath seemed to take an age to pass his lips. Maybe he was a coward and this was fear manifesting itself in him, or perhaps everyone felt this way before a battle; to ask his fellows would be to expose a possible weakness, and what man could do that? To be known as a coward before his men was not something he could live with. Anyway, he knew that as soon as that signal came, and he was running towards the Greeks with his fellow soldiers, things would begin to move fast; sometimes too fast to control. That was the reason for the old saying: *even the best-laid plans last only until the first arrow is in the air.*

The line spread almost five hundred metres from the walls with four hundred men to the front ranks, and Drussos with his command spread wide in a second rank, to finish any fallen. There would be no enemy survivors from this mission. Arimnestos felt very exposed out on the right flank. Even though he knew the position to be necessary, and had two shield-bearers covering his back, he was keenly aware that he would be first to be hit if the Greeks formed quickly.

Looking forward across the space in front of the wall, straining to catch a glimpse of Achenia forming up opposite him, he was shocked at how many Greeks were there. There must be ten or twelve thousand of them around those fires. It was lunacy! They were just asking to be slaughtered. But who would be stupid enough to attack an army of one hundred thousand with what was left in Troy? Laughing to himself, he thought '*Achenia*, that's who'.

There was no sign of Achenia; of course not, he thought. If he could see the other Trojans, they'd be far too close and in clear view of the Greeks; drunk as they were, the Greeks wouldn't miss something so obvious. Looking back at the walls, he wondered what was keeping the signal; it had to be time. There! Just a faint flickering, the lamp lighting. It flashed brighter; Heraclitus would be holding his polished shield at an angle to increase the lamplight. It was time.

Adjusting the shield on his arm with a spare spear gripped in that hand, he hefted his first spear in an overhead grip. The time for silence was over. He lowered his helmet over his face; looking out of the Y-shaped slot narrowed his vision on the enemy. Taking a deep breath, Arimnestos called down the line.

"It's time, men. Helmets down, let's get moving, forward at a trot," he shouted and began to move forward.

Like a tidal wave of flesh and bronze they surged forward, five hundred pairs of sandalled feet slapping the sand, making a lot of noise with the jingling of harnesses and armour. The gap between them and the revelling Greeks was closing fast. What had been mere blurred shapes only moments before were transforming into men like himself, doing everyday things: drinking, laughing, talking. None knew what was coming towards them.

At thirty paces away, the first Greek faces turned toward the sound of their advance. There was just time for shock to register and then they were among them. The first one Arimnestos took with a spear to the throat, flicking out like a viper's strike and knocking him flat with a punch to the face from the sharp edge of his shield. Swinging his shield wide, he clubbed the man to the ground to spear him through the ribs. As he pulled out the spear, the tip broke on a rib. He threw it away and caught the second spear from behind his shield.

The narrow breath he took gave him just enough time to look down the line and see his group open around the fires as they pushed forward into the unprepared Greeks and close up again as they passed around the flames. The distraction nearly cost him his life as a poorly-swung sword landed on Xenos' shield, wielded by a drunken Greek who had recovered from the shock faster than the others, and his other shield-bearer's spear took the man in the neck.

Concentrating on the battle again, he moved forward and lanced a fleeing Greek in the upper back. They had all begun to flee now, running from his advancing force. Inside his copper helmet, Arimnestos heard the faint echo of screams from further across the plain and could just make out firelight glittering off polished bronze which was moving slowly toward them.

Chapter Five

It was like watching the sea from a high cliff, the way a wave reverses after it has crashed against the headland. Two small, indefatigable waves were rushing back out around a headland to meet again in the centre; only this time the wave was of bronze, and the headland consisted of unarmoured Greeks being crushed between the rushing waves.

Heraclitus watched it all unfold from high up on the walls of Troy; as cold as it seemed even to his own mind, that is what it reminded him of. He remembered well his days before the great war, when he had been fishing with his father. His father owned a fleet of thirty fishing boats and three biremes, or at least he had done so before the Greeks arrived. As his sons grew up, he had insisted on their being able to do the job themselves. The Greeks had ended his chances of following his father into that career, and had thrust him into the role of a soldier of Troy.

In a way, this life suited him better. Yes, he loved the sea, but he'd never had the patience for fishing. Sitting in a small boat all day watching the surface of the water for signs of a shoal? No. Here he had his shoal, all marching up for him to plant his arrows in. If it weren't for the food shortages in the city, it wouldn't be a bad life.

The lamp and shield he had used to signal Achenia and Arimnestos lay near his feet, tucked behind the crenellations of the wall. Looking left and right, to make sure that none of his men was visible above the wall, he saw all five hundred archers hunkered down, laying out arrows and checking bowstrings. He smiled to himself; he had trained them well.

Another look over the wall showed the Greeks who had run from one front or the other beginning to realise that they were trapped between the two forces. Some had the presence of mind to run towards the ever-narrowing gap, back towards the Greek camps; some might even make it. It's amazing how quickly you can sober up when your life depends on it.

Others were forming themselves into small fighting bands, organising whatever arms they had between them to resist, attempting to strike back at their attackers before they died. Unarmoured men were no match for an armoured and well-led phalanx, though he did see a few bronze-clad figures go down under a hail of swords, knives and fists as they tried to break through the lines. Every time a Trojan went down another bronze figure stepped into the gap, and a few Greeks were falling every time, even when they outnumbered the Trojans they brought down.

Even as Heraclitus watched, the gap at the far end of the waves was closing. Achenia on one side and Arimnestos on the other were bringing their respective pincers together, positioned at the outer edges of their consecutive lines in order to control how deep they went. The Greeks, not realising their position, were still running for their lives. They came together, shield-bearers watching their backs, and started pulling in their lines closer to the wall, closing the pincers on the beleaguered Greeks.

Something caught his eye in the cluster of panicked Greeks, a few armoured men. They must constitute the ineffective watch that had been set near the gates. A group of five sober men, judging from their movements, wouldn't be enough to save the Greeks, but if they could organise the panicked ones they could still do damage to the Trojan line. They were pulling the fleeing

Greeks to a stop, getting ready to try to punch a hole in the Trojan lines, a pathway to freedom.

Pulling an arrow from his quiver, he brought up his bow. Things change fast on a battlefield; the Greeks were moving. Arrow to string - fifteen Greeks running - arrow drawn back to his cheek. He aimed for the leader of the Greeks, whom he could identify from the crest on his helmet. The Greeks crashed into the Trojan line, which was thickening with soldiers moving back from further out, where they were compressing the Greeks. The arrow left his string, flying through the air for a breath, and seemed to hang there for an eternal heartbeat, before the feathers were just visible in the armoured back of a man falling on his face.

By then, Heraclitus already had another arrow fitted to his bow. Aiming at this point was useless, however; too many people were crammed into too small a space. He would be as likely to take a Trojan as a Greek. He dropped his arms to his sides in disgust, forced to watch matters play out without his interference. Scanning the field for other possible targets, he saw a blood-soaked Achenia striding through a field that was completing its slaughter. The last of the Greeks were falling fast.

Achenia clasped hands with Arimnestos, and they seemed to be talking; then both looked towards the place where the Greeks had tried to break out. Heraclitus followed their gaze; the Greeks were all down, but so were five or six Trojans.

Even from this distance, the shock on Achenia's face was visible, and he started running towards the fallen Trojans, as fast as a man can move in full armour. Arimnestos was hard on his heels. Being on the wall was annoying; it was difficult to guess what was happening from so far back. He looked again at the fallen Trojans, and saw a crest.

As he tried to work out what was happening, the sound of

rhythmic tramping of feet came to him from further out on the field, where many men were running together. Looking out, all he could see were shadows, as if darkness were moving in firelight. Then the truth struck him and he began to shout.

"Myrmidons! Myrmidons incoming! Archers at the ready!" he bellowed.

Achenia didn't even break his stride but Arimnestos was hesitating, glancing back out to the field. Arimnestos it is, then.

"Arimnestos!" he screamed, pointing with his bow outstretched, "Myrmidons coming; form up!" The message finally seemed to get through to him.

***

"Myrmidons, to me," Achilles shouted, running towards his tent. "Armed and armoured in thirty seconds. Eudoros, where are you, damn you?"

"My lord," called Eudoros.

"Everyone up," said Achilles. Ducking into his tent, he buckled on his sword belt, to the sound of men making quick preparations outside. Picking up his shield and two spears, he rushed back out; his men were ready for him.

"At a quick trot, form up into ranks five abreast and fan out as we get there. Ready to move?" he asked. "Good, then follow me."

He took off at a steady trot over the sand toward the front gates of Troy where a constant stream of Trojans seemed to be swarming out of the darkness. Those Greeks sober enough to realise what was happening were in full retreat, as most weren't even wearing armour; any who stood were being brought down fast and trampled under a stampede of Trojan sandals.

Through the light cast from the numerous bonfires lit by the revelling Greeks, Achilles tried to work out what was happening. The main gates were closed, yet there were hundreds of Trojans charging through the Greeks, slaughtering everything in their path. It was like a bloody nightmare. Then he saw them, sweeping in from the sides along the walls of Troy. Of course, they were using the side gates to launch their attack. He looked at the walls and saw that they were supported by an almost invisible long row of archers, waiting on top in the dark.

Anyone who attacked would find flight after flight of arrows raining down on them, while the Trojans moved back to the safety of their walls. If enough of the Greeks were sober, they could storm the gates, taking acceptable losses to gain entry, but even from the walls, any fool could see that most could hardly stand.

At this point in any battle, the decisions made could mean the difference between winning and losing. The lack of light made things harder; judging distances became more difficult, which was the main reason most commanders avoided night battles. However, the moment Achilles saw the duelling ring he had left earlier, he made his decision.

"Spread out left from me, five deep," he called to his men.

In the files in which they had been running, like a tide the Myrmidons swept left from the point where Achilles had stopped.

Seconds passed that felt like minutes to Achilles, until the last of his Myrmidons swept out from him, the final one stopping almost where he stood. That was how well-trained men behaved, knowing exactly where they should be.

"Shields together!" shouted Achilles. The almighty crash of shield on shield announced their arrival on the field.

"Spears down!" Every one of two thousand spears was levelled towards the walls of Troy.

The Trojans had not yet noticed them, in their joy at slaughtering the unarmed Greeks who had been besieging their city, and they were still rushing towards them with hundreds of Greeks caught between the two forces.

"Forward at the step, on my mark," and they went forward, a solid black shield wall. A depth of five men wasn't much, but Achilles made his decision in the hope that the Trojans would be unable to ascertain their numbers in the dim light, balanced against the need for as wide a front as possible.

Panic entered the faces of the fleeing Greeks as they realised where they were trapped, and knew that Achilles would give no ground for their escape, since it would leave him with gaps for the Trojans to exploit. He could see the panic building in them and understood their fear. It was a fear every man in a phalanx had felt at some time. He could feel his own men looking at him, wanting to save the Greeks, but the Trojans had what could be anything up to three times their numbers on the field. In the dark they couldn't know his ranks were so thin, but if he gave them any weak points, they would exploit them and he knew he would be driven from the field.

"Hold the line," he shouted at the top of his lungs. "Eudoros, spear the first man to give ground or open ranks."

"Yes, sir," shouted Eudoros and Achilles could hear his feet crunching on the rough ground as he walked the length of his line of men shouting orders. "Come on, you lousy maggots; hold that line tight. Do not make me come up to you, Acemes!" Achilles could feel his own men take comfort in their commanders, in that they knew what to do.

Greeks who had any sense left in their panicked heads began pushing out, left and right, hoping against hope to make it to the end of the line so the outnumbered Myrmidons could hold off the slaughter, but he watched a few, too far gone in their panic to think straight, run directly into the spears of some of his men. Spears pierced chests here, blood pumped from a neck there, and still another, further back, was running towards them only for a spear to sprout from his chest.

One man was directly across from Achilles, running towards him, thinking he was free; he was only a dozen metres away from safety around their lines when suddenly his head left his shoulders in a spray of crimson blood. The body remained standing for half a dozen heartbeats, as if stunned and wondering where its head had gone, before dropping to the ground.

Out of the darkness, behind the fleeing Greeks, came a golden wave of Trojans in shiny bloodstained armour, screaming bloody murder as they stalked forward after their prey. Seeing the Myrmidons lined up and waiting for them brought the Trojans up short, and more than one head swivelled, looking for their commander, looking for their ranks, looking for inspiration as to what to do next. Killing unarmed fleeing soldiers was one thing; facing the most infamous, unmistakable jet-black armour of the Myrmidon phalanx in battle order was something else entirely, and Achilles decided to take the risk of pressing the advantage of surprise, in the hope that whoever was commanding this assault would be inexperienced.

"Forward at a step, on my mark," he called, and the phalanx moved forward slowly, closing the distance between themselves and the Trojans, and further squeezing those unfortunate enough to be caught in between.

"Hold!" A call came from behind Achilles, sounding hollow and washed out in the echo of his Y-faced helmet.

"Hold, damn you!" The shout came again; this time Achilles recognised the voice as that of Agamemnon, and he silently cursed the gods.

"Hold the line," he screamed across at his men. "Hold the

line! Shields up, brace for incoming." He watched the Trojans who were forming up into ranks, instead of chasing the few remaining trapped Greeks.

"What are you doing, trapping men against them like that?" bellowed Agamemnon. "Let them through; you're killing half my bloody army here!"

Feet shuffled in the Myrmidon ranks. "Hold your positions!" screamed Achilles. Turning to face Agamemnon, his voice dropped dangerously low. "We are not opening up. They have time now to run around us, but if we open ranks to let them through, the Trojans will tear through our ranks. We're not deep enough to take that."

"Then why didn't you make the ranks deeper?" Agamemnon snarled in Achilles' face, engulfing him in wine fumes.

"Because I am trying to protect the entire front of your army," Achilles said, softly and menacingly. "If your men were disciplined and not so drunk, I wouldn't need to protect them. Anyway, the last of them are out of there now. If you have any men sober enough to hold the right side of a spear, this would be a good time to fetch them." Shouting from the Trojan phalanx announced the arrival of whoever had commanded this raid.

"At the step!" Achilles shouted again and the front moved slowly forward towards the Trojans. Orders were shouted from the Trojan front, and they began to back away just as slowly, slightly faster than the Myrmidons followed: ten steps, fifteen, twenty paces. "Hold the line!" and the Myrmidons stopped as one, while the Trojans continued to back away from them towards the city walls.

"Now you don't even intend to follow them? Are you not going to revenge your countrymen?" Agamemnon laughed, taunting the Myrmidons. "Cowards!" he finished and spat on the sand.

Rounding on Agamemnon, Achilles pulled back his helmet, his eyes burning with hatred. "My men lined up, alone, to protect your drunken fools, and you think we should attack? Maybe you need to sober up yourself, Agamemnon. Look at those walls; another ten paces or so and those archers lining the walls would wipe out my men."

"Those archers are too far away. Wipe these Trojans from the field, Achilles, or by the gods I'll-"

"Forget it, Agamemnon. I won't throw my men away for nothing," replied Achilles, glancing at his line of Myrmidons who had begun to shuffle a little uncomfortably under Agamemnon's abuse. "Hold your ground, men."

Some shuffling from behind announced the arrival of more Greeks who had finally managed to stagger into their armour, too late to have saved anyone, had Achilles not blocked the Trojan advance. Unevenly, they shuffled into place around the Myrmidons.

"Form up in three phalanxes, ten deep, in front of the cowardly Myrmidons," shouted Agamemnon, staring at Achilles when he saw how many Greeks had arrived. Achilles held his gaze and clenched his jaw against a retort.

The Greeks began forming up unevenly in front of the Myrmidons, looking over their shoulders. The Trojans looked a little less certain now, but had stopped backing away and were bringing their shield wall solidly together, spears hefted to their shoulders, faces grim as they watched the Greeks form up. More than one of their heads swivelled to look back at their gate and their walls, no doubt wishing they were back inside them.

The Greek phalanx finally seemed to find some coherence, coming together in three large blocks to face the much smaller Trojan force; this was now trapped between the walls of Troy, with the gate locked tight against the Greek multitudes, and three times their number of Greeks lined up outside them.

Still holding Achilles' gaze, without even looking at his men, Agamemnon roared at the top of his lungs, "Forward! Destroy the Trojan scum!"

***

The line closed, and Arimnestos finally lowered his spear, but held the shield braced to his shoulder as he looked around. To his right, those Greeks who had managed to get away before the line closed were running towards the main Greek camp. To his left, Achenia's line had just touched his. The outside pinched first, to trap as many Greeks inside as possible.

Since the immediate area seemed secure, he pushed back the helmet on his head. Achenia was pushing back his own helmet. He seemed to have had the rougher side of the vice. He had only one shield-bearer left, and had a deep cut on his left thigh along his bronze guard, and a nasty dent on his breastplate. Glancing around, Arimnestos saw that some of his men were in bad shape, too.

It was hard to tell yet who was actually injured, as a liberal coating of blood seemed to decorate everyone and the ground was churned underfoot to a red, sandy mud that sparkled ominously in the light of the glowing fires. Achenia was coming towards him, favouring his right leg slightly. It demonstrated very clearly how tired he was that he'd allowed his limp to show.

"Well met, Arimnestos," he said. "Congratulations."

"It was your plan, Achenia; we just stood where you told us to."

Achenia looked around and shook his head. "You did a lot more than that. Where's Priscus?"

"I placed him halfway in to the wall with another two shield-bearers. The greatest danger was out here, so he is to form the men up if anything happens to me," replied Arimnestos. "He should be closing up the line and finishing them off by now."

"Casualties?" asked Achenia, looking back to where the slaughter was still going on.

"I'll need to do a full count, but as of now I know of only three we lost on this side. You?" answered Arimnestos, following Achenia's gaze to where the last Greeks had been surrounded.

"A dozen, that I'm sure of. We were slower to attack than you. I got delayed by a few Greek sentries; when you hit that side, they all ran in my direction. We actually had to brace the line with the second ranks, but they soon broke."

In seconds, the last thousand or so Greeks were down to the last hundred.

"You did well out there, Arimnestos. You've come a long way from the spoiled lording I was sent to train so long ago." Achenia clapped Arimnestos on the arm, an unusual gesture from this man.

"You trained me well." Arimnestos broke off in mid-conversation. Watching the battle progress, he had noticed the arrival of a few armoured Greeks, dragging the others with them in an attempt to break out of the Trojan lines. They had obviously stumbled across a watch detail, but the Greek soldiers were charging hard towards the Trojans, a little over a hundred yards away.

The Trojans were now clustering together into deeper and deeper ranks; there was no escape for these Greeks. Ares himself would have trouble getting out of there now, thought Arimnestos, but as he watched, he realised that they had hit the line exactly where Priscus' red-and-black horsehair crest had been just visible over the heads of his comrades, and now it had disappeared. The Greeks were down; in the press of Trojans it was difficult to see much, but short as Priscus was his crest should still have been visible.

While Arimnestos was still trying to make out what was happening in the confusion, Achenia had already begun to move. The limp was gone in an instant, as he broke into an awkward run, his greaves and thigh-guards restricting his movements. In seconds, Arimnestos was in an all-out sprint. His family's money had bought armour which fitted much better than Achenia's and he was twenty years younger, so in a few seconds he had caught up.

The orders given to their men were to leave nobody alive, hence the second rank of men to finish off any living wounded so they couldn't be healed and rejoin battle. This produced an eerie quiet on the field. Over the laboured breath of tired warriors, the jokes to ease their nerves, the clapping of each other on the back was - nothing. No cries of pain, no begging for mercy, no struggling last breaths; none of the sounds associated with a battlefield. In that silence Arimnestos heard his name being screamed, a sound he caught only because his helmet was still pushed back from his conversation with Achenia.

Looking up quickly, he could make out Heraclitus on the wall, gilded bow pointed out beyond them. Still running, he glanced over his shoulder as the shout reached his ears: "Myrmidons!"

Almost falling over his own feet, Arimnestos looked at Achenia, who was still running, and decided to turn. The Greeks were still stumbling away from the end of the Trojan lines, and, through them, he could see only darkness; but he could hear the tramp of many feet. Grabbing every Trojan soldier he could along the way, he finally concentrated their attention in the right direction, but most started chasing after the fleeing Greeks in an uncontrolled mass of groups of three and four. They were churning through sand mixed with the blood of thousands, forming a gruesome mud which clung to each man's legs, all trying to catch a few more Greeks.

Xenos and Orestos, his second shield-bearer, were Spartans and stood at his shoulders like ridge cats, eyes up, alert, searching for any threat. They understood what was coming, having heard the call, and looked with cold condescension at the Trojans throwing themselves forward.

Brasides, Bulos and Drussos trotted over from the side to ask what was going on, just in time to see the first Trojans slow suddenly and then stop, looking less eager for a fight when faced with dark, looming figures in tight ranks. Even in firelight they were difficult to discern as the armour gave no reflection; indeed, it seemed to drink in the light. The question remained unasked, as the commanders saw what they faced and immediately moved back out to take control of their men.

The training which had seemed lost a moment ago as they gloried in the slaughter reasserted itself in the men, and they didn't even need the orders from their commanders as they began forming ranks in straight lines, eight deep. Survival instinct brought their training to the fore, and Myrmidons brought out their survival instincts more quickly than anything else. The only threat as great would have been the scarlet cloaks of Spartans forming up opposite them.

Arimnestos took up his position on the far left of the line. From here, the Myrmidons could be seen much more clearly: the toughened black leather of their armour sculpted tight to their bodies, aspides tilted back, and each man's shield covering the man on his right from waist to neck. Spear points glistened in the cool night air, all held at the exact same level, sloping down over the shields.

Looking down his own line, the Trojans seemed just as

impressive, shining in the reflected firelight as the Myrmidons' armour drank it in. Directly across from him, Arimnestos saw the commander of the Myrmidons. Taller than the others, muscles glistening in a light sheen of sweat under his armour, curls of ghostly pale hair spreading out from under the rim of a helmet, with a horsehair crest so dark it was lost in the night as it rose above him: Achilles.

Though he couldn't see the man's eyes in the shadow of his helmet, he could feel the weight of his stare in the darkness: weighing, judging, deciding.

The air on the field seemed to drop a few degrees, as the two sides faced one another. Time seemed to flow more slowly. The need to urinate became the most important thing in the world; if it came to blows he would let it flow down his legs as he went into battle, but until then he did not dare to exhibit such weakness to the enemy.

Just as it seemed that the Myrmidons must come for them, another man moved up beside Achilles; a big man. He was obviously a warrior, judging from his build and the way he carried himself. This was someone important, judging by his self-assured stance and the way he seemed to be giving orders to Achilles.

Arimnestos couldn't be sure, but he thought he caught a hint of amusement from the helmet of Achilles. Eyes still fixed straight ahead, he was studying the Trojan lines and Arimnestos. There was a very subtle nod of the head in his direction, and Achilles relaxed. He relaxed. Achilles straightened and turned from the lines to face the newcomer.

Salvation is hard won on the battlefield, but in that moment Arimnestos thought he glimpsed it as Achilles argued with the newcomer. The hands of the gods, perhaps, had brought the other man there, and Arimnestos grabbed at the chance like a drowning man grabs a log.

"Backwards at a shuffle," he shouted. "Rear ranks turn and guide us through, front ranks keep shields up ready; let's go!" And they began retreating slowly from the Myrmidon line.

Slowly at first, twenty paces became thirty, then forty, and then they began to pick up the pace; forty became sixty, which became a hundred. Then Arimnestos heard the sound he had been dreading.

"Forward! Destroy the Trojan scum," was shouted from the distance.

Still facing backwards, Arimnestos was confused by what he saw. The Myrmidons didn't seem to be budging at all. There appeared to be no movement from the lines. If he hadn't known better, he would have thought them statues. Then he saw a stream of brightly-clad Greek warriors in bronze armour pouring out from around the Myrmidon flanks, sweeping around them to form up facing Troy.

The pace of the Trojans picked up again and Arimnestos found himself looking behind. They were a mere two hundred paces from the city walls, but those Greeks would close on them well before they all managed to get through the gates. Some would have to stay behind to hold them off outside while the gates were closing. Arimnestos felt the fates tighten around him, as the wall of Greeks ran towards them at a heavy pace.

***

The solid thump of six thousand hobnailed sandals took that first marching step towards the Trojans. Three thousand spear points glistened in the reflected light from the bonfires which still burned around the area. Three thousand grim sets of eyes stared down the heavily-outnumbered Trojans. The Trojans began backing away slowly as the Greek phalanx moved towards them with increasing speed and confidence.

Suddenly their backs were pressed against the walls of Troy, with only a hundred paces between them, and Achilles saw a glimmer of light between the gates, moments before the screams began. At this distance, it was almost impossible to see the arrows descending. The first signs were Greeks falling, screaming, in the phalanx. Not knowing what was happening, the Greeks in the back continued to press forward as those at the front suddenly pushed back from the walls, and the entire phalanx degenerated into a confused mess of men and bodies milling about and shoving one another. Then all three phalanxes, what was left of them, were in full retreat, being struck down all the while as men ran and were cut down with arrows in their backs.

Watching the massacre, Achilles and Agamemnon had moved forward together ahead of the Myrmidons to get a better view. The retreating Greeks streamed by them, forced back by a constant stream of arrows landing just short of where they now stood. Turning to Agamemnon, Achilles said, "I told you; if we'd moved any closer, their archers would have had us."

Agamemnon held his gaze for a minute before flicking his eyes towards the wall as an arrow struck the ground five paces from their feet. Eventually he gave a loud harrumph, turned and walked away. Achilles looked back towards the wall, to see the Trojan phalanx slipping through the main gates back into the city. The gates closed behind them with a thud that could be heard four hundred paces away, and Achilles looked back down the length of his shield wall bristling with spear points, then at the bodies littering the ground between his men and the towering walls of Troy.

"Stand down," he called.

***

The hail of arrows taking down thousands of Greeks at a time caught them totally by surprise at the beginning; men fell with two or three arrows protruding from their chests, neck or legs. The running Greeks hadn't concentrated on keeping their shields up as they charged the Trojan line, leaving themselves very vulnerable to the arrows. The second, third and fourth ranks, unable to check their headlong sprint, went down in a tangle of limbs over the felled front row.

The mass of bodies writhing on the ground were like one large shooting target for the archers, as more and more volleys of arrows launched into them. The few who survived the first volley, or subsequent ranks who managed to leap over their fallen comrades, soon found themselves almost alone. These few hundred searched in shock for their own ranks, then looked at the Trojans before turning to run. Their attack descended into chaos, as they ran for all they were worth back to safety.

Arimnestos breathed a deep sigh of relief as he turned and looked up at the wall where Heraclitus was pulling back for one last launch of an arrow; he waved down at Arimnestos with a wide smile on his face, one that had rarely been seen over the last few months.

"Pick up our dead and wounded," shouted Arimnestos. "Everyone inside, now!"

Surprisingly, though the last fifty yards had been taken at a veritable sprint, the front rank had turned and faced what would have been the Greek horde in good order. Shields were up, forming a solid wall, and spears were lowered. Faces were hard to see inside helmets, but the fear in the set of the jaw was not, nor was the sweat dripping from those chins; the same fear that Arimnestos had himself felt just a few seconds ago. Despite their fear, if the Greeks had kept coming these men had been ready to die to allow their friends in the rear ranks to get to safety inside.

The knowledge made Arimnestos swell with pride.

The massive gates of Troy were already open. Inside rank upon rank of soldiers lined the sides of a massive path for the men returning. They were all prepared for battle themselves, ready to defend the open gate if things had gone differently during the raid, and they were now struggling to get the gates closed once more.

The soldiers now resembled an honour guard for returning heroes. They were cheering and coming forward to clap the shoulders of friends, calling out greetings and looking to see who was returning and who was being carried through the gates. Arimnestos saw more than one wife crying over a body, as the friend, comrade or brother-in-arms who had carried him through the gates tried in vain to comfort her.

The returning soldiers did not resemble the heroes of legend. Heads low and shoulders hunched, the adrenaline which had carried them sprinting in full armour to the gates slowly drained away, leaving men exhausted and literally covered in blood. There was gore from their shields to the tips of their spears, dripping down their arms and torsos, and their legs were caked in a bloody, sandy mud which was just beginning to dry and harden into clumps, as blood is wont to do.

Arimnestos felt the exhaustion, too. His legs were barely strong enough to hold him upright, and his shield arm felt as if it would have fallen off if not for sheer strength of will. His spear arm – oh, how his spear arm burned, from the shoulder right down to the elbow! His forearm was a numb lump of flesh, and liquid fire ran through the veins in his legs. Even the type of slaughter they had engaged in tonight took its toll on the body.

But he kept his head up and his back straight, the shield levelled across his chest and spear straight up, held off the ground. The men had to have faith in their commanders, to see them as more than ordinary men; they had to have something to strive to emulate.

The gates swung shut as he passed through, one of the last to come off the field. Only his Spartan bodyguard were at his back: two men he barely knew, men whom some thought should be back with their own, bred by the enemy they now fought. He had just trusted them with his life, leaving them to guard his back as he fought men from their own country. It felt like madness, but, after that, he would trust them implicitly to guard his back or the lives of his family and friends. They had just proven their loyalty, if it had ever come into question.

Arimnestos looked around at the injured, the dying and the dead they had carried back. He looked at faces, remembering them. Some names came to mind but more did not. He walked among them, and talked to their families a little, as grieving mothers came to collect their children's remains, as wives and daughters came to see to husbands and fathers. It was the least he could do to honour the sacrifice they had made to defend their city: let their families know that what they had given would not be forgotten.

Then he passed through a cluster of soldiers, towards the inner side of the great square. Achenia was kneeling over the prone form of Priscus as his mother took solace in the arms of her husband, who was standing a little to the side. Her body was shaking with silent sobs, her face buried in his chiton.

Heraclitus came running up to Arimnestos, laughing. He had not yet noticed Priscus, and his mood was jubilant.

"Hey, Arimnestos, what a victory! That was spectacular!" He threw his arms around Arimnestos and nearly knocked him over with his rush. Arimnestos barely acknowledged the hug as he stood staring blankly at Priscus.

Priscus was pale from loss of blood. His body seemed to

have abruptly deflated. Lying flat on his back, breathing shallowly, his shoulders didn't look nearly as wide as they had done earlier that evening. His helmet was thrown to one side and his breastplate removed by the physicians in order to inspect his wound. His chiton, once white, was now a sticky wet red. Hair was plastered to his head with sweat; blood dripped from his mouth as he breathed and coughed it out of his lungs.

Achenia knelt at his side, holding his hand. He occasionally murmured to Priscus but mostly he simply held his hand in a strong grip, as if he could force him to stay alive through the strength of his will alone. Priscus was looking at him, maybe just gazing and seeing nothing, but the blank stare of the dead was not in his eyes just yet. Arimnestos knew it was coming, though. Priscus' lungs were filling with blood as he lay there and his breathing became more ragged.

"What is Achenia doing there? He should stand back and let Priscus' parents say goodbye to their boy. He's nearly done for," said Heraclitus a little too loudly to Arimnestos when he finally noticed that his friend was lying on the ground, dying.

Arimnestos grabbed his arm roughly, dragging him a little further away. Nobody had responded to his comment, but it was impossible to believe they hadn't heard him.

"Are you blind, Heraclitus? Have you never looked at them? Does Priscus look anything like his father? Cassandra's parents would never have let her marry Achenia. Her family were broke when they agreed to the marriage with Deiphobus, and he prefers boys so he never complained that he wasn't the father. Now shut up and let the man grieve for his son."

Heraclitus couldn't have looked more stunned if he had been hit between the eyes with a wooden mallet. His eyes flicked from Achenia and Priscus back to Arimnestos more than once, his jaw working but with nothing coming out. Finally, he seemed to find words again, though all he could manage was "Really?"

Arimnestos nodded. "You know what it would mean for him if anyone found out, Heraclitus. Never mention it, not even to him!"

"I won't, Ari. I won't," promised Heraclitus.

Arimnestos turned away and walked over to Achenia. Cassandra had moved closer to Priscus' other side, taking his hand, with Deiphobus standing behind her, holding her shoulders. Priscus was labouring to breathe now, and Arimnestos could actually hear air sucking in the puncture wound on his side as he exhaled. Arimnestos knelt with an arm on Achenia's shoulder as Priscus breathed his last. Nothing dramatic, no cries, no kicking; he just breathed out, and that was it. There was nothing more. He was gone.

Arimnestos knelt at Achenia's side for a few minutes, before realising silence had fallen behind them. He turned to see a circle of soldiers quietly watching them. Any who hadn't known before could probably guess what had just happened. Rising, he turned to the soldiers.

"Right, you maggots, listen!" he said, in a loud voice. "Double the patrols on the walls tonight and throw out burning torches every half hour so you can see anything moving beyond the wall in the darkness. We had a very successful evening raid, but only because we caught them by surprise. Let's not return the favour. Anyone caught drinking or sleeping on duty will be hanged immediately. All those who were out with us tonight are off the watch rotation, but everyone sleeps in their armour tonight. Keep your weapons to hand."

He wandered over to Heraclitus. "Any word on Pedasus?" he asked.

"I haven't seen him since we put him to bed," replied Heraclitus.

Arimnestos shook his head. “Can you take first watch, Heraclitus?” he asked. “Come and get me in three hours and I’ll do rounds until morning. Something tells me that Achenia won’t be much use for a day or two.”

“Sure, that’s no problem. I’m a little too worked up to sleep yet, anyway.”

Arimnestos made his way back to his rooms in the barracks, where he fell back onto his bed, taking his own advice about the armour. Even with that discomfort, he was barely in bed before he fell asleep.

Chapter Six

Grainy-eyed, Diomedes watched Achilles sleep from his pallet in the corner. Although just a pallet, it was of better quality than the bed back in his mother's house. In fact, it was better than his mother's own bed, but the fact that a prince could afford a better bed for his slaves did not make them free. Diomedes was still enslaved.

Sleep had come late to Diomedes. He had stayed awake in terror, watching his enemy who surely intended to have him killed. He wouldn't let Diomedes return to fight the Greeks, no matter how long or how well he served. The night had been terrifying. Never before, even after losing his father, had Diomedes felt so alone. He felt ashamed of his fear. No matter what Achilles said, he wouldn't trust him.

He had arrived late in the afternoon, surrounded by these huge men in black. Achilles was bigger still; the legends about him told only half the story. Then Agamemnon had arrived, which hadn't improved Achilles' temper, but he soon calmed down. He had actually been laughing with the one he called 'Eudoros' about their king. Eudoros was older, with a horribly-scarred face and only one eye, like a monster come to life, but it seemed that Achilles had tamed this monster, as they laughed and joked like friends.

Achilles obviously had some clever plan, for although he told Diomedes to pour their wine for them, he seemed to have no other use for the boy, and told him to eat as much as he wanted.

Diomedes ate a little cautiously. Achilles watched him from the corner of his eye, pretending not to notice him as the men talked. Eudoros didn't even pretend; he grinned at the boy, as if wanting to laugh. There was something funny about his eating; maybe that was the plan, to poison him! But no, Diomedes had watched Achilles swallow huge hunks of the food himself while talking to Agamemnon.

So that meant the meat wasn't poisoned. He ate a bit more. He tentatively tried a little bit of this and a little bit of that, things he had never seen before inside the walls of Troy. His stomach growled, reminding him that he hadn't eaten all day. There was nothing in his mother's house to eat, and the excitement of the duel had sent all thought of food from his head. The noise brought a raucous bout of laughter from Eudoros. Hadn't he ever heard a stomach growl before?

Nerves getting the better of him, his stomach tied in knots, Diomedes had eaten little more and crept back to his pallet to hide with a heel of bread that he picked at for an hour or so. Achilles and Eudoros stripped from their armour; naked, they were not at all what Diomedes expected. The hated enemy whom Diomedes had spent his childhood hating, thinking of as monsters, looked just like those he had grown up with. Eudoros was horribly scarred in the face, true, but no more so than some of the veterans in Troy. Ten years of continuous war tended to do that. They were paler of skin than the Trojans, even after ten years in the sun of Asia Minor, but other than that they were just men.

They left soon afterwards, talking about Hector and Agamemnon, leaving Diomedes to consider his position. He couldn't see any good choices. Well, if he was going to die anyway, there was no point in worrying about the food being poisoned. He made his way back to the big trestle table at the side of the tent.

There were so many strange things there. For nearly six years, since food had started to run out, Diomedes had tasted little other than heavy dark bread, occasional hard cheese, and whatever tough donkey meat or half-rotted food Pedasus managed to bring back from the army mess halls. This feast reminded him of stories he had heard of Troy before the war, a time he was too young to remember.

Even trying just a few bites of different things, it wasn't long before he felt full. Well, if Achilles was silly enough to leave all this food lying around unprotected, which would not have happened in Troy, then Diomedes was going to take advantage of his stupidity. Wrapping as much as he could in a white cloth he found near the wash basin, he hid it under his pallet before Achilles came to his senses and started to restrict his slave to scraps of bread left lying around.

He was surprised to find Achilles managing without dozens of slaves to do his bidding for him. He was a prince after all, but Diomedes found himself alone. There must be some more, since his bed had been made up when he'd arrived in the tent. Diomedes would probably have to share the pallet when the other slaves returned from whatever duties they'd been occupied with. After some thought, Diomedes decided he should find a better hiding-place for his stolen food in case he had to share his pallet.

Pulling back the carpet at the back of his bed revealed sand, stamped smooth from the years that the tent had been here; it was packed tight, but was still just sand. It took some time, but eventually the surface broke enough for Diomedes to dig a small hole in the sand into which he placed his food. He covered it over carefully, but the extra sand from the space the food took up caused a slight bulge under the carpet, and some sand from his digging was scattered over the area; however, it was the best he could do.

Lying down on his pallet, time seemed to Diomedes to pass laboriously slowly. Although the seconds crawled, sleep wouldn't come; he lay there, looking at the dark pattern of the animal hides making up the tent roof as day turned into night, and tried to make sense of the day. He had been given up as a slave by his own uncle; worse, given up as a slave in front of all Troy. His dream of taking his father's place in the phalanx was gone, as was his bow. His life had changed completely.

He considered running, attempting to escape, trying to make his way back quietly to the city walls of Troy. Surely the soldiers among whom he had spent so many days would let him in, take him back to safety and the life he knew. However, the sound of men outside the tent convinced him that he would be recaptured and punished severely. Besides, he had come here because he had cost Hector honour, and he would repay that debt. He would be honourable, although everyone believed that Greeks knew nothing of honour.

Hours passed; he wasn't sure how many. He listened to the sounds of the party which had been going on all day, ever since Hector had died; that couldn't have been this same day, he thought, so much has happened since. Over the sounds of the camp, something else became audible: screaming from far away and angry shouting. Something was happening.

Running to the wall of the tent, he tried to have a look outside to see what was going on. The sound of concerned voices came closer; not worried or panicked, very much in control, but anxious to know what was happening and asking questions. All this was overlaid with a more familiar sound, that of a lot of men getting ready to fight, their armour straps being tightened.

One concerned voice materialised into Achilles, clad as always in his black armour, coming over a sand dune; he was followed by Eudoros and a large group of men. They were talking animatedly, but the only words he could discern were 'Trojans attacking. ' This was spoken in Eudoros' harsh accent.

Diomedes fled from the door of the tent back to his pallet as he saw them coming and tried to hide under the thick soft blanket spread across it, vainly hoping that Achilles would forget about him in his rush. Through the tent flaps he came like a whirlwind, his cloak falling from him before the flaps had even settled back into place. As he was donning the dirtier, faded black cloak to blend in with his armour, he called to Diomedes to bring his shield and spear.

His armour was adjusted next, in the fast, efficient movements of a man who had done a thing so often it came naturally to him without thinking. It made Diomedes wonder again where his other servants were, since there was no one to help him with such things. Diomedes became annoyed with himself for hoping that Achilles would bring Diomedes with him, but he excused himself with the thought that he just wanted to see the Trojan attack, to witness for himself what was happening. Achilles' bark brought him back to the present very quickly.

"Not the bronze one, that's just a prize taken in battle. I wear the black of the Myrmidons," he said.

Looking down, Diomedes flushed to see that he had brought a Trojan shield. Habit had made him pick up the bright shield, similar to that his father and Pedasus used.

He ran back, finding that, despite himself, he wanted to make Achilles happy. He laid the polished bronze shield back in its place, picked up the toughened, black, layered leather aspis and brought it to Achilles.

"That's better," he said, strapping it onto his arm. As he made his way to the door he glanced back. "I expect you to keep your word and be here when I get back."

Then he was away, shouting at his men, and the deep, earthy

sound of many, many sandalled feet hitting the ground together rumbled like far-off thunder.

It was about two hours later, well into the night, when Achilles returned. He didn't seem angry, but neither was he particularly happy when he came back. There wasn't so much as a single scuff mark on his armour, and no blood on his shield, his spear or any other part of him. *Had he been too late?* Diomedes wondered. He didn't look like he'd been in a battle. Maybe that was why he seemed annoyed; he had missed the battle. Everyone knew Greeks were bloodthirsty.

Diomedes lay still on his pallet, again hoping he wouldn't be noticed. He watched as Achilles stripped off his armour, placing it with care back on its stand. He removed his black tunic for washing and replaced it with the white one.

Cringing as Achilles said his name, Diomedes lifted his head.

"Come over here, Diomedes," said Achilles. His tone was not unkind, but this was not a request either. He climbed off the pallet and came over to stand in front of Achilles, who bade him sit on a stool beside the table and popped an olive into his own mouth. He was looking at Diomedes with a curious interest in his eyes.

Sitting on the stool, Diomedes felt very uncomfortable under that stare. "Do you drink wine?" asked Achilles, pouring himself a drink.

"I never have," he answered. Achilles looked at him as if expecting an explanation, so he decided to supply one. "There hasn't been much wine in Troy for many years, and Pedasus says I am too young for the grain spirit they drink now. I was to be allowed a cup of it today at the duel, but something happened, and I had to give up my cup."

Since Priam had taken such care with his disguise and

leaving the general at the palace to pretend to be the king, he obviously didn't want people to know he had been there, and Diomedes wasn't going to reveal his secret to an enemy. He was no traitor.

"Priam took your cup, then," said Achilles. "Don't look so surprised, lad. I spent a few summers in Troy training with Hector, and later fighting for the great king with him. I know Priam too, and he was at every duel Hector fought in Troy. I didn't think he would wait at the palace for this one."

Diomedes only realised that his jaw was hanging open when Achilles put a strong, rough finger under his chin and closed it for him.

"Fair is fair," intoned Achilles. "You were supposed to have your first drink today, and so you will. You're lucky; this is from my own vineyard back home." He poured some for Diomedes before adding almost as much water again. "We can't have you falling over from your first drink. Now, we must talk about your time here."

Diomedes hesitantly accepted the offered cup, looking into it with both hands wrapped around it.

"I'm no traitor," he said harshly. "I won't tell you anything to help you beat Troy." He took a large swallow, half-choking on the unfamiliar taste.

Achilles laughed. He was laughing at Diomedes! That made him angry, but then Achilles disarmed him completely.

"So you've got some spirit! That's good." Achilles clapped him on the shoulder.

"Firstly, I am the only man in this whole army who wouldn't gut you for speaking to him like that. Secondly, if I wanted information from you, Diomedes," he said, looking very intently into Diomedes' eyes, still smiling, though now as a wolf smiles at a sheep, "*if* I wanted that information from you, I would make you squeal until you told me. And you would tell me, Diomedes; never question that. Even the strongest man, even I, will break and tell his questioner all he knows under a few days' torture. Everyone breaks."

Diomedes felt the colour drain from his face. There was no hint of humour in Achilles' voice. The grin was still there, but Diomedes knew he was in deadly earnest. Achilles took a drink of his wine and Diomedes gulped down another mouthful before resuming his study of the inside of his cup, unwilling to meet those cold, hard eyes.

"I have no need of you to tell me about Troy, lad," he said, his voice light again. "I told you, I lived there for a while. I know all I need to know, but even if I didn't, I wouldn't torture a child to give that bastard Agamemnon the price of a loaf of bread in Troy."

At that Diomedes' face shot up, staring at him. He couldn't believe what he had just heard. Achilles' jaw was clenched and he looked like murder, talking about his king.

"So what do we need to talk about?" Diomedes finally managed to ask.

Achilles seemed to snap out of his unpleasant thoughts, and smiled at him. "We need to talk about your place as my servant. I have never had a servant while on campaign; several back at the palace, but never before on campaign."

Diomedes thought a moment before asking. "Then why take me as a servant?"

"Would you have preferred to have taken Hector's honour without atonement, lad?"

"No," he admitted sullenly.

"Then this is how it is going to be. When outside this tent, or inside if I have visitors, you will keep your mouth shut. There are those who would kill you just for your Trojan origins; they blame all Troy for us being stuck on this beach these last ten years. Nobody will argue with me about you, but they might take the opportunity to hurt you when I'm not here." He let this sink in, watching Diomedes' face for comprehension.

"And there are some, even among my own men, who will think I should have killed you for the shot you took at me during the duel. Keep your mouth shut and they may not even know you are Trojan."

"Okay," said Diomedes meekly, eyes cast down, looking at the pattern on the carpet as he thought this over. "But why should you care if I'm hurt or killed?"

This question was obviously not what Achilles expected because, for a second, he seemed thrown, as if looking into the sands of time. "Let's just say that I owe a debt, and taking care of you might help."

"Now, even in front of my own men, you are not to question me; you have seen how a servant behaves, and that's what I will expect in public. But while we are here, alone, you are basically free. Eat what you want, but don't get drunk or act the fool with me. This tent will be your dwelling-place for a while, so make yourself at home."

Diomedes couldn't believe what he was hearing. The rules he had to follow in Troy were stricter than this. As much food as he wanted, and wine to drink! Suddenly a thought occurred to him. "If you have no servants, whose is the other bed? It was here before I came."

"You're quick," said Achilles quietly, looking at the bed, and Diomedes thought he had caught him out in a lie; this was some form of trap, though he didn't understand the purpose. The silence dragged on as Achilles stared at the bed. Diomedes could have sworn he saw the man's eyes moisten before he eventually said in a low tone, "It belonged to Patroclus, my brother, until

Hector killed him."

What was there to say to that? Diomedes felt a fool for having brought it up. Mouth dry with worry over Achilles' reaction, all he could force from between his lips was a rather inadequate, "Oh." He might not like or trust the man, but he had just lost his brother.

Eventually Achilles looked at him as if he had forgotten he was there and said, "If you're no longer hungry, I think we should try to get some sleep." He rose to go to his own bed. As he removed his tunic and lay down, he looked back at Diomedes and said, "One last thing: the food hidden under the carpets will attract vermin. Eat it or get rid of it, but get it out of there."

Diomedes was so surprised that Achilles had noticed that he didn't even reply, just stared at Achilles as he rolled over to go to sleep. Diomedes finished his wine in one last gulp. Moving towards his own pallet in the corner, he blew out the one lamp left alight and felt his head swim from the wine as he stumbled to bed. He lay there, drifting in and out of sleep, having nightmares until exhaustion finally took over.

***

Agamemnon was fuming when he returned to his tent, which was in effect a portable villa. The arrogance of Achilles was astounding. The nerve of him! If the Myrmidons had attacked at the same time as the rest of the forces – well, yes, they would probably have been slaughtered along with the rest, but at least then he wouldn't have that arrogant prick to worry about.

In truth he was annoyed with himself; he should have expected this attack and been ready for it. But the men needed an occasional outlet for their frustration from staring at those damn walls, and he'd assumed that it would take the Trojans at least two or three days to recover from the loss of Hector. That mistake had cost him dearly.

Odysseus was waiting in his tent when he arrived, sitting back comfortably on a bed of pillows, drinking his wine. The sight of him, so seemingly carefree, while the army had suffered a massacre, inflamed Agamemnon's temper further. "Where the hell have you been?"

He walked over to the large trestle table, and poured himself a cup of wine. Odysseus said nothing; he knew better. Agamemnon went on. "It was a bloody slaughter."

"How many did we lose?" Odysseus finally asked.

"Far too many!" the king replied gruffly, but Odysseus had always had a disarming way about him; he was ever the negotiator, able to calm tempers with no apparent effort, and he had always advised Agamemnon well. "At least fifteen thousand men are dead. We don't know for sure yet, there may be more; it'll be morning before we can get anything resembling an accurate count," he said, throwing himself down on the cushions opposite Odysseus.

"A bloody night," mused Odysseus. He always fancied himself a bit of a poet. Agamemnon had read some of his drivel, and subsequently brought his own poet from Mycenae to write the story of their victory over Troy, a fellow called Homer. Still, it wouldn't do to offend someone as cunning as Odysseus.

"Bloody? That's one way to put it. I'll send back to Greece for more men in the morning," he said. "That arrogant fool Achilles blocked their advance, but refused to engage them." Watching Odysseus over his wine cup, he added, "You have something on your mind, old friend. Out with it."

Odysseus was obviously reluctant to speak. "I haven't yet worked out all the details, but I wouldn't advise sending ships for more men just yet."

“We lost fifteen thousand men, if not more. That’s a serious blow. We will need more men,” replied Agamemnon.

“No; what you *need* is to get through the walls. You still have about a hundred and twenty thousand men here; there are no more than thirty thousand fighting men inside Troy.” Odysseus looked and sounded as if he had said something incredibly clever. The man could be really difficult at times; getting a straight answer out of him was like drawing blood from a stone.

“Very well, so what do you want to do? Fly us over the walls on a flock of seagulls? Do you think that if we ask nicely, the Trojans will just open the gates and let us in?” said Agamemnon irritably. “You know as well as I do that to take a wall like that, you need almost ten attackers for every one defender. We don’t have that; that’s why we’ve been sitting here trying to starve them out for ten years.”

“Which hasn’t worked,” commented Odysseus, leaning forward. “It’s time to try something else, Agamemnon. Something unexpected.”

“What ‘something’, Odysseus? You’ve obviously come up with an idea. What is it?” Agamemnon’s patience was starting to wear thin.

“First I need to know something: exactly how many ships did Hector burn on the day he attacked the beach?”

Agamemnon thought back to that day. Yet another surprise attack; all the Greek heroes had been attacking the eastern wall of Troy, and only a shield wall led by lesser men had blocked Hector’s path and prevented him from laying waste to all their ships, leaving them stranded on this god-forsaken strip of beach.

“Sixteen triremes burned that day,” he eventually replied.

“Sixteen?” Odysseus responded, musing. “That means that we have about fifty-nine ships, too many to sail home with full oar banks?”

"Well, I haven't done a full count yet, but that sounds about right."

"I need you to hold fifteen, Agamemnon," he said, looking around warily to make sure nobody else had come in. "Do we know anyone who's leaking information to the Trojans inside the walls?" he asked.

"I'm sure we can find someone, and if not, there are ways of getting it in. What do you need to leak out?" Agamemnon was interested now. A light glowed in his eyes. He had known Odysseus a long time, and when he got like this he tended to have a particularly sneaky plan up his sleeves.

"I want them to believe that some of our lands back in Greece are being attacked from Gaul, or those steppes animals; it doesn't matter exactly where," said Odysseus.

"Don't be stupid, man; if they think that they will resist twice as much, knowing that we'd have to leave soon. What sort of blind fool are you?" Agamemnon almost choked on his wine as he assimilated this idea.

"That's exactly what I want them to think, Agamemnon. Then we will attack all out for a few days; hit them hard in numerous places around the walls." Odysseus obviously liked this idea or he was drunk, because he was gesturing wildly as he spoke.

Agamemnon cut in sharply. "Are you intent on destroying my army, Odysseus, or have you finally lost your mind?"

"Just listen, Agamemnon. We want them to think us desperate for a quick victory, because our homelands are under threat and we have to leave. That way they'll understand when we do."

"*What*?" bellowed Agamemnon.

"It's a ruse, Agamemnon, just a ruse. Listen, you know the way those boetian animals up the beach worship the great rider?"

Agamemnon nodded, gritting his teeth in impatience to see what the old man was getting at. "Well, every year they build a wooden horse and burn it as a sacrifice to their god. What if they built a huge horse to watch over their trip home, and didn't burn that one?"

"What then? We build a huge wooden horse and just sail off home? Odysseus, how does this help me?"

"No, no, you don't understand. We build a huge wooden horse and stuff it full of soldiers! Think about it." Odysseus' eyes were bright; sitting up straight on the cushions, he was almost hopping with excitement.

"Fine, but it will just sit there on the beach, Odysseus. Won't they leave it there, or burn it themselves? Achilles did sack the temple of Apollo, so that seems the most likely outcome." In spite of his words, Agamemnon's interest was growing.

"You've met Priam, Agamemnon. He's one of the most pious men you are ever likely to come across. He wouldn't burn it, for fear of offending any god, his or another's." Odysseus leaned forward, pointing at Agamemnon with his wine cup. "He will drag the thing inside his city as part of their celebration of the end of the siege."

Agamemnon thought about it. From the few times he had met Priam, this assessment sounded accurate. He might even have done the same thing himself. Looking at the old man again, he considered him. Odysseus was a good councillor, but he was too clever by half. Would he have tried a similar trick on him? He'd bear watching, but the king liked this idea.

"All right, they get inside the city that way and then what? That few men couldn't take the city, let alone hold it, and we will be halfway across the Aegean!"

"That attack tonight worked only because we were celebrating, Agamemnon. Think about what Troy will be like if the siege is lifted and they see our ships on the horizon heading for home! There won't be a man in that city able to stand for celebrating. The soldiers wait till dark of night, then sneak out of the horse. Their work should be minimal - a few drunken guards in the square. Then they signal to us, and we have the rest of the night to get back."

"Yes, Odysseus. Yes, I can see it now. By the time they wake up, there will be a hundred thousand Greeks inside. It will be a massacre; the streets of Troy will run red. They will pay in blood for every Greek life they cost, for every day I have wasted outside those accursed walls!" Agamemnon's eyes took on a distant look as he spoke, seeing the scenes as he painted them with his words: his dream of destroying Troy finally coming to fruition.

They sat there long into the night, discussing the number of men who could fit inside the wooden horse and how they would need to be armed; they must also provide water, to keep the men alive during the heat of a summer day inside a wooden box. All such details had to be finalised before an operation this size could be carried out.

As the first fingers of dawn were reaching the sky, and they were running low on wine, Odysseus broached a dangerous subject. "You had another fight with Achilles tonight, Agamemnon? I heard something from a few drunks passing before you returned."

"That useless degenerate? Yes, I had an argument with him. He disobeyed a direct order to attack the Trojans when it might have made a difference to the outcome."

"Are you sure it wouldn't just have cost the lives of himself and his men, along with the other soldiers you sent after them?"

"How dare you? I gave him an order; his duty was to obey it. I don't care if it kills him."

"He is a good soldier," said Odysseus placatingly, "and in

his shoes, you would have done exactly the same. He resembles you too much, Agamemnon, that's why you rub each other the wrong way."

"I am nothing like that pup!" thundered Agamemnon.

"He is almost exactly as you were at that age, Agamemnon: loyal to your men, wise and a great leader. I want you to apologise to him."

At this, Agamemnon looked as if he had been struck. Jumping to his feet, he thundered, "Never! I will never apologise to that arrogant little prick."

"You don't have to mean it, Agamemnon, but you *must* apologise; say it was the drink and the shock of the attack that set you off."

"Why would I do that?" growled Agamemnon.

"Can you think of anyone better to hold the gates, Agamemnon? And if we are wrong and Priam does just burn the horse where it stands – well, is there anyone you would rather lose? Make no mistake, Agamemnon, this will be the most risky mission you have ever entrusted to a warrior." Odysseus looked Agamemnon in the eye. "A single reflection of armour, a noise, a movement, a single sneeze, and they're all dead."

"Very well, but he dies when this is over," answered Agamemnon sullenly.

"As you wish," replied Odysseus eventually, breaking off eye contact and looking down sadly at the thick carpets.

Chapter Seven

Achilles woke later than usual, but still early. The sun was a finger's breadth above the horizon on a bright summer morning. This far down the beach, there was little trace of the slaughter of the previous night. Achilles had wisely chosen his campsite at a distance from the city, for precisely that reason. Nothing put a man off his breakfast more than the smell of death warming in the morning sun.

Diomedes was lying awake on his pallet, pretending to be asleep, but his breathing was irregular and gave him away. It looked as if their talk last night had not completely alleviated the boy's fear. With a clean chiton pulled on over his head, he called to Diomedes. "Time to get up, lad! And you should have my breakfast ready when I wake up." Diomedes' head rose up, and he stared at him, but Achilles was smiling mischievously.

"You'd better get something to eat quickly. Pull on a chiton and take a few of those towels," said Achilles, pouring himself some watered wine. As an afterthought he poured Diomedes a cup too, but he'd noticed how quickly it had taken effect on the boy last night when it was only half wine and half water, so this time it was mostly water slightly flavoured with the deep red wine.

Diomedes was ready quickly, and brought over the rough woollen towels. Achilles grinned discreetly to himself at how nervously the boy looked at him when he reached for a slice of cold pink beef, and then shoved it into his mouth as though afraid

Achilles would stop him.

"How far had your training progressed?" asked Achilles, as a third slice of beef disappeared into a sleep-deprived face. A busy day would leave him too tired to stay awake worrying at night.

Diomedes was trying to choke down the beef, and when enough of it was gone to get his tongue around, he started attempting to speak, until Achilles was forced to stop him. "The first thing you need to learn, boy, is not to speak with your mouth full. Take smaller bites when you are eating, it'll make it easier. I can wait until you finish your mouthful." Diomedes nodded his comprehension and chewed for nearly thirty seconds before he was ready to answer.

"Well, I had done a lot of archery. I won that bow."

Achilles raised a hand to forestall him. "I know all about your archery skills; I meant swords and spears."

"I had some training on the sword, sir, but my uncle said I was too small yet for the phalanx, so refused me the spear and shield." As he spoke, Diomedes lowered his head, staring in shame at the thick carpets, barely resembling the boy who had looked so excited about his archery skills only a second before.

Achilles nodded in understanding. "Have any of the other boys your age been permitted to join the phalanx?" he asked.

"Not in three years, sir," replied Diomedes, still looking at the carpet. "Back then, all boys training with the spear and shield started at thirteen to fourteen, but they haven't since then."

"That makes sense," replied Achilles, putting a hand under Diomedes' chin to lift his head up so that he could look him in the eye. "The siege, Diomedes: that's exactly what it does in the long term." Diomedes' eyes widened as he tried to understand. "There has never been a siege of this length before, but it makes sense that all the meat and the best food goes to the fighting men to keep their strength up. When is the last time you had meat?"

Diomedes didn't even have to think about it. "My uncle got us some donkey meat only last Thursday," he replied. Under Achilles' stare he continued, "I've only had a few bites before that."

"As I thought. You will never reach full growth without eating properly." He tapped the table with his finger. "While you're here, eat all you can. I'll see you fill out. Don't just take the meat, though; eat the fruit too."

Diomedes looked at the platter of fruit in confusion. He had obviously never seen such food before and very cautiously chose an apple. Achilles smiled, picked one out himself and took a bite before standing and moving to the tent flaps. Eudoros was outside waiting, as usual, when Achilles emerged. "Who do I have today?"

A small tilt of the head was as much of a bow as Achilles allowed from any of his men, and so Eudoros' head dropped that fraction as he answered. "Abydos, my lord."

"A good man; how has he been doing since he was given the command?" asked Achilles, looking over at some of the men standing to attention. Abydos had obviously taken his new command very seriously; his men were turned out without a buckle out of place. "After last night, I think we might need to double the usual guard."

Eudoros snorted a laugh. Almost all his laughs had come as snorts in the years since his nose had last been broken. "Already done. Abydos wanted to treble it but I managed to talk him down; I think he just wanted more of the men under his command. The lad's capable, but he might be a little too ambitious. The rest are waiting spread out around the ridge so as not to look as if we're preparing for battle."

"Good. He might not be wrong, though, given how

Agamemnon reacted last night. Anyway, we can worry about that when it becomes a problem. Can we trust him?"

"You know his background as much as I do or better, Achilles. He saved your father's life against the Thracians, which is why you let him join the Myrmidons," replied Eudoros a little uncomfortably.

Achilles looked across at the waiting men. "I suppose so. I just wish I'd had him with us in Persia; any man who was there is a man I would trust behind me in a shield wall." He looked back towards the tent, frowning. "Diomedes!" he shouted. "Come out here."

Diomedes' head poked nervously through the tent flaps, followed by a scrawny arm holding the remains of his apple, the rest of him almost tripping on the tent flap, in a tunic made for a boy with a lot more meat on his bones. The sight still made Achilles' fists clench at the reminder of the loss of his brother. "What's done is done," he thought, as his hands grasped each other around the apple core, behind his back, and tears blocked his vision for a moment, before he wrestled his anger and loss under control. Agamemnon would pay, but this was not the time.

"Yes, my lord?" said Diomedes, when he came within a yard of Achilles, bowing so low that he almost fell over in his haste, though his eyes were fearfully scanning Myrmidon faces to both sides.

"Relax, lad." Achilles put a hand on his shoulder, forcing him to straighten up. "We don't bow on campaign; save that for palaces and such. Dip your head only; that way, you're not pointing me out to every potential assassin in the area." Diomedes reluctantly straightened his back, rising to his full height, which was more than Achilles had expected it to be. He would make a fine man one day, if he ever managed to build up some muscle.

"Now," Achilles went on, looming over him, "you say you have started to train on the sword, so let's see what you have learned. Choose a blade from the rack over there." He pointed to some weapons which lay in neat rows on a rack.

"You're giving the boy a weapon? Have you seen how he looks at you, Achilles? It's a confused mixture of terror and hatred. He will probably stab you with it as soon as he gets a chance," whispered Eudoros as soon as the boy had turned his back, his eyes never leaving the boy as he spoke.

"So now you fear that the mighty Achilles can't defend himself from an untrained boy?" laughed Achilles. "Fear not, old friend. I'll train the lad, but I'm no fool."

Diomedes went over to the rack, seized the first sword in the row and turned to return to Achilles, who held up a hand to stop him in his tracks. Diomedes shied away.

"Did you actually choose that blade or lift it up? Feel the weapon, boy; you should experience a connection with it." Taking the blade from the boy's hand, he gave it a few practice swings. "It's a good sword, you have an eye for that, but it's not for you. Look through the rack; these aren't barbarian blades, they are primarily for phalanx fighting, and the blade should be the length of your forearm for balance. This is nearly as big as you are."

Achilles walked to the end of the rack and picked up a much smaller blade which looked like a large hunting knife in his huge hand, and Diomedes looked apprehensive as Achilles approached him. "Try this," he said, holding the sword reverently. "It belonged to Patroclus when he was younger, and it should be a much better fit for you until we can have one made." Diomedes took it from his hands. The sword looked made for him with his short, scrawny arms, and his eyes lit up as he looked at it, then up at Achilles and back at the sword. "If you prove yourself, maybe you can earn the right to carry that blade."

Achilles went inside his tent, and emerged a moment later, carrying his own sword. Compared to the one he had just given Diomedes, it looked monstrous, but in his hand, it was dwarfed to a normal size.

"All right," he said, after a couple of practice swings, "come at me."

Diomedes looked down at the sword in his hand, and then at Achilles. He stepped forward slowly, left foot leading in the way he had been taught, sliding his foot forward along the sand and dragging his right foot behind to keep his balance stable.

Achilles watched him hesitantly move, watching for Achilles' reach, and trying to judge how close he could come. His moves were classic trained motions, just the kind that he remembered Hector making at around the same age, when they had first met. Diomedes darted a slash low at Achilles' leg, which Achilles easily brushed aside, but Diomedes lashed up with the backlash of the cut towards Achilles' exposed forearm. Again, Achilles swept up his sword to knock it aside, but the move had surprised him. Had Diomedes been an adult with full reach and a full-sized sword, Achilles would have taken at least a scratch on the arm for his inattention.

Diomedes took two more quick swings before stabbing his sword straight towards Achilles. Achilles slid his blade along that of Diomedes, twisted his sword underneath and lifted, wrenching the sword out from Diomedes' grip and flipping it into the air. The sword came to a clattering halt on the ground a few feet away from them and Achilles nodded respectfully to Diomedes.

"Not bad at all. You've had a bit of training, but there are a few things that you need to work on." He went over to pick up Diomedes' sword. "For the present, I want to work on building up your muscle. See that post over there?" He indicated one of a number of poles which were two foot thick and about eight foot high, standing just beyond the weapon racks. “Take one of the dull practice swords, and Eudoros will show you how to work with the post. I expect you to do one hour on the post every morning after breakfast. If I ever catch you using a good blade on it, you will never hold a sword again.” The last words were said with intensity, as he stared hard at Diomedes.

The boy shrank away from the stare and looked nervously at Eudoros, who nodded to him. Together they moved away towards the posts, and Achilles put the swords away and picked up the apple he hadn’t yet finished. He crunched into it as he watched Eudoros showing Diomedes the swings and strokes for training against the post.

The shock of the blunt sword repeatedly hitting the solid wooden post would hurt Diomedes’ arm, and send shock after shock of pain up the arm until his muscles hardened to the effort, but it would build the muscles the lad would need if he ever hoped to be a great soldier.

Distractedly noticing movement round one of his large barrack tents, Achilles bit straight through the core of his apple. He looked at what was left and spat out the mouthful, glancing back at the approaching group.

Surrounded by his own Mycenaean bodyguard, and his usual group of hangers-on and advisers, Agamemnon was approaching. Stretched across his bulk was a bright, pristine white chiton trimmed in gold leaf with scroll-work all along the edges and belted gold coins, presumably bearing the faces of the gods. He looked every inch the Greek king, with his oiled and curled beard and expensive clothing.

Achilles looked back at Eudoros with Diomedes, then checked to make sure Abydos was paying attention. Yes, he already had the bodyguard closing the ring a little tighter.

Achilles could see them more obviously now between the tents, helmeted heads cresting sand dunes. Catching Abydos' eye, he made a subtle gesture to hold the men back a little. He was strongly tempted to bear a sword himself, but turned away from them and walked towards Agamemnon's group, exuding all the confidence he could manage.

"Agamemnon, what brings you here?"

"I want to talk to you, Achilles. Might we step inside?" asked Agamemnon.

Achilles let his eyes roam slowly across the mass of faces. "I'm not sure that my tent's big enough."

"Just us, Achilles; the others can wait out here." He gave the others a pointed look before they could argue the point.

Achilles watched the reactions, which ranged from relief, on the faces of his servants, to disappointment, on those of some of his closest advisers; there was outright anger on the face of Ajax of the Locrians, but he was clever enough to keep his mouth shut, and his face averted from Agamemnon as he sneered at Achilles. The Mycenaean bodyguard knew better, and their faces betrayed none of the thoughts that went on behind those eyes. Achilles took all this in as his eyes swept suspiciously across the group looking for the trick, the hidden trap.

"I'm honoured that the great Achilles thinks me worthy of such worry." Agamemnon boomed a great laugh from deep in his huge chest; it was a laugh that sounded genuinely amused, one which carried honesty. That laugh finally convinced Achilles to find out what this was about; he had plenty of men scattered about, ready to sort out any problems that might arise.

Standing to the side, Achilles dipped his head in a shallow bow, sweeping his arm in the direction of his tent by way of invitation for Agamemnon to enter. He would have preferred to enter first, taking that honour from Agamemnon, but he felt safer not having the man at his back.

Achilles' men, the Myrmidons, like true soldier ants, showed no such worries about Agamemnon as Agamemnon's own servants had about Achilles, but then every man Achilles had brought was a soldier first and foremost. He didn't intend holding court on the beach, so why bring servants to war?

As Agamemnon reached the tent entrance, twin spears slanted down to block his way and a third man stepped forward. "Your sword, my lord," he requested, looking Agamemnon in the eye.

Again Agamemnon smiled, twisting his head around to watch Achilles as his hand drifted down to his sword-belt to remove it. Achilles came up to stop him, saying, "That won't be necessary."

Abydos held Achilles' gaze for a second, obviously uncomfortable at letting another warrior into his master's tent, alone and armed. Although well past his prime and grossly overweight, Agamemnon was still considered a warrior with few equals. Abydos must have seen something in Achilles' eyes because he broke his gaze, looking down quickly before putting a hand to one of the spears to lift it up. Both guards took their cue and stepped back to their posts at the edge of the doors, spears held up perfectly straight, and Agamemnon stepped through the door flap of the tent without hesitation.

Entering the tent behind him, Achilles swept his eyes around outside, catching Eudoros' one good eye watching closely while he appeared to oversee Diomedes as he trained. Even one-eyed, he could probably still do both.

"Your men are protective," said Agamemnon over his shoulder, still smiling as he made his way over to the trestle table. "May I?" he asked, indicating the wine cup and jug sitting on the table, beads of condensation rolling down the side.

"Help yourself," replied Achilles, moving to one of his recliners. He picked up the cup he had left there earlier while talking to Diomedes and sat back, watching as the bigger man poured himself some wine and moved to the other recliner.

The wood creaked under his bulk, but he must have been used to such a reaction from his furniture, since he seemed not to notice. He sipped from his cup, giving no indication of his opinion of the wine, as his gaze slipped from place to place around the tent, taking everything in. Eyes a little bloodshot, it was obvious that he had been drinking late the night before, though he bore the effects well.

"A very impressive tent you have here, Achilles; almost a palace away from home."

"Thank you, Agamemnon. It was a gift from my father when I went away to fight for Troy and the Persians, and has stood me in good stead. But you didn't call over to make small talk and compliment me on my tent, did you?"

"Straight to the point as always, Achilles," replied Agamemnon. "I can rely on you for that." He seemed ill at ease as he looked around the tent once more. "This isn't an easy thing for a king to say, Achilles, but I am sorry about last night." He was looking down now, unwilling to make eye contact with Achilles; he lifted the cup towards his mouth, but stopped, looking deep into the wine before dropping his hand again.

"It was the wine, Achilles; that and my rage at losing those men. When you didn't follow orders it made me angry, but you were right." He took a sip of wine and shook his head. "It is difficult for a king to admit he is wrong."

"A king, most of all, should admit when he is wrong, Agamemnon," said Achilles, "because more rests on his decisions than on those of other men. The lives of other men depend on what you decide to do."

"Don't you think I know that, Achilles?" Agamemnon looked up with fire in his eyes, but it faded quickly as he dropped his head again and continued in a lower voice. "When I closed my eyes last night I saw that field of red, littered with the bodies of my loyal soldiers."

He took another drink and a silence stretched out as both men sat there tensely grappling with their thoughts. At last Achilles asked, "How many did we lose last night?"

Agamemnon had the grace to look uncomfortable. They looked across the room at each other for a while, but eventually he spoke. "Twelve thousand from those who were celebrating outside the gates; they were killed almost to a man. A few survived, just enough to give us a rough picture of what happened. We found the sentries killed by arrows near the corners of the city." Here Agamemnon found it hard to go on, but said, "The tally is not complete, but probably another four thousand that I sent in were killed with arrows. Achilles, I need you to advise me, to tell me when I am in the wrong; I need more than the 'yes' men who attach themselves to me. Can I depend on you, Achilles? Can I be sure you are on my side?" asked Agamemnon.

"I fight for Greece, if that's what you mean, and I don't think you can doubt my willingness to tell you if you're in the wrong," responded Achilles in a prickly manner. He knew he should be politic and tactful, but something about Agamemnon made it almost impossible for him to be so.

Agamemnon nodded, and took another drink. "Good, because I need your opinion on a plan which Odysseus has come up with. I want to know what you think of its chance of success, because I cannot let this bloody siege go on forever."

Now he had Achilles' attention. Was this the plan Odysseus had intended to discuss before the battle had interrupted them last night? It certainly explained why Agamemnon was apologising and being pleasant this morning. Suspicion flared in Achilles, but he put it aside, because he wanted to hear the details of the plan. This was the bait, he knew; now he needed to find the hook.

"Very well, Agamemnon; you have my full attention," said Achilles.

"First of all, this must stay between us for the moment. The men have to believe what we tell them, or the plan will fall apart."

"Of course."

"Well, Odysseus has a plan to get us inside the city walls."

"Are we receiving the help of the gods for this?" asked Achilles sceptically. The walls of Troy were legendary for their sheer size and impregnability. Nobody had ever managed to breach them.

"In a manner of speaking." Agamemnon laughed at his own joke. Achilles watched him, wondering what he had missed. "Are you familiar with the boetian god, the horseman?"

"I have heard of him," replied Achilles, confused. Agamemnon continued to speak.

***

Eudoros watched Achilles disappear into his tent with Agamemnon. Even with only one eye he could continue his sword work while watching them; he knew where the practice stake was from hundreds of hours of training.

Ajax of the Locrians was still there with Agamemnon's bodyguard. Eudoros had had to work with the man many years before, when Achilles was still a child, before he had taken over the Myrmidons as his birthright. Ajax had a taste for cruelty that Eudoros had not seen before in any man; he seemed to enjoy the pain he inflicted on others.

In the years he'd worked beside him, he had known Achilles

to fight for many things, for the glory and honour, the riches gained through war and the protection of his homeland, but Eudoros had never seen him take pleasure in killing. Each death weighed heavily on his conscience. It was one of the things that tied men to Achilles; they knew their lives were more than numbers to him. He would risk their lives only in order to protect a greater number.

Ajax was a different animal, and in Agamemnon he seemed to have found a kindred spirit, tying himself to the king like a pet dog. Since Agamemnon had begun this war against Troy, his loyalty to his men was gone. To him, life now held nothing more than beating the Trojans. He would throw everything away to beat them, including the lives of his soldiers. The well-being of the men in his rank and file meant nothing to him.

Eudoros felt a wave of shame for the faint hope that, here in the middle of their camp, Agamemnon might try something stupid and give them a chance to attack. Even Agamemnon's Mycenae bodyguard would not be able to stand up to the Myrmidons, and Eudoros would be aiming his sword straight at Ajax. He felt fairly sure that Achilles could take Agamemnon, though Achilles hadn't brought his sword in with him and Agamemnon had.

A quick check showed that Abydos had his eyes on the tent and his men in a tight formation, secluding the extra men from the direct view of the Mycenae. At a signal they could all fall on the bodyguard in seconds, but to the casual observer they seemed relaxed and merely sharpening their tools.

Eudoros turned back to Diomedes and corrected some of his positions. Every half an hour or so, he gave the boy a break. It would take time to build up the muscles he'd need to be a warrior, and he would only hurt the boy if he pushed him too hard, too fast. After three such cycles, he decided to give him a meal break.

Looking back at Achilles' tent and listening for raised voices, he brought Diomedes away to the mess tent, since he couldn't eat in Achilles' tent while Agamemnon was there.

Another hour passed, incredibly slowly, as Eudoros cast glances at Achilles' tent between bites of food. The boy was eating slowly, but that wasn't surprising. Having been in a siege on a little town on the borders of Thrace in a previous battle, Eudoros had some idea of how little food the Trojans would have. The boy probably hadn't eaten much more than porridge or broth in his whole life, and the only meat he was likely to have seen were the weevils in his black bread.

Eventually, the flaps of Achilles' tent were tossed aside, as Agamemnon emerged, with Achilles one step behind; for a wonder, they were laughing and joking together as if they were the best of friends.

Rising from the table, Eudoros began walking back towards Achilles' tent to find out what was going on, and arrived just in time to witness a sight he'd never thought he would see: Achilles and Agamemnon embraced and kissed one another's cheeks in parting. If he didn't know better he might have thought them fast friends, but as they separated his friend met his eye with the slightest shake of the head, barely visible.

Eudoros stood in the background and noticed how Ajax's face hardened as if he were gritting his teeth when they hugged. Eudoros waited silently as pleasantries were exchanged, and Agamemnon departed with his entourage in tow; the men looked sweaty and disgruntled at being left to wait outside in the heat of an early sun for nearly two and a half hours.

Following Achilles back inside the tent, Eudoros waited till they were alone to enquire, "What the hell happened?" Achilles looked at him with a sly grin on his face and made his way to the table to pour a cup of wine. Handing that to Eudoros, he filled another for himself. Eudoros could contain himself no longer. "What's going on? Are you best friends now, all of a sudden?"

Achilles raised a hand to forestall him. "Peace, Eudoros; you know me better than that. Sit down, friend, and I'll tell you all."

They talked for a while, interrupted at one point by Diomedes' putting his head in through the tent flaps; Eudoros sent him back to the training post while they finished their conversation. By the end of it, Eudoros was smiling too.

"You know you can't trust him," he said, more statement than question. "Even Odysseus has said Agamemnon won't let you leave Troy alive."

"I'm not a complete fool, Eudoros," replied Achilles smiling, "but he needs me till he has men on the gates and inside the city. That means we can trust him until then." Eudoros looked confused for a second, then Achilles added, "I'll be inside the horse, Eudoros; the fool wants me to hold the gates for him," and they both laughed.

"Now," said Achilles when they had regained control of themselves, "you have had the men out collecting wood in the forest?"

Eudoros nodded solemnly. "I've had a steady stream of two hundred at a time going to the forest all morning, sir. We should be ready in an hour or so."

"Very well, then it's probably time we thought about getting him ready. Call the boy inside."

Eudoros ducked out through the tent flaps, and returned a few minutes later, leading a sweating Diomedes. "Have you eaten?" Achilles asked him.

"Yes, sir. Eudoros brought me for some food earlier," he mumbled in reply.

"Have you ever seen a dead body, Diomedes?" asked Achilles.

Diomedes nodded, looking a little paler. "I have watched a few battles from the walls, sir, and seen some of the injured and dead being dragged inside."

"Well, this may be a little different. This body won't be as freshly dead as those you have seen before, and it will be a lot closer than watching from the walls." Diomedes looked a little shaky at the thought, and Achilles put a hand on his shoulder to steady him. "You are going to help me to prepare Patroclus' body for his funeral. If you are still hungry, eat now, because you probably won't feel like it for some time afterwards."

Diomedes looked frightened and shook his head slowly. "Good. Go back to the mess tent where you ate earlier and bring me a bucket of hot water. We will be in the smaller white tent when you return."

"Do you trust him not to run away?" Eurodos asked as Diomedes disappeared out through the tent flaps. "You saw his face; the lad's terrified."

"If he were going to run, it would have been last night, I think." Achilles looked thoughtful for a moment. "Everyone would recognise him as mine now if he tried to leave; he wouldn't get far," he concluded as he left the tent with his friend.

In the small white tent where lay the body of Patroclus, still wearing the armour he had died in, Achilles was a different man. Gone was the relaxed warrior Eudoros knew. Even a blind man could see he was struggling with what he saw. He had protected his brother all his life, even taking beatings from his father for the boy when his father had been in a drunken rage. Now this beloved brother lay dead before him, his skin waxy white as if he had been carved out of a thick candle, cold to the touch even in the heat of the day. The smell of meat left too long in the sun permeated the air as soon as the tent flaps closed behind them.

Standing at his side, Eudoros could see that Achilles wasn't even looking at the body; his eyes had the far-away look of a man who saw far beyond what was in front of him, and his jaw moved constantly, the only sound inside the tent that of his grinding teeth.

Diomedes entered hesitantly, looking around, holding the bucket of water. Glancing back, Eudoros caught the hint of a wry smile on Achilles' lips, as he softly murmured, "I told you." He turned and beckoned Diomedes to come closer with the bucket. "Eudoros, would you leave us now and see that the pyre is built and ready?"

"My lord." Eudoros bowed and backed slowly out of the tent. As the flap closed behind him, he heard Achilles speaking softly to Diomedes, saying, *this was my little brother, the one Hector slew.*

Chapter Eight

The fire from the torch caught the straw stuffed between the logs and slowly began to spread through the timber stacked twelve feet high, gaining speed and momentum as it spread, and heat began to build in the pyre; the snap and pop of the burning wood was audible to the two thousand watching men lined up in full armour.

Many similar fires were springing up simultaneously all along the beach, as men gave up friends and family members who had died in the slaughter of the previous night, so that, from a distance, the beach must have looked like the stars in the sky. Patroclus, whose pyre held everyone's attention, was the north star.

His men had worked hard all day, collecting the wood, and Achilles was satisfied with the result. It was a pyre worthy of a king, and Patroclus would have been proud of it. Achilles himself hoped to have one as splendid when he passed. Silence enveloped him, as it did most of the beach, while he watched the flames reach up through the pyre, lighting more wood as it wove its slow route up through to Patroclus, wrapped in a sheet of the finest Egyptian cotton, to take him on his final journey across the river Styx.

The heat on his face built up from warm to hot to uncomfortable. He barely noticed the discomfort, though part of his mind knew he couldn't stand there indefinitely. A hand on his arm pulled him back to reality as a tear dried on his cheek. He looked into the worried face of Eudoros, but his friend wasn't looking at him; his eyes slid away from Achilles to his other side. Achilles followed his gaze to the small form of Diomedes, one hand up to shield his face from the heat, glancing between Achilles and the blazing pyre with a terrified look on his face.

Coming back to himself, Achilles laid a big hand on Diomedes' shoulder and turned him around to move them back from the fire to where the entire Myrmidon phalanx was lined up in full battle formation. As Achilles walked towards them, two thousand spears clashed against their shields, as if in signal; one final battle salute from the men to one of their own, followed by a huge reverberating war cry that echoed across the plains to the walls of Troy.

As Achilles turned to watch the pyre burn, his eyes passed over the walls of Troy. Rising above the walls into the dark night were flickering flames, trailing smoke up into the twilight sky to disappear into darkness. His eyes were still locked on the walls of Troy when Diomedes pulled on his hand, and he looked down into the confused eyes of a boy whose world had been turned upside down. "Hector?" he asked; one simple word. Although Diomedes had seen him fall, he had only now realised that Hector must be on the Trojan pyre.

Diomedes' head lowered, and his shoulders slumped forward. Achilles understood what must be going through the boy's head. At around the same age Achilles had killed his first man, but that was a different time; children of this generation were a little softer than when he'd been a boy, as their fathers had fought all the major battles for them. He well remembered his first swordmaster falling; a man whom he had respected and emulated as he grew up, a man from whom he had wanted praise and respect as much as from his own father.

Achilles dropped to one knee by the boy and said softly, so

that no one else would hear, "Offer your prayers to the gods for him." Diomedes' head snapped up at that, eyes searching Achilles' for signs of treachery. "He was a good man, Diomedes," Achilles said softly. "He was my friend, too." Looking back at the pyre of Patroclus, he whispered, as if to himself, "If he hadn't killed my brother, I would be offering him prayers myself." He looked back at Diomedes through eyes glazed with tears, and they came to an understanding. Standing together, they offered up their prayers and sent them with the flames carrying the body of Patroclus high into the heavens.

Much later, as the flames from the fire began to die down, and Diomedes began to yawn, Achilles lifted a skin of wine lying near his feet; pulling the stopper from the skin with his teeth, he took a long pull from the skin, before splashing some on to the sand. Looking at Diomedes, he hesitated before handing the skin to him.

Looking at Achilles, Diomedes took a mouthful of wine from the skin, then a longer drink, gulping it down till Achilles' large hand pressed down the bottom of the wine skin. "Easy, there," he said. Diomedes was abashed and his cheeks reddened, whether from the warming effect of the wine or from embarrassment, Achilles couldn't tell.

"Now offer a libation for the shade of the fallen," he said, subtly indicating Troy to Diomedes. The deep red wine poured from the skin and soaked into the sand, reminding Diomedes of the blood flowing out of Hector as he'd died in the circle the previous day. Achilles stopped the flow, and snapped Diomedes out of his daydream. "Time you were in bed," said Achilles and sent Diomedes to the tent they shared.

The day's activity had taken its toll, and Diomedes was tired, but fear of what might happen when he fell asleep spurred him to take some food and a cup of wine from the trestle table and bring it back to the door of the tent, where he sat and watched the men drink and talk late into the night. Some time later, strong arms lifted Diomedes and he woke to see the face of Achilles as he carried him to his pallet in the corner and covered him gently with blankets.

***

The morning dawned hazily, or maybe that was just Diomedes, whose head was full of wine fumes. As the sun crested the horizon, Eudoros had Diomedes out working his sword against the large wooden post and the haze burned away as he began to sweat.

Entire days passed in this way: swordplay in the morning until his muscles ached, then he was sent running on the beach with the other soldiers till his legs felt like they were going to fall off; there was swimming to wash off the sweat before they ate their lunch. Afternoons were the same, with the addition of some diluted wine with his meal. This was almost the first meat Diomedes had had in his life, and there was as much as he could eat every time he sat down.

Nights were almost a blur as he stumbled back to his cot, too tired to do anything. Even the ever-present danger of living in the middle of an enemy camp wasn't enough to overcome his tiredness, but every morning he woke with a jump and looked around in confusion, as, once again, he had to come to terms with being Achilles' prisoner.

Days turned into weeks in this manner, but slowly Diomedes felt his muscles growing stronger; he was able to slice the practice post for longer before his shoulders began to burn. After the second week, Achilles took him aside for his evening practice and trained against him instead of sending him to the post.

More than anything, that first lesson taught Diomedes what he didn't know. He was fast, and his muscles had hardened from two weeks of training and from being properly fed for the first time in his life. Swing as he might, however, his practice sword never came close to Achilles; after disarming Diomedes for the fifth time, he stopped and corrected Diomedes' grip on the sword and the position of his feet.

More days passed, and Diomedes began to realise just how good Achilles was, and, slowly to appreciate that his uncle Pedasus had never had a chance of defending him against this god. Pedasus was a good soldier, but that was all he would ever be, a good soldier; he could never have matched Achilles. Diomedes began to question if even his hero, Hector, had had any chance in their duel. During those long days, the boy decided to train hard, and learn everything Achilles could teach him, against the day when he might have the opportunity to kill Achilles in battle.

Some days were broken by battles, troops passing the Myrmidon camp on the way to attack Troy's walls, then troops returning carrying their wounded. Trojans sometimes came out from behind their great walls to give battle.

The Myrmidons themselves were rarely called into action, but, when they were, Achilles refused to allow Diomedes to come along, and always left a few men behind to train him, though he guessed they were actually there to watch him to make sure he didn't try to escape. It didn't matter; with a battle being fought in the space between the camp and the city, there was nowhere to run to.

The longest month of his short life passed; then, one day, while eating his lunch, Diomedes overheard some of the other men grumbling angrily. He wasn't close enough to hear what they were discussing without making it obvious that he was listening, but he caught something about an attack, and families, which sounded like they wanted to go home. Asking Achilles about it later, he was told that reports were arriving from their homelands of tribes attacking their cities from the north; these were horse tribes for the most part, but there had been numerous similar reports from different cities.

"It's nothing for you to worry about," said Achilles in a light voice, "but with an entire generation of young men here in Troy to wage Agamemnon's war, our usual home defences have been left fairly weak. It was only a matter of time before some of those barbarians decided to take advantage of that weakness."

This reply was given while Achilles strapped on his sandals; he didn't look up and didn't seem particularly concerned. "Doesn't it worry you that your home is being attacked?" Diomedes asked, shocked by Achilles' apparent lack of reaction.

Achilles looked up with a quizzical expression. "Worrying about Greeks now?" he asked with a smile. "They're not attacking *my* home, Diomedes. I am only here because refusal would have had Agamemnon's armies at my father's gates instead of at Troy. Thessaly is far enough south for safety; they would take years to reach my people."

For the first time, Diomedes realised that he had always seen the Greeks as one huge monster attacking his home; listening to Achilles now, he began to think about how the Greek camp was divided. He rarely saw the troops mix, apart from a few distinct groups, and tensions seemed to rise in the Myrmidons whenever Agamemnon or another prince of the army came to visit. They weren't one big army at all; they were numerous small armies, forced together through distrust of each other and fear of Agamemnon.

Suddenly the monotony of training was broken. Diomedes looked around more, and began to see patterns to the groups:

places where certain sets gathered, places where men from the same groups came together to drink and talk in hushed tones. He paid more attention to the snippets of conversation he overheard, men grumbling about home and the war. As the days passed, the grumbling changed in tone; men started talking seriously about going home to protect their lands and families. Fathers worried about children being killed before they'd even reached an age where they could fight to defend themselves.

The effect was like a boulder rolling downhill, starting with slow movements and whispered comments; as more and more men discovered they were in agreement they became braver, their grumbling became louder and they didn't try to hide it as much, talking openly about their worries. Three weeks after Diomedes had asked Achilles about what he'd heard, a group of the men approached Achilles to talk to him about returning to defend their homes.

Diomedes was sitting on his pallet in the corner of the tent, eating, when they came. Achilles was sitting at the trestle table, having his breakfast, and didn't rise as the delegation came to talk to him. Calmly, he listened to them, taking an occasional drink from his cup. Finally, he set his cup on the table and slowly rose.

The fact that his sword was strapped to his waist spoke volumes about his expectation of this meeting, and its symbolism was not wasted on the men, as they nervously shuffled back a step. Achilles walked towards them, smiled, and clapped the leader of the group on the arm. "Thank you for bringing your concerns to me," he said, "I understand and share your fears; I worry about my family at home also. I will seek an immediate audience with Agamemnon."

Although these were Achilles' own men, men sworn to him, whom Achilles had frequently shown himself willing to die to protect, the relief in the tent was palpable; he hadn't taken offence at the demand being made on him. They seemed to release a collective breath as they thanked Achilles and made their way out of his tent.

As they left, Eudoros stepped forward; he had been waiting just inside the door of the tent, his hand continually resting on his sword hilt. For a split second, Diomedes saw a ghost of a smile pass over his face, as he exchanged a quick nod with Achilles, but it had vanished as he followed the men out of the tent.

"At last!" Achilles mumbled to himself as they left. "I thought they'd never build up the courage." Sitting down, he gestured to Diomedes. "Bring me my armour - and my good cloak," he added as an afterthought. "I'm going to meet a king, after all."

Dressed in his finest garb, Achilles kept his word and left for a meeting with Agamemnon without delay. On his return a little later, his mood was a little less buoyant. Agamemnon was apparently unenthusiastic about leaving Troy, thinking of it as admitting defeat against the Trojans, Achilles told his men. He didn't take kindly to acceding to demands from his soldiers.

Achilles explained that he had not been the only Greek prince to approach Agamemnon about their men's concern; almost all the captains had had a similar approach from their men, worried about reports of attacks on their home. They had told Agamemnon that they, and indeed he himself, could eventually be left without a home to return to if these raids were allowed to continue.

The Myrmidon host gathered before Achilles' tent erupted into a frenzied cheer as Achilles told them that Agamemnon had finally acceded and ordered them to begin preparations for their return journey to Greece.

Chapter Nine

Preparation for the return voyage was hectic. Without the option of getting fresh food along the way, every town and village for miles around was being stripped of any food available. Diomedes barely had time to think about what this could mean for him.

His mornings were still spent slashing at the practice post; instead of the run he had grown accustomed to before lunch, however, he was being sent out with foraging parties to stock up for the journey; running, yes, but neither for exercise nor pleasure. They still jogged out, but more often than not they were laden down with supplies on their way back to the camp, with, occasionally, the result of a hunt in one of the forests on the lower hills to carry also.

With so many groups from the army trying to stockpile food, those runs were becoming longer and longer. By the third day, his swim on return was already taking place in the dark. He would have been scared of swimming in the dark but for the forty other men from the foraging parties in the water with him. The splashing and dunking of the men became a bonding experience for Diomedes.

By the time he had eaten afterwards, he was ready for his bed. On the third such night, however, one of the members of the foraging party at his table mentioned something being built further down the beach by the light of numerous large bonfires. Tired though they were, the group of five decided to climb one of the dunes to have a look.

The sand beneath their feet slid down as they climbed, making the dune seem twice the height it really was, but a sense of competition between the five drove their legs. Reaching the top, they collapsed on their backs, staring at the star-filled sky as they caught their breath. Slow moments passed as they sucked cold night air into their lungs.

As their breathing slowed and returned to normal, Alekander, the shortest but heavily-muscled dark young Myrmidon, pulled a small amphora of wine from a bag strapped to his back. The friends (against Diomedes' wishes, that's what they were becoming) looked at each other, and laughter exploded, as they realised he had pilfered the amphora from the quartermaster's stores. It seemed they were going to make a night of it.

Diomedes rolled over onto his stomach after he'd had a mouthful of wine, to see the beach below lit by a myriad bonfires around a central platform upon which something was being built. Four large pillars were being erected from each corner of the platform. Judging from the size of the men working on it, who appeared tiny in the distance, Diomedes estimated the pillars as rising to four times the height of a man.

"What is it?" he asked, awe evident in his voice. He might have felt stupid after he had asked the question but for the fact that he could see the same curiosity reflected in the faces of his companions.

"I heard it's a temple," replied one.

"Someone said something about the boetians building a horse to honour their great rider," replied Aleksander, but he didn't sound convinced.

"Don't be stupid," replied another youth. "It's the pillars of a temple; the roof will be going on any time now that the pillars are finished."

"I'm only repeating what I heard," replied Aleksander sullenly. That mood didn't last, as they returned their attention to the amphora, casting occasional glances back at the beach. By the time they finally went to bed, they had forgotten completely about the construction. Had they kept looking, they might have seen hundreds of men labouring to raise the huge hull of a bireme to rest on the four upright pillars.

The next day dawned bright and hot, the sun a shimmering agony to bloodshot eyes unused to the effects of a night spent drinking. With a pain behind his eyes and a thirst which wouldn't go away no matter how much he drank, Diomedes made his way to the mess tent, preferring not to exhibit his suffering to Achilles.

A quick look at his companions from the previous night showed that he wasn't the only one suffering from the effects of their night's debauchery. Sitting at the table with them, he tried to eat as he did every morning but although he felt he had been starved for a week, the food didn't seem appetising. He forced some down but became aware it wouldn't stay there, and ran to the latrines to the sound of laughter as bits of breakfast made their way back up.

Red-faced, both from emptying his stomach and shame at doing so in front of the other men, Diomedes wiped his mouth on his sleeve and made his way back to the table; he sat there, looking into his cup of water, unable to think about food. His friends around the table laughed and joked, telling him their mothers held their drink better, and Diomedes hung his head in shame.

A hand on his shoulder brought him out of his thoughts. He realised the table had gone quiet and a quick glance up showed him why; the hand was Achilles', Eudoros standing behind him. Shame gripped him anew and he wanted the ground to open up and swallow him.

Rather than giving out to him as he expected, Achilles laughed, and called across in a loud voice, "As if any of you fared better your first time! Ha, I remember Aleksander's not even making it to the latrine, and having to clean the ground afterwards." Raucous laughter met this anecdote and Achilles sat down beside Diomedes. It was the first time Diomedes had seen their leader in the mess tent.

Leaning in close to the boy, he said in a much quieter voice, "Don't eat too much and eat slowly, but you have to eat something; it's a busy day and you'll need your strength. Don't worry about the others; they always make fun of the new guy, but I don't want to see you making a habit of your activities last night." Relief swept through Diomedes as he realised that he wasn't in trouble, mingled with gratitude to Achilles for drawing attention away from him.

"I won't," he mumbled.

"Good. Now, what did you see from the dune last night?"

Diomedes' head shot up in surprise as he realised that Achilles knew what they'd been doing; he instantly regretted the action as the blinding headache which had receded a little returned with a vengeance. Achilles was waiting for an answer, so after a moment he managed to gather some of his wits about him. "The bo-boatians, sir," he stuttered, "or at least I was told that's who it was. They're building some sort of big wooden temple; while we were there, they'd got as far as erecting four big wooden pillars to hold the roof."

"The *roof* was finished before you left," said Achilles in a very deliberate tone. "You were all obviously too distracted to notice." He sat thinking for a minute, tapping a finger on the table, and then rose. Looking around the tent where the men had gathered for breakfast, he judged there to be forty men present, but the message would pass quickly to every Myrmidon he had brought with him.

"Myrmidons!" he shouted. In reply came a roar from forty throats as they all turned to give him their attention, and other men who were passing the tent stopped at attention to hear what their lord had to say.

He looked around at the waiting faces. "For ten years now, you have followed me; ten years away from your families and homes. For ten years we have tried to gain these city walls," he pointed at the huge walls of Troy through the opening of the tent, "for someone else's war. Tomorrow those ten years end."

Silence fell; the noise of work from other Greek camps drifted across the sands, but from the Myrmidons there was no sound. Diomedes watched as more and more Myrmidons paused in their work to draw closer to the tent; others, further back, saw the movement and followed suit. Diomedes heard anvils fall silent and men stop sword drills; the silence seemed to spread like a fire until it felt as if the tent was surrounded by a tight press of men.

He had them in the palm of his hand, a sense of anticipation thick in the air as they waited for his next words. They were not disappointed. "Tomorrow, men, tomorrow we sail for home."

There was a pause, as men looked at each other briefly with a sense of disbelief, took a breath and then another; then came a crescendo of noise, as if all the sounds of a battle had erupted around them. Men were shouting, cheering and wrapping their arms around their comrades, as they realised they had made it through the most famous war the world would ever know; they had survived to go home.

Men whom Diomedes had seen returning from battle covered in blood and gore with grins on their faces were now on their knees crying with the sheer joy of knowing they would soon see their families again.

Diomedes saw something else too, though he couldn't explain what it meant. He saw a look pass between Achilles and

Eudoros, sadness in their eyes. It lasted only an instant, but it had been there.

Chapter Ten

It was well before dawn when Eudoros came to the tent. Bleary-eyed and half awake, Diomedes had seen Achilles rise half an hour earlier. Most of his possessions had already been packed away in his ship the day before.

Diomedes lay where he was, pretending to be still asleep, hoping for a little while longer in bed. He was still trying to work out what this would mean for him. Achilles was going home; would Diomedes be set free to return to Troy, or would Achilles take him back to Greece with him? He shivered at the thought. He had never been out of Troy before Achilles had taken him, and the thought of travelling to a foreign land, the land of these barbarians, terrified him.

He had to admit that he had developed a certain grudging respect for Achilles over his two months in captivity, and he longed to continue the training he was receiving from the only legendary hero left walking the earth since the death of Hector. He could never receive such training under Pedasus.

He could feel Eudoros' eye on his while the man stood there and tried to keep his breathing slow and regular, hoping that they would leave him alone for another little while, and he might manage to get back to sleep.

"Don't worry," said Achilles softly. "He hasn't stirred since I got up. Are all the chosen men ready?"

"They're all fully armed and waiting for you outside," came the gravelly reply. "Sir," he continued more hesitantly, "I don't feel comfortable with this. I would rather come with you."

"No, Eudoros! We have already discussed this," came the reply. Tired though Diomedes was, this conversation had captured his interest; he almost forgot to control his breathing as he strained his ears to catch everything that was said. "I'm sorry, Eudoros, but you're the only one I can trust to get the men home, and if this goes wrong, father will need those men. Besides, we have handpicked those who will accompany me, and one more sword will make little difference."

"I know, but that doesn't make me feel any happier about leaving you here. Your father will have my hide."

"My father will know you were following my orders, Eudoros."

"What about him?" Eudoros asked, clearly referring to Diomedes as he was the only other person in the tent.

"I'll take him with me," was the reply.

Silence reigned for a while. Eudoros obviously didn't agree with whatever Achilles was planning, but Achilles was his lord in all things. The way they spoke about it sent a shiver down Diomedes' spine, and he was going to be brought along.

Finally Eudoros spoke again. "You had better wake the boy then and get him ready. I'll make sure the men are ready to move out with you." He gripped Achilles' forearm in salute, but Achilles pulled him into a more familiar embrace. This lasted only a moment before they moved apart again and Eudoros turned to leave the tent. "Take care of my men," Achilles called after him, his voice thick.

"Always, sir," was his reply as the tent flaps fell back into place.

Diomedes hadn't been given long to get ready. Achilles had come to wake him with a cup of well-watered wine, telling him to eat and dress quickly, in dark colours. Nerves killed his appetite, but he managed a few handfuls of meat with some fruit, all washed down with the cup of watered wine, and stumbled out of the tent two hours before dawn broke.

Achilles was already there, checking the ranks of men whom Eudoros had ready. Rank upon rank of dark-clad men in black leather armour stood to attention like wraiths in the dark night, the creak of leather punctuating the call of cicadas in the night air.

As soon as he'd emerged from the tent, Achilles had handed him a knapsack, and they'd all set off through the night like shadows, moving together in perfect step. Achilles set a hard pace, a steady ground-eating jog which they could keep up for hours, but one that was unusually fast for men in full armour unless they were going into battle, leading Diomedes to believe that they hadn't far to go.

They crested a sand dune, and Diomedes became even more lost. Below them on the beach was the construction which he and the others had seen while drinking a few nights previously; what they had thought to be temple pillars were in fact the legs of a giant wooden horse. It being still dark, he could make out only the outline from this distance, but the proportions were amazing.

Diomedes might have been embarrassed that he'd stopped dead to stare like a country boy in the city for the first time, but, as he recovered himself, he realised that he wasn't the only one. All the men standing around him, fully-grown fierce warriors, had the same stunned looks on their faces; all except Achilles.

Achilles looked rather smug as he surveyed the faces of his men, their ranks and position forgotten in a momentary lapse of discipline as the men in front stopped, dumbstruck, and those behind crowded forward; they all wore the same look of awe on their faces.

"The boetians worship the 'great rider'," he explained. "A

barbarian belief, but they obviously felt it would be helpful to make an offering to him for his protection on the voyage home." Diomedes had the feeling he was holding something back; that small smile indicated there was more to this than he was telling them.

"Right," he called, "enough gawking. Get back in formation." They continued their walk towards the beach.

It was a long way to the place where the Thebans were still working on their creation. Agbo had been right, thought Diomedes; crazy as it had seemed at the time; they *were* building a huge horse. As they drew nearer and nearer, the sheer scale of the edifice became clear. He had thought it big when they'd watched from the dune that night, but up close it was immense; colossal. The entire structure was the size of one of the temples to Apollo in Troy.

Diomedes looked in awe, trying to figure out how many trees it took just to make the legs. The entire Theban contingent of the army must have been gathering this wood for days. As they arrived on the beach, Diomedes could see how the chest of the horse dipped down almost to a point like a huge ribcage, sweeping down from the neck between the front legs and running all the way to the back, where the wood which was being used to form the tail had been covered in loose straw to make it look like real hair as it moved in the breeze.

The hair of the mane seemed to be coated in that too, but the straws were more tightly bound and shorter, so that it stood straight up, and looked as if the horse had been perfectly groomed and made ready for battle, like the huge Andravida warhorses of old, of which Diomedes had seen tapestries, when his uncle had brought him to the palace in Troy on one occasion.

As they arrived, with workmen all around, finishing the construction of the horse, Diomedes didn't notice the other men already standing there in full uniform. Another army unit, roughly the same size as that of Achilles, waited at attention near the head of the enormous wooden horse; distracted as they were, Achilles' men were almost upon them before they answered his call to stop.

Looking around, Diomedes was surprised to recognise Ajax as the man leading the other contingent, one of the most hated men in all of Troy. Standing beside him was the hulking figure of Agamemnon, standing at his leisure talking calmly with Ajax Telamon. Diomedes' hand went reflexively to his sword hilt; he knew he wouldn't be able to take either man, but the smooth wooden grip was comforting in his hand.

A large hand closed over Diomedes', and he looked up into Achilles' eyes: not the friendly face he had seen around the camp but the cold eyes of a killer, framed by the narrow Y-slot of his helmet. Diomedes felt his throat close, understanding suddenly the fear felt by all the men who had faced Achilles in battle. The urge to soil himself was strong, but he suppressed it with an effort and dumbly nodded his head.

The hand dropped away as Achilles strode forward to meet Ajax and Agamemnon and greeted them both like long-lost friends. Agamemnon threw his arms around Achilles, and embraced him in a massive bear-hug. Ajax Telamon was a little more restrained, exchanging a soldier's grip with Achilles. He looked grave; worry lines creased his face and he didn't join in the laughter between the other two men.

"What do you think of my offering to the gods?" asked Agamemnon, laughing loudly

"It certainly looks the part," replied Achilles, "but will it hold enough men? It looks quite solid."

"Can't you see it, Achilles?" asked Agamemnon, genuine surprise in his voice. "It's understandable; they made a good job of it. See the body?" Agamemnon stood back a pace and pointed up at the main section of the horse. "It's a bireme, Achilles! The entire thing is a bireme, with benches inside for a double bank of rowers. It should comfortably take all your men." He laughed.

Never having been to sea, Diomedes didn't know what they were talking about, but Achilles seemed to recognise the lines of the boat now that they had been pointed out to him. A slow smile spread across his face and he removed his helmet to take a better look. "This is marvellous work," he murmured quietly.

Diomedes looked up. Although he was amazed at the size and scale of the horse, he couldn't see what had caught Achilles' attention until suddenly a hatch opened in the bottom of the horse and a man's head poked over the edge, fifty foot in the air.

"Let us be clear on how this is going to happen." Agamemnon's demeanour had changed quite quickly and he was all business. "You are going to be first into the city, so it will be up to you to hold the gate for us. After the signal, we should take about five hours to reach you. With the war supposedly over, most of them should be drunk, so it shouldn't be too difficult a task, but I would recommend that you try to keep things as quiet as possible. Once we get the army inside the gates, it should all be over in a matter of hours."

Suddenly Diomedes knew the real purpose of the giant horse and shock filled his whole body. He had to get away, to warn Troy what the horse really was. Without realising he had started, he was running. There were shouts behind him and suddenly he was on the ground, squirming under a huge weight.

"Are you sure about bringing the boy with you?" asked Agamemnon.

"Yes," replied Achilles. "I want him to witness the fall of Troy, to know there is no going back to his old life."

Diomedes could feel rough hands holding his arms behind his back as they were bound tightly and he looked up at Achilles with undisguised hatred. Agamemnon was laughing in the background, but it didn't matter. One day he, Diomedes, would kill Achilles for this.

Chapter Eleven

The last thing Diomedes remembered before everything went dark was looking up at Achilles and wanting to bury his sword in the warrior's stomach. He opened his eyes but couldn't tell if he was actually awake or having a semiconscious dream, for he could see nothing; it was dark all around him.

Turning his head slowly, he could make out points of light as his eyes adjusted to the darkness. He could do no more than turn his head, for when he attempted to touch his head where he had been struck, he found that his arms were tightly bound and a damp cloth was tied tightly around his mouth, gagging him.

A quick, panicked movement revealed that his legs were also securely tied. Since he couldn't even roll around, he assumed that he had been tied to one of the benches to keep him from making any noise that might give them away.

As his eyes adjusted, the gloom receded and he began to recognise the faces of the men closest to him. An eerie silence filled the place as they all sat quietly.

"You're awake, then," said a voice on the other side of his head and he turned to see Achilles sitting in the front, with another huge shape who could have only been Ajax concealed in shadow. Diomedes tried to shout something at him but it was smothered by the gag, and Ajax rumbled a laugh in the background. Achilles glanced back at Ajax in irritation and turned back to Diomedes. "I'm going to take this gag off now for a few minutes to give you some food and water, since they haven't yet left the city. Once they do, I won't be able to risk letting you loose till this is over, so there will be no point in your shouting or trying to attract attention. Do you understand?"

Diomedes nodded sullenly. There was no point starving or dying of thirst out of stubbornness when there might be some opportunity later to help his people. Achilles' big hands deftly undid the binding on the gag, and pulled it away from Diomedes' face. Diomedes sucked in air through his mouth, and realised the relief of actually being able to breathe through his mouth.

"Better?" asked Achilles, and Diomedes looked at him with hatred in his eyes. The sweet air coming through his mouth, and the thought of starving while waiting for a chance to do something useful, stilled his tongue. He just sat and glared at Achilles, and Ajax again rumbled with laughter.

"He's got spirit in him, this one, Achilles," commented Ajax, looking at him with the kind of interest he'd have in a horse. Curiously, he enquired, "Are you sure he's not too spirited? Looks to me like the type of dog who would turn and bite his master's hand."

"We will see what happens after today," replied Achilles, holding a skin of water to Diomedes' mouth; it released a stream of warm, stale water which he tried to gulp down as quickly as he could, but some spilled out around his mouth. As he finished that, Achilles fed him strips of dried meat. It was like eating leather but it was food, and still better than he'd been used to before he was taken from Troy.

Chapter Twelve

The room was still dark; it wasn't full morning just yet, but something had wakened him. Lying there, staring at a dark ceiling, he waited to hear another noise. Maybe they were being attacked, but there didn't seem to be enough noise for that, unless it was far away on the wall.

Then he heard it again, a shout from the wall; it still didn't sound like an attack, but he could hear the slap of running sandals on hard-packed dirt approaching down the street. The door swung open and Heraclitus stood there, panting from the run. Arimnestos sat up quickly, knowing only a major event would bring Heraclitus himself instead of his messenger.

"Well? What's the panic about?" asked Arimnestos.

"They've gone!" said Heraclitus, gasping for breath.

Now he had Arimnestos' attention. "Who's gone? What are you talking about?"

"The Greeks, Arimnestos! They've gone."

Arimnestos jumped from the bed, pulling his chiton from its peg on the wall. He called "When? Tell me everything!" as he pulled it over his head.

"When first light broke over the beach, all there was to see were sails almost to the horizon. I wouldn't have believed it myself if I hadn't been on the wall. I don't know any more yet. I sent a messenger for Achenia and came straight for you," he replied.

"Are you sure they're gone? It's not some trick?"

Arimnestos couldn't believe the Greeks would just give up after so long. It seemed too good to be true. Ushering Heraclitus outside, he said, "Come on. I have to see what this is about," as he moved into the faint gloom of the false dawn.

"Of course I'm not sure," Heraclitus muttered, plodding along beside him; the night watch, followed by his sprint to Arimnestos' house, were beginning to make themselves felt. "Do you think I went out to check and had a quick wander around the beach before I told the rest of you?"

"No. You did right, Heraclitus; thank you." Arimnestos wasn't in the mood for Heraclitus' having mood swings this morning after being rudely awakened about an hour before dawn, but held his tongue and refrained from provoking his friend. Heraclitus was a good officer and soldier, but he needed someone to keep him in line from time to time.

Reaching the wall, Arimnestos took the steps two at a time in his hurry to see this marvel, and found Achenia already there, looking as if he had just fallen out of bed. Arimnestos should have expected him to be there first, as he almost always stayed in his quarters in the barracks instead of going to his house further up the hill.

"Morning, Achenia," greeted Arimnestos, as he looked out over the great bay. "What do you make of it? It has to be a trap of some kind, surely?" he said, but there was hope in his voice.

The masts were now little more than pinpricks on the horizon, but from what Arimnestos could see, it seemed to be the entire fleet on the sea. The beach seemed deserted, at least those parts of it he could see from here. Achenia took his time answering, as if making up his own mind.

When he spoke he sounded tired, though that wasn't unusual in the days since losing Priscus. "Those ships need every oar manned to move that fast, and to my old eyes it does look like the entire fleet. If this is a trap, I can't see to what purpose. They're gone." He shook his head slowly, "I have sent runners to tell the king, but we 'll have to organise a group to go and check the situation before he gets here in case there is some trap that I can't see."

"I'll do it," said Arimnestos. Achenia turned as if seeing him for the first time.

"No, no, I'll go myself," he said after a moment. "I ought to be able to tell Priam what I myself saw."

"No, Achenia. If it is a trick, the city can't afford to lose you. If there is a trap, let me spring it."

Holding Arimnestos' gaze for a long minute, Achenia finally nodded. "So be it. Get your men together. I'll form up the rest of the men to offer what support we can if we need to get you back inside the city quickly; and tell Heraclitus to line up his archers on the wall." Arimnestos made for the steps, calling orders as he went.

Ten minutes had barely passed before Arimnestos was back in front of the gate, and the last of his men were falling in. Heraclitus was already on the wall, and Achenia was emerging from the barracks in full armour. Arimnestos called out an order, and the gates began to swing in. A quick nod to Achenia started his men marching out through the massive gates, as the last of his men were falling into rank from the barracks, where they had been awakened only moments before.

The sun was just a line of light on the horizon as they left the city. It felt ominous to Arimnestos. It had been ten years since he had walked this road in peace, without fighting Greeks filling the entire horizon. He had been little more than a child then, and the world had been full of wonder and promise. The Greeks, he realised, had taken the best years of his life: the time when he should have been learning how to live and enjoying himself.

Now his life was half over, and the Greeks seemed to have disappeared, leaving him empty. They had taken his life, his chance to make something more of himself, and left him with nothing. Half a lifetime spent in training for a war; when that war is over, what do you do next?

These and other thoughts filled his mind as he marched slowly down the road meandering across the plains to the sea, until he rounded a large dune just before the beach. He stopped dead in his tracks so suddenly that the soldiers behind him had walked into his back before they realised he had stopped. Coming to his senses, he shouted "Halt," before the entire flank ran him over.

Rising over the dip in the sand where the beach ran down to the sea, the huge head of a horse rose to break the horizon. As Arimnestos watched, the rising sun behind him spread the first rays of light on to the head of the horse, and his eyes opened wide at the wonder of what he saw: the mane moving gently in the breeze coming off the sea.

He only realised that he had begun moving forward again when he felt Xenos' hand on his arm; Orestos was half a pace behind, frowning inside his helmet. The Spartans never seemed fazed by anything; they were as amazed as the rest of the men, that much was obvious from their furtive glances at the horse's head, but, unlike the others, they didn't allow it to dominate their world, and their heads continued flicking left and right, looking for possible threats. It was like watching a hawk hunting, which normally made Arimnestos smile; now it brought comfort, as he knew that he had allowed himself to be distracted.

"Okay," he shouted, "when you've finished gaping like country hicks at a market, spread out. I want two men on each of those dunes. Let's go."

Everyone seemed to recover from the shock then, and they

were moving almost before the words were out of his mouth. Training kicked in, and the preselected scouts took off up the dunes, their sandals showering down sand as fast as they climbed so that they ended up taking two steps instead of one as they made their way up the dunes.

Arimnestos returned his gaze to the horse while he waited for the climbers to reach the tops of the dunes. He couldn't quite believe that men could make such things. "All clear," shouted one set of scouts, echoed seconds later from the other dune. They inched forward furtively from here as the scouts moved from dune to dune, checking for any signs of the enemy.

They moved forward until he was standing on the lip of the plains looking down on the beach, where the horse could be seen to rise to an incredible height. When the scouts called out from the beach that everything seemed clear, Arimnestos began moving his troops down on to the beach proper.

It was nothing like he remembered. The whole beach was a jumbled mess of broken wood, warm camp fires, a huge abundance of broken and scattered amphorae and the bones of innumerable animals. Its resemblance to a huge graveyard made Arimnestos a little uncomfortable. Everywhere sand had been tramped into a compact from the feet of two hundred thousand soldiers over the course of ten years.

It all seemed smaller than he remembered, too, but that could have been the fact that he'd been a child when he'd last been on this beach, or that a horse a hundred feet tall seemed to dominate the beach to the right of where he now stood.

He moved forward, aware he was staring as his men spread out onto the beach. They went to check further along the sands while he had a better look at the horse, shadowed by Xenos and Orestos. Priam and Achenia would want to know all about this, whatever it was.

The ground beneath had been flattened to packed earth, on which a huge display board had been laid out. The horse seemed either to be attached to this, or just sitting on it as a solid surface to support it. He couldn't tell; he was no carpenter, and could only imagine how much wood it had taken to build something of this size.

The legs, as far he could tell, were about the height of six or seven men, so he estimated that they were about forty feet in height before they reached the main body of the horse. The tops of the horse's legs swelled out to look like bunched muscle at its haunches, as if it were about to spring into motion at any second. This in turn moulded around the huge rounded chest of the horse, tapering almost to a point as the chest narrowed up towards the throat.

The head of the horse would have been a feat on its own, thought Arimnestos. Even having seen the head peering above the dunes from halfway up the road, the view up close was still something to behold. A strong equine jaw swung down, overhanging the neck and tapering out to a well-rounded muzzle, then up to two pointed ears half the height again of a man.

The mane stood straight up on the head between the two ears, working its way down the back along the spine; it was actually moving softly in the breeze. Arimnestos had thought from a distance that it must be an optical illusion, but as he walked around the monument, close enough to touch the rough wood with his hands, he could see it moving gently. As he worked his way around the horse, the tail was moving considerably more as the wood had been wrapped in what looked like loose straw.

All of this he learned in one slow walk around the horse, wondering why they had made such a creation. It was an immense task, and the freshly-hewn logs indicated that the horse had been completed shortly before they'd jumped in their boats and apparently sailed away. Just then, he heard shouting coming from further along and turned to see his men dragging someone up the beach. There was no point rushing, thought Arimnestos as he sat on the edge of the horse's platform. He removed his helmet, setting it on the platform beside him, removed the stopper from his water bag and took a long pull as his men made their way to him with their burden. They dropped the man on the sand only a few feet away from Arimnestos, and he saw that the captive was little more than a boy. Clad only in a loincloth, whip marks across his back, the boy was in bad condition. He had obviously been hiding in the dunes for a day or more and was suffering badly from exposure and dehydration, having had nothing to eat or drink over the long hours he had hidden there.

Arimnestos reached out and lifted the boy's face with his hand. Looking into scared, bloodshot eyes, he offered his waterskin. Slowly, hesitantly, the boy's hands reached for the skin. When he realised it wasn't a trick, that it wasn't going to be snatched away, he grabbed it and quickly began pouring its contents down his throat until Arimnestos had to take the skin away to prevent him from drowning in what he saw as his salvation.

"Do you have a name?" he asked when he'd taken his waterskin back.

"Sinon," the boy replied through cracked lips.

They sat looking at each other for a minute. Arimnestos' face indicated a lack of understanding; on Sinon's, it was difficult to make out much beyond the fear in his eyes and the hostility he felt towards his captors. Here was a man abandoned by his fellow Greeks, but raised to see all Trojans as the enemy, and the conflict was evident on his face.

Finally Arimnestos asked, "What are you doing here?"

"Hiding," was the reply.

"Why?" asked Arimnestos. "Why didn't you leave with the rest of the Greeks? You obviously have no love for Troy."

Sinon deflated a little, losing what little defiance he had managed in his sorry state. "They wanted to sacrifice me to appease Minerva," he admitted, tears leaking from his eyes. "I only arrived from Athens three months ago to join the war, and they wanted to sacrifice me for a safe trip home. I escaped; I ran away while they prepared the pyre and hid in the dunes," he gasped out between choking sobs. "I couldn't come out, or they would have burned me."

Arimnestos sat there watching him cry for a few minutes before he spoke again, giving Sinon a chance to pull himself together. This boy was the enemy, but watching him cry he couldn't help seeing him as just a child, no different from any inside the city walls. His story made sense. If the Greeks thought Minerva was annoyed with them, they would do whatever was necessary to appease her before setting out on a voyage of this scale.

"Why did they go?" he asked eventually. Sinon dropped his head sullenly and Arimnestos coaxed him. "They are gone, Sinon, so what harm can it do to tell us why?"

"There have been attacks at home," he told them. "We brought news of it when we arrived from Athens. That's why they picked me for the sacrifice; Agamemnon said I was to blame."

"Who is attacking them?"

"Horse tribes from up north," replied Sinon, a little surprised that they had to ask. "They have been raiding up and down Greece since most of our men are over here fighting this war. They have been pushing further and further into Greece. Agamemnon is bringing the army home to wipe them out and make sure they never set foot on Greek soil again."

Sitting in stunned silence, Arimnestos thought about what

this could mean. The Greeks really had gone. Looking up, he could see the same realisation on the faces of those soldiers close enough to hear what had been said. He steeled himself, determined not to be influenced by his desire for this to be true.

"What about this?" he asked, indicating the horse with a casual gesture of his hand.

Even Sinon, a Greek who must have watched it being built, could scarcely look at the horse without a certain amount of awe. "The Boeotians built it," he replied hesitantly. "They worship the great rider, Agamemnon said. Agamemnon wanted it as an offering to Athena for her hunt, and he ordered it built within the week. Its completion was supposed to coincide with - " he swallowed hard as he continued, " - the sacrifice."

"I see. Well, you're not going to be sacrificed, Sinon," said Arimnestos, trying to reassure the boy. "You will have to come up to the city with me and repeat all this to the king," he added when Sinon seemed to have calmed down a little.

"No, no, please!" pleaded Sinon. "Just let me go, please. I'll run away, and you'll never have to worry about me again." Tears running down his face, he pleaded as if they had just told him he was to go on the pyre.

"I'm afraid the time for running is at an end, Sinon." Arimnestos gestured to the waiting soldiers who took Sinon in rough hands and dragged him upright, as he continued to beg for his life. "Did anyone find anything else?" he called out to the rest of his waiting men. Negative replies and shakes of the head greeted his question, so he shouted "Get in formation; we're heading back to the city."

Chapter Thirteen

Priam stood tall above the highest tower of the city gates. He had been told of the ships having sailed away, but by the time the messenger had arrived at the palace, there had been nothing to see from his balcony.

By the time he was dressed and out of the palace, rumours had sprung up, and the people of Troy were coming out on the streets to find out what they could. Most made space on the road when they saw him coming, but his royal guards had been forced to remove those few who didn't move fast enough.

Rumours had reached the city days before about attacks on Greek soil, northern horse tribes attacking the settlements all along the borders of the largely-undefended lands. It was a fair assessment that they would send some men home to bolster their defences, but a complete withdrawal seemed unbelievable.

Achenia stood beside him, hardly the same man he had known for years. Since Priscus had fallen a few weeks previously, the years had begun to tell on Achenia, in a way Priam had never imagined. Instead of the tall, broad-shouldered bear of a man Priam had always thought him, now his shoulders slumped, and his armour seemed to hang on him rather than form the second skin which it had always done. Even his grey eyes, almost constantly angry, were now sunken, and his expression was distant and aimless. His job was now being done by rote and habit, by continuing a routine which he knew as well as any.

Fortunately, though, he hadn't completely fallen apart in the way Pedasus had. Ever since Diomedes had been taken by Achilles, Pedasus had been worse than useless, turning up for duty drunk and rarely leaving his room otherwise. Where he was getting the drink, no one knew. He'd had to be relieved of his command; they couldn't risk losing men because of an unfit commander when they had barely enough to defend the walls, regardless of his previous record.

No, Achenia had been badly shaken by the loss of Priscus, but he still performed his duties as well as any man Priam had ever known. He already had Arimnestos down there, investigating the beach, to confirm or deny the rumours. Priam would have liked to relieve Achenia for a few weeks, to deal with his personal issue, since he knew about Achenia's relationship with the boy, but they simply didn't have the men to replace an officer like him.

From the report Achenia had given him, Arimnestos must have been gone almost an hour already; plenty of time to cross the plains of Troy and reach the beach. If he didn't return soon, Priam would be forced to assume that this was all an elaborate trap set by the Greeks. Achenia had reported that the majority of the ships had left, if not all of them, and Priam wasn't inclined to doubt the man, but he would have preferred to witness it for himself.

The walls were thick with watching soldiers. Achenia had had to threaten those whose job it was to patrol the walls just to get them to leave the front wall, in case this was a distraction to get the Greeks in over another section of the city walls.

Yet more soldiers were inside the wall in the square, holding back the ordinary citizens, in case Arimnestos came back in a hurry, pursued by a host of Greeks; that way, the soldiers would fit through the gates with space to close them before any pursuers caught up. Priam was looking down on the square when a shout went up. Turning to face the front as a cheer erupted along the wall, he could just make out shapes moving along the road on the far side of the plains.

"What's happening, Achenia?" he asked. "My eyes are struggling at this distance." He would never have admitted it freely had there been other people there, but with only Achenia as a witness he felt a little more comfortable.

"It's Arimnestos, lord," he replied.

"Is he being pursued? How do things look?" Priam asked, a little annoyed at being told what he could have guessed.

"They look calm enough, sir; no sign of pursuit, though their ranks look slightly off." There were a few moments of hesitation before he said, "They seem to have brought someone back with them."

He turned to look questioningly at Priam, who shrugged. "Perhaps he found someone who can make sense of this. All the better if he did."

Some fifteen minutes later the huge gates swung in, and Arimnestos and his men poured into the city. Achenia had already sent orders for Arimnestos to be brought straight to him so Arimnestos dismissed his men, apart from the two holding Sinon. He left them on the top steps of the wall as he went forward to tell the king what they had found on the beach.

Priam allowed him to make a full report, waiting patiently, though he wanted to ask questions of the man as soon as the horse had been mentioned. After thirty-five years as ruler of the greatest city of the world, he had learned that silence is often the wisest course. So it appeared this time; although Arimnestos took his time to explain everything, he gave quite a detailed account of the horse and everything else on the beach.

When he'd finished, Priam asked that Sinon be brought forward. The boy was barely able to stand, and Priam felt a certain amount of pity for him, but he wouldn't allow it to show. Achenia questioned him, and he repeated more or less everything Arimnestos had told him. Regardless how often or how differently a question was asked, his replies were the same; his fear was plain for all to see.

"He is to be held in the cells beneath the palace, until we decide what all this means," Priam decreed. "See that he is fed, and his injuries treated. I must consider his future."

Sinon was quickly led away by the soldiers Arimnestos had brought with him, and Priam turned to Arimnestos to ask, "What are your thoughts on the boy? Do you trust what he has to say? The horse, too; what do you make of that?"

Arimnestos hadn't expected to be asked any more questions, and was caught slightly by surprise, so he said the first thing that came to mind. "Your Majesty, we saw the ships sail away and there was no one on the beach when we checked." He shrugged his shoulders. "The boy's story sounds reasonable, but I don't trust Greeks, even when they bring gifts."

Priam nodded slowly. "Wise words. Very well, you may return to your men."

Arimnestos bowed low, saying, "Thank you, lord," and backed away towards the stair before descending.

Priam stood looking out over the bay for a long time, thinking. When he turned back to Achenia his expression was resigned. "Organise work parties, Achenia; the horse is to be brought in. We shall use it for our celebration as a symbol of the end of the war, then make an offering to the temple of Apollo in reparation for what the Greeks took from it when they attacked."

Achenia looked shocked, but it was not for him to question the will of the king. "Yes, lord. And I'll organise lookouts to patrol the beaches. They may be gone, but I still cannot bring myself to trust those Greeks."

Priam smiled at him. “You’re in charge of the city’s security, Achenia. Take whatever steps you deem necessary.” With that, he turned and made his way back towards the palace, already thinking about the breakfast he had missed.

Within two hours, Achenia had sent scouts to patrol the area. He also had a group of two hundred volunteers looking at the largest wooden horse he could ever have imagined. Even after Arimnestos’ description, it was still a shock to see it at first hand. He wasn’t the only one stunned into silence; a hush had descended upon the entire group when they’d arrived on the beach.

His help consisted of a large group of civilians from the city. It was unusual to have so many volunteers for any form of manual labour, but he had had to refuse most of those who had wanted to come. Of course, it was the first time in ten years that most of them had got out of the city; along with the rumours which had flown through the city faster than Achenia had thought possible, this had ensured his workforce, as no one was yet allowed outside except these volunteers.

Priam had sent three of the city’s engineers out with them to decide on the best method of moving the monstrosity, and they were currently trying to estimate the length and number of log rollers required to move the object.

Achenia had sent fifty men with axes to begin working on trees suitable for rollers, as soon as he had arrived and realised what would be necessary. The fact that the Greeks had already built the horse on a platform would make their task somewhat easier; still, moving this to the city promised to be a monumental task.

If it had been left to Achenia, he would have burned the thing right here on the beach, but the king was a pious man; he wouldn’t desecrate an offering to a god, even a foreign one he didn't believe in. He paid respect to all gods. He was probably right, thought Achenia with a sigh; there's no point in pissing them off unnecessarily.

Ropes had been brought along when they'd left the city, an excessive amount of rope in Achenia's opinion, for dragging the horse on the rollers. As they began to fasten the ropes to the horse's front legs, however, he realised that they had barely half the amount required, and was forced to send men back to the city to get more. It would take ten of them just to carry the thick, heavy coils.

By the time the first logs were being hauled down the beach, the ropes were arriving and being tied to the legs of the horse. Two hundred men provided a lot of pulling power on the wrist-thick cables of rope, but Achenia thought at first that he might have to send back to the city for more volunteers. When they started pulling, nothing happened; the sand held the horse fast. Eventually there was a movement, then another. Once the front of the platform had been hauled onto the first roller, it started to move much more freely.

By the time the platform was completely on the logs, Achenia had sent for another two hundred volunteers, realising that they were going to have to work in shifts. No one could keep on pulling for the length of time it was going to take to get this thing into the city.

Hours passed as they dragged the horse along, inches at a time. Achenia kept expecting to hear the sentries call out that the Greeks were attacking, but the call never came, and, as night fell, the horse was two-thirds of the way to the city. The following morning Achenia was back at the horse with a different set of volunteers. Most hadn't returned now that they knew what the task would entail.

The walls of the city were tightly packed with people

wanting a view of the huge horse everyone had been talking about, and you could feel the anticipation building with every step that brought the horse closer to the wall. By midday, the horse was passing under the gate.

The new temple of Apollo was just across the square from the main gate. It had been built and dedicated after the Greeks had violated and desecrated the original temple, half-way across the plains of Troy. The horse was dragged close to the temple, which it dwarfed completely.

The smell of roasted meat had entered Achenia's nostrils as soon as he'd entered the gates, and as they'd moved forward he had seen why. The entire main square had been transformed as if for a festival, with huge spits of meat, freshly caught by a hunting party, roasting around the sides, and people were already starting to drink. A large thoroughfare had been left to be kept clear by a group of disgruntled soldiers who obviously would have liked to participate in the festivities.

The gates had been left open after they had passed through, which made Achenia uncomfortable, after so many years of controlling the security of the city, but they had maintained constant patrols of the area, since the Greeks had disappeared and there had been no sightings. He had to assume that the Greeks really had left, but he would still have preferred to keep the gates sealed for the time being. Unfortunately, with the war over, he was being overruled by the nobility who wanted to show the world that Troy was back open for business.

As Achenia oversaw the manoeuvring of the horse into its position in front of the temple of Apollo, a messenger arrived from the palace. Achenia broke the wax seal on the parchment and opened the message. It contained an official request from the king to attend festivities in the palace to celebrate the liberation of the city.

Chapter Fourteen

Priam stood in the throne room, surrounded by his generals and advisers and half the court of Troy. Many younger members of the court had preferred the idea of leaving the city to celebrate, having only vague memories of the world outside the walls. Those who were in attendance were decked out in all their finery. Had the city been free all along, the clothes they wore would undoubtedly have been regarded as outdated, but as things stood they were the height of fashion.

Nerves rarely affected Priam, but today wasn't a normal day, by any standards, and he wasn't certain of the best way to approach the gathered crowd. They wouldn't like what he had to tell them but that made it no less necessary, and he must retain control of the nobility to have any chance tonight.

Achenia was the last to arrive, unsurprisingly, since he had spent the better part of two days having that damned horse dragged inside the city from the beach. It was also not unexpected that he was still in full armour, but Priam could see that he had been home for a wash and change before answering the summons.

He was wearing a very fine Egyptian cotton cloak, probably the finest he could afford. Achenia hadn't been captain of the guard when the war had started and trading had all but ceased in the city, so Priam could only assume that he had traded some possession for the cotton with one of the nobles since his promotion.

His ease seemed on a par with Priam's own this evening. He slipped in very quietly through the huge bronze-clad doors, shutting them silently behind him, and moved uncomfortably along the wall. When he took a goblet of wine from the servers, he used it to keep his hands occupied, but didn't try to interact with any of the other guests. He'd been a commoner before the war, but, as the old saying went, war makes kings and paupers. Achenia had raised himself to the lower nobility, but had no heir to whom to pass on the title.

Priam snapped himself back to the present and the task at hand, realising that he had been procrastinating. He stood up on to the raised dais, and, before he had turned around, he could hear the noise level drop in the room as the guests noticed him there, and anticipated a speech. The silence spread like ripples in a pond as everyone turned to face him.

"Ladies and gentlemen of Troy," he began, his natural parade-ground voice echoing around the huge vaulted ceiling of his throne room, "you are all here to celebrate the fact that the Greeks have finally left our shores." This was greeted with raucous cheering, and Priam could see that some people had already overdone the celebrations.

He gave the cheering a little time to die down before he went on. "However, I am sorry to have to tell you that the war with Greece is not over." There were a few ragged cheers, but as his words sank in they died away and confused looks were exchanged.

"Earlier this week I received information that the Greeks were going to leave, but I didn't believe it until I saw it for myself." Silence still reigned in the hall and he could feel their confusion, their anticipation weighing on him. "This source also informed me about the horse they were offering to their gods and their hopes for it, and I can tell you now that by tomorrow morning every one of those Greek ships will be back on our beach."

The silence had now turned from confusion to shocked disbelief. Muttering started up in small groups, spreading fast around the room till people started shouting at him in disbelief and outrage. Those of military breeding held their peace and looked around, perplexed but thoughtful as to what this would mean for them. A glance at Achenia showed him setting his goblet aside, looking at the ground in thought, his face flicking slowly to the great doors time and again.

The noise in the chamber began to rise to a clamour as people became argumentative and rowdy with alcohol. Priam lifted his sceptre and rapped the large round base on the marble floor. The resulting gong reverberated around the chamber, echoing out to drown all other sound. This worked just as it had been designed to do, allowing the king to control noise in the room from the throne dais. It was modelled on the stage in an amphitheatre.

As the vibrations settled, and a shocked silence descended, royal guards stepped out from behind the curtains, their bronze armour polished until it glowed. Unlike most guards inside a palace, they all bore the full panoply of battle, shields held to the front and spears upright at their sides. It was a clear message to everyone in the room, reminding them who was in charge. Priam had given the court a voice for most of his reign, allowing them to offer advice freely and question him openly, but now they were to see the iron king who had built up Troy from the village it had once been.

Everyone in the room knew better than to question this. To the military personnel this was normal, but the civilians and traders among the court suddenly looked very uncomfortable; cups were set down and people looked from one to another.

Priam looked directly at Achenia. He had spent many years holding court but even now he was more soldier than courtier, and felt more comfortable talking directly to one person than making speeches. “No one outside this room is yet aware of this, and that’s the way I want it to stay.” He looked around the room at the shocked faces. “Every city has spies,” he said, interrupted by claims of loyalty, and rapped his sceptre on the floor again for silence.

“Every city has spies,” he repeated, “and I don’t want word carried to the enemy that we know of their plans, so you shall all be guests of the palace tonight. The military men will return to their barracks and have all their men hidden and ready around the area of Apollo’s temple and the great wooden horse for midnight.” A shocked silence filled the air. “No move is to be made on the horse until your new general gives the word.”

He swept back his arm in a sweeping gesture towards the balcony, and from around the curtain strode six feet of muscle dressed in the finest armour any of them had ever seen. Black curls tumbled from his head on to the blood-red cloak on his back. “May I introduce - Romulus?”

Chapter Fifteen

Three hours after Diomedes had been fed, Achilles came rushing back to his side and retied the cloth that acted as a gag on his mouth. He moved with sure steps, and quieted the other men in their benches. Even Ajax seemed to accept Achilles as his leader, waiting quietly.

Twenty long minutes passed while Diomedes lay there, straining his ears, before he heard the faint noise of people talking outside. He could make out speech, but hearing anything coherent in the low buzz of voices was impossible, even though it was silent inside the horse.

He strained at his bonds, knowing that to shout with the gag in his mouth would be less than useless when he couldn't hear those outside talking at normal volume. Testing the knots holding his arms around the bench behind and then those on his legs, he found there wasn't an inch of give in the ropes. He kept trying till his arms burned with the strain before giving up, and lay there trying to think of how he could warn his people, but he could think of nothing and his inadequacy tormented him.

Around half an hour passed before the sound of the voices faded again. He hoped that that meant that they had decided to leave the horse there, but around two hours later, his hopes were dashed, as, again, he heard voices outside. This time there were a lot more, accompanied by the deep commanding bass tones he knew all too well: Achenia's voice.

Even that strong voice was barely audible so high up, but he could make out a few words such as 'forest' and 'ropes' and his heart began to sink. The sound of voices didn't fade this time, as he'd hoped they might, but carried on for what felt like an eternity. The heat inside the horse increased, as morning turned into afternoon, and the sun turned the horse into a sweatbox.

Diomedes felt his mouth dry up and thought he might die of thirst, as the soldiers around him silently passed around skins of water, and he realised they wouldn't risk removing his gag to let him drink. Achilles eventually came over and poured a little water over the gag, which nearly choked him as it splashed over his nose, causing him to cough uncontrollably into the gag; but some of the water eventually soaked through. It didn't quench his thirst, but it brought a little precious moisture to his lips.

As Diomedes was sucking on the gag with all his strength, he heard a screamed 'Heave!' and felt the first vibrations as the horse shifted. On the ground the horse had probably not moved at all, but a hundred feet up in the air, any movement felt as if the horse was about to tip over. Terror filled Diomedes at the thought that the horse was about to fall over, causing them to crash to the ground in a mangled heap of splinters and broken wood.

He could see the same fear barely controlled on the faces of some of the soldiers, but Achilles was quickly among them and a quick word here or a hand on a shoulder there seemed to steady their nerves somewhat. They believed in this man leading them, and Diomedes could understand why as he watched him move among them. They held fast, if only to avoid shaming themselves in front of Achilles, and even Diomedes wanted to hide his fear from the hero.

The shaking continued, accompanied by shouts of 'Heave!' and the movements grew more extreme, but the swaying seemed to pick up a rhythm; tied to the bench, unable to move off his back in the almost complete darkness, Diomedes was being rocked to sleep. With his stomach still full from what Achilles had fed him, and the hot air trapped in the horse, combined with the rocking motion, Diomedes drifted into sleep.

Hours must have passed like that, as he drifted in and out of sleep, swaying and constantly hearing the creak of wood and the command to heave, over and over. When Achilles eventually removed his gag, it came as a shock. The dim light that had previously filtered through the boards was gone, and the blackness around him was complete. Diomedes felt cold fingers of fear touch his back as he pieced together where he was and why he was tied up. As the fog cleared from his mind, his sense of helplessness returned.

The darkness receded a little, as two or three very heavily-shuttered lamps sprang to life, and he could just make out the shaded form of Achilles bending over him with a waterskin. Before he could say anything, Achilles was pouring the liquid into his mouth, and he just had time to register how dry his throat was before the water rushed down his gullet. It was warm and stale from their day in the horse, but Diomedes could never remember tasting anything so good.

The toilet, however, was another story. Odysseus had worked out a system with pig's stomachs tied at the top to try to seal them as makeshift portable latrines, but with so many inside the smell was still beginning to build in the confined space. Air vents hidden on top were a welcome addition, but nowhere near adequate in the heat, and the fumes occasionally made Diomedes' head swim. "How can they not smell this outside?" he kept asking over and over in his head.

He swallowed all he could before Achilles took the skin away and began asking questions as soon as his mouth was empty, while Achilles was guiding a strip of meat towards his mouth. "Are we there?" he gasped. "Are we in the city?"

"Not yet," replied Achilles. "We are yet some distance from the walls. Tomorrow." That was all he said before the dried meat was pressed between Diomedes' lips. Achilles was eating the same food himself. A quick look around showed Diomedes that most of the soldiers were doing the same, standing to stretch tight muscles as much as possible in the confined space and squeezing their heads into the air ducts to try to see what was happening outside as the horse moved. Every shift down below, creating terrifying swaying motion this far above, felt like being on a ship in a storm.

Diomedes was afforded no such luxury. He lay there eating the dried meat, followed by another few mouthfuls of water, before the lamps were doused again. After a day of no physical activity and dozing off in constant heat, Diomedes lay awake for hours into the night, listening to the slight movements of hundreds of men trying to get comfortable. Eventually he drifted into an uneasy sleep.

Achilles awakened him in the dark hours of the pre-dawn, and the same cycle repeated itself. Achilles had replaced Diomedes' gag barely half an hour before he heard voices from the ground and the slow swaying motion of the horse began again.

By midday, the heat inside the horse was stifling. Shortly after that a shadow passed over, slowly forming a solid line across the horse as any tiny gaps which were letting in light darkened, then lightened again as the shadow passed. Diomedes knew instinctively what it was and once again tugged at his numb hands, still tied tightly behind his back.

He wanted to scream, to call out to them not to bring it inside the city, but all he could do was rock back and forth on the bench to which he was tied. Black despair engulfed him and he sobbed into his gag. By the time he'd regained some control, the rocking and heaving of men had also stopped. Light was still getting through cracks in the floorboards, so he assumed that they'd finally reached their destination. Presumably Priam had decided to offer the horse to the new temple of Apollo.

It was fitting, he thought, as only the gods could save his city now. He sat there silently, tears dripping from his eyes as images went through his mind of the violent death of everyone he knew: Pedasus, Achenia, Heraclitus; his own mother would probably be raped and sold into slavery. With these thoughts, he drifted into a haze of slumber. Only the gods could save them now.

Drifting in and out of sleep began to feel like a fever dream. The smell of roasting meats drifted up, along with the sound of music and song, sounds Diomedes had heard only rarely during his life in a besieged city. He recognised almost none of the songs he heard. The smell made him remember that he hadn't had anything to eat since the dried meat strips this morning, and, though they would keep up his strength, they did little to satisfy his hunger.

The soldiers inside the horse were becoming restless, too. He heard more than saw them moving around in the darkness, trying to get a look down at the festivities; feeling safe in the knowledge that the sounds of merry-making down below would cover any noises they made. Occasional phantom shapes drifted into his line of vision, merely different shades of black in the darkness.

The sounds from below lessened as the night wore on, and it became evident that those remaining down there were becoming very drunk; even they began to quieten after a while. The soldiers in the horse quietened proportionately with the crowds below, some of them falling asleep on their benches, until, finally, all was still.

Time passed slowly now. Achilles stood up at the front of the horse and crept down the central walkway to pass instructions to the men. The hatch in the back of the horse was slowly opened, and allowed in the first breeze of cool night air. It was a welcome relief after two days of stifling heat in a sealed wooden box in the sun with two hundred others, and the sweat on Diomedes' tunic quickly cooled.

Two soldiers began dropping silently to the ground through the hatch. Three moved back beside Diomedes; one sliced the bonds holding him to the bench, while the other two held his arms, and lifted him to a sitting position. His hands burned as the blood rushed back to his hands and feet with a painful tingling.

***

Achilles stood silently in the darkness. His eyes had adjusted to the dark as much as possible the previous day, and yet he could still only make out the vague shape of everything around him. He quietly moved down the catwalk between the benches and ordered the hatch at the back to be opened, and ropes dropped down. Two men were sent sliding silently down the ropes to deal with anyone lying asleep near the horse, to prevent them waking to find two hundred Greek soldiers in their midst, and raising the alarm before he could secure the area.

The boy was the problem now; he couldn't leave him here, as there was a good chance the horse would be on fire before the night was over, but he had to keep him quiet for the moment. His men knew what they had to do, but this was going to leave them short of assistance if anything went wrong. Still, he knew what must be done. He instructed three men to take charge of Diomedes and get him down to the ground safely and quietly, then he slipped out through the hatch into the cold night air on to the rope.

Achilles knew he was brave; he had fought on a hundred

battlefields, staring death in the face a thousand times from the point of sword and spear, but only a fool enjoyed heights and a fifty-foot drop from a great wooden horse certainly qualified. He couldn't let his men see him afraid, however, so he looked up at the sky, wrapped his legs around the rope and kept moving arm over arm until he was down.

His armour, arms and shield weighed him down, and, even with his great strength, his arms were burning by the time his feet touched the wooden platform. Shaking out his arms, he had a quick look around. The two first men he sent down had indeed secured the area. Around fifteen civilians were lying where they had dozed off; they looked as if they were still asleep in the dark until you noticed the thin red line at their throats. Achilles hated killing civilians, but occasionally exceptions had to be made; from the few messages he had received, these should be mostly prisoners released as part of the celebrations.

Moving forward into the shadow of the horse's front legs, he ducked down and looked around the area, trying to get a feel for the place, as the rest of his men made their slow way down the ropes and moved into place in the shadows, waiting for him to give the orders. When the last of them had dropped down, after lowering Diomedes in a sling, still gagged and with his hands rebound, he gave the signal and they started across the square. Moving stealthily from building to building, they made their way towards the huge gates of Troy. The siege might be over, but the gates would still be closed for the night and manned by guards. Even in peacetime it would have been so, and, after ten years of constant war, old habits die hard.

They moved carefully from shadow to shadow, all clad in dark armour; they were hardly visible unless sharp eyes spotted the dark steel of the small knives they were carrying to silence anyone who noticed them. Spread out as they were, they consisted of a rough mixture of Ajax's men mixed thoroughly with those of Achilles; in the dark, it was difficult to make out who was where, but Ajax shadowed Achilles closely, the three soldiers holding Diomedes taking up the rear.

As they reached the borders of the huge square surrounding the main gate, Achilles signalled the men to halt in cover. He sat there in complete silence for a while, just watching. The guards on the gate passed over, slowly and diligently, moving in regular patterns and completely intent on their work. Anyone attacking Troy from outside would find their task all but impossible. If they had been his men, Achilles would have been proud of them.

Unfortunately for them, they were completely focused on enemies attacking from the outside. There were a few men inside the gates, but they weren't expecting anything and seemed content to let those on the wall keep watch. Achilles rose to his feet to signal the others into action and, like a slowly-moving wave, they moved forward around the square.

Moving silently around the last building, he had less than fifty yards of open ground in the square to cover before they were on the Trojans. He looked at the men around him and ran his finger slowly along his throat before continuing forward. Swords were being drawn at this point, as everyone knew that if the warning went up to the Trojans they were finished.

Ajax had his huge war-hammer in his hand and was running forward slowly, soon outstripping Achilles. Achilles watched him from the corner of his eye and gained on him in ten paces. Men were choosing their targets. Suddenly Achilles' arm snaked out like lightning to plunge the tip of his dagger into the gap in Ajax's armour between breastplate and backplate. The knife went in, puncturing the lung deeply. Ajax stumbled, twisting in shock to look at Achilles as his hammer came round hard.

Even though he was expecting it, Achilles narrowly avoided

the huge reach of the hammer by throwing himself back. The big man staggered again. As Achilles pulled the knife free, he could hear air sucking from the wound; looking around, he saw the last of Ajax's men falling to his Myrmidons. Ajax saw it too, as blood oozed out of his mouth to dye his beard shockingly red, visible even in the moonlight.

The fight went out of him then; his hammer dropped from his fingers and he sat heavily on the ground. His hand went to the wound and blood dripped between his fingers. He looked at Achilles with confusion in his eyes, sucking gasps of air through his mouth only for it to escape through the hole in his side.

"Why?" asked Achilles. "You're my cousin, Ajax!"

Realisation dawned on Ajax. "My family," he gasped, the pain audible in his voice. "I'm sorry, Achilles. He had a ship ready to go to kill my family, my children, if you left the city alive." Achilles moved closer, kicking away Ajax's dagger from his hand on the ground beside him. "I'm sorry, Achilles. I had no choice."

"You should have come to me, Ajax," replied Achilles, tears in his eyes. "We could have worked something out. It didn't have to end like this."

"I'm sorry," gasped Ajax again. "What else could I do?" He slumped in Achilles' arms as his lifeblood dripped onto the ground where he lay. The Myrmidons had quickly finished off the completely surprised Athenians, and moved in closely around the place where Achilles lay on the ground with Ajax.

After a long moment, Achilles used the two first fingers of his hand to gently close the lids of Ajax's glazed, staring eyes and whispered, "I'm sorry, too, cousin." Gently he laid Ajax down on the sand before rising.

As he stood up, he realised why his men had closed in around him. Trojan soldiers were pouring out of the gaps between every building to surround them in a wide circle. Burning torches were being held up at regular intervals, providing a circle of light to illuminate the entire square.

The watching men showed no fear, but he could see confusion on almost every face as the men scanned the square, taking in the Greek bodies littering the area.

Diomedes was close behind him now, and he took a moment to untie the bonds on his wrists, and cut the rope holding his gag in place. "You see, boy? I told you to trust me". The boy looked around at the surrounding Trojans and still looked unhappy, probably thinking that he was about to be cut down as a Greek sympathiser.

The wall of Trojans parted just in front of the main gates, and a small group of three men stepped forward from the group. Two of these were regular soldiers, but the man leading them was obviously someone important, judging by his brilliantly embroidered cloak, the shining bronze armour engraved with silver, and the bright red horsehair crest rising high above his head.

The three men walked straight towards the Myrmidons encircling Achilles. The Myrmidons bristled, unsure how this was going to play out, and prepared to sell their lives dearly. A few cast nervous glances at Achilles, who stood there casually watching the approach of the trio, exuding confidence he didn't feel in order to calm his men's nerves.

He had decided on this course of action and gambled with the fate of his men; men who put their faith in him, men who would follow him to Hades if he asked them, safe in the knowledge that he would always do whatever he could to bring them back alive. Looking at the surrounding Trojans, he wasn't certain he would succeed this time.

The commanders kept coming till they were only ten yards

from the Myrmidons. They were certainly brave; from here the Myrmidons could cut the head from the Trojan snake if they so desired before the encircling Trojans would have time to react. When they'd reached that point, the leader stopped and looked them over. Without saying a word, he turned his head to the man on his right, who immediately stepped forward.

A loud bass voice called out, "Drop your weapons!" in a voice which was used to command and expected instant obedience. At his side Achilles heard Diomedes whisper, "Achenia," and pull his arm in the direction of the Trojans. Achilles held on and looked down at the boy, giving a slight shake of his head, and Diomedes relaxed again.

No weapon so much as wavered as the Myrmidons stood with shields locked and spears pointing out, ready to move on Achilles' order. The eyes of the leader were still watching them from inside his helmet. Slowly and deliberately, his hands came up to his head and began raising his helmet.

There was a collective gasp from the Myrmidons, and Achilles released a breath he hadn't even realised he'd been holding. "Stand down," he called to his men as Diomedes shouted, "Hector!" in a combination of fear and amazement, and broke from Achilles' grasp to run forward between the Myrmidons, stopping just before Hector. He stared at him in awe for a moment before throwing his arms around Hector's waist in a hug.

Hector smiled down at the boy, placing a big hand on his head. He looked up at Achilles. "Achilles," he said, "well met." He gestured around the square. "Your handiwork, I presume?"

"Good to see you too," replied Achilles, stepping forward from the ring of dubious Myrmidons and approaching Hector. The two men stared each other in the eye for a few moments before stepping closer to throw their arms around one another, laughing. “Thank the gods you survived,” said Achilles. “I didn’t know if they’d get the medicine into you in time. Then there was the big pyre that night, and I wondered.”

“The gods had nothing to do with it, Achilles.” Hector slapped his back. “It was that antidote you gave them; otherwise I would have been on that pyre with Priscus and the other men we lost that night.” He looked at the circle of Trojans surrounding them and signalled them to lower their weapons. Glancing down at Diomedes who was still at his side, he said to Achilles, “What you did for me was very brave, Achilles. If Agamemnon ever found out, he would destroy your homeland; you know that.”

The love and gratitude between the two men was evident even from a distance, as they both fell quiet for a moment. Achilles broke the silence, saying, “Then we’d better make sure he doesn’t have enough soldiers left to do any more damage, Hector.”

“Well, I’ve decided he shouldn’t find out I’m alive, so no more mention of ‘Hector’. Anyone here whom I don’t know and trust personally knows me only as the new general, Romulus. If Agamemnon survives, he won’t know you betrayed him. Now, what was the signal for their return?”

“Romulus?” Achilles laughed. “That seems like a good idea. Hector is dead. The signal is two flaming arrows from the top of the north gate. There are men stationed along the coast to relay the signal.”

Hector nodded to the man on his right who had given the previous command; he disappeared immediately to relay the orders. Hector turned back to Achilles. “After two days in that horse, I imagine you could do with some relaxation for a little while before it begins again. Come to the palace with me now for some food and wine.”

Chapter Sixteen

Diomedes was allowed to go home to see his mother, but she wasn't there when he arrived, so he stayed only long enough to change into a clean chiton and sprinted back to rejoin Achilles and Hector as they arrived at the palace gates. The guards on duty looked askance at the grubby child following the prince of their city, but Hector waved them away and he passed through with his heroes.

King Priam was waiting for them when they arrived in the palace forecourt. Not knowing how to behave in the presence of his monarch, Diomedes followed his elders' lead by dropping to one knee with his head bowed, watching Hector and Achilles out of the corner of his eye.

"Up, up," said Priam as he walked towards them, a smile splitting his face, and pulled Achilles into a powerful hug. "It has been too long since you graced my palace, Achilles. You have my eternal gratitude for saving my boy from the poison." He looked at Hector with fierce pride in his eyes. "The antidote was a welcome sight."

"My lord, you are too kind," replied Achilles. "I was anxious in case it came too late. When we were surrounded down at the gates, I feared too much time might have passed. As for saving Hector, I owed him my life many times over when we were in Persia. I hope we may soon count my debt paid," he said, with a smile and wink for Hector.

Hector smiled back. "There are no debts between friends."

The reunion was cut short, however, when Priam spoke. "What happened in the square, Achilles? Ajax was your cousin."

The smile fell quickly from Achilles' face as he explained about the warning Odysseus had given him, and what Ajax had told him before he died. "This is one more item on the list of crimes for which Agamemnon must pay," he finished.

"You realise that you can never go home now?" said Priam gently.

"No," answered Achilles shortly, his lips pinched. He had spent a long time considering that fact before he had agreed to this mission. "I am now dead to them, or soon will be." He looked thoughtful for a moment, before going on. "The hundred men I have with me are all I can offer you, Priam. I have sent the rest of the Myrmidons home under Eudoros' command, to protect my father's lands and people if Agamemnon returns to take revenge."

Priam looked at Hector before answering. "You have already given me more than I could have hoped, Achilles, more than I could have dreamt possible." He turned away from them to think for a moment, and when he sought their gaze again he looked ill at ease. "Since you cannot return home and are now officially dead, I think I should adopt you as a prince of Troy for the services you have rendered to the city. You should choose another name, as Romulus has done, since Agamemnon may follow the trail if your name surfaces again."

"My lord, you honour me," responded Achilles, taken aback. He recovered quickly and looked across at Hector. "From now on I shall be known as Remus, brother." The two embraced as brethren.

"Welcome home, brother," replied Romulus, "and now let us drink in celebration."

They retired to Priam's private chambers, where a small fire glowed in the hearth to ward off the chill of the night. Servants had placed warmed wine in large silver jugs on a table in the corner of the room before they arrived. Priam reclined on a couch before the fire with a chased silver goblet full of wine, and allowed the others a moment to settle in before he spoke. When they were all seated, he asked, "How long do we have before the ships come back?"

Achilles thought for a moment before replying. "The signal will be with them within a few minutes of its having been sent. They had men placed all along the coast to relay it." He looked into his wine, thinking. "I estimate that Agamemnon will be back here within five hours. That is the fastest speed at which the ships can travel, and we must assume that he's ready to cast off the moment the signal arrives."

Priam nodded thoughtfully. "That leaves us little time to prepare," he remarked, strolling out through the double doors to the balcony. He looked out over his city, his life's work, wreathed in darkness, and turned back to Romulus and Remus. "I issued orders before we went down to meet you, Remus. The city is being prepared for their arrival as we speak."

"Good," replied Remus, glancing quickly at Romulus. "What do you require of us, my lord?"

Priam looked at them then with sadness in his eyes. "I will require your armour and that of your men." Shocked silence met his words. "We will find bodies aplenty down by the gate, and some will fit your armour. Achilles must die upon the wall if Agamemnon survives, and he *will* survive." Both men stood up to argue, but Priam forestalled them with a raised hand.

"Make no mistake, Troy will fall; that has become clear. We have bled for ten years while Agamemnon brings in fresh men with each new season. We grow what we can, but are rapidly running out of food, and two of our wells have been poisoned by spies, while he sits outside our walls with all the bounty of our country to feast upon." Priam had never felt so old, so exhausted and beaten as he did now, his shoulders drooping and his head lowered to gaze at the floor.

Admitting defeat rankled, especially in front of his son. Lifting his head, he found the old mettle he had used to build his little country, and strength flooded through him as he looked at Romulus. "We can make sure that whoreson's army is destroyed, that he has too few men left to hold this land. Our gold is long since gone to pay for mercenaries. He will gain nothing from this war."

Looking beyond Romulus, he gave a barely perceptible nod to the guards behind and ropes looped quickly over Romulus' head, binding his arms to his sides. Romulus struggled and shouted in shock and Remus reached for his sword but Priam was faster, clamping a hand over his on the pommel of the sword and forcing it back inside the scabbard as Remus looked at him in confusion.

"I have lost thirteen sons, and am about to lose my city," he said, looking from one to the other with anger in his eyes. "I will not lose my last son here." He spoke in a tone which brooked no nonsense, one he had used to them many times when they were children caught doing something they shouldn't. In a milder voice, he continued. "The phoenix, the symbol of our city, is being taken down as we speak; it is the last gold in the city. As long as the phoenix remains in Trojan hands, with the sword of Troy, the Greeks can never win and our city, our people can live on - but not here."

"But, my lord," Remus tried to interrupt as Romulus cried "No, father! You can't do this."

Again Priam gave them no chance to object, rolling straight over them. "You asked what I would have of you," he said to Remus. "Only this: this is my city; I built it and I will lead it in its final battle. My son would die at my side, which I will not allow. You are to take him with your Myrmidons and his own men, along with some civilians who are already on their way, to five ships which Odysseus has hidden in the Hellespont. He has also supplied a captain to lead you to a new home. The captain's name is Aeneas; you are to meet him in a few hours. We shall distract them with this last battle while you get away, thus guaranteeing the survival of our people."

"No, Father! Don't do this!" bellowed Romulus, fighting simultaneously against both the restraints and the two big palace guards.

"I can and I will. I have some surprises ready for Agamemnon; I have fought enough wars to know how to destroy an enemy, but with the numbers he brings, I can only hope to destroy his army." He turned to Remus. "Your orders are to escort Romulus and those civilians waiting in the courtyard to the ships. Can I depend on you to do that?"

Remus looked sadly at Romulus, struggling and shouting at Remus to free him, then looked back at Priam and nodded heavily.

"Good." He released his hold on Remus' hand and turned back towards the balcony. "Then I can go to battle without worrying that Agamemnon has won, knowing that my family is safe." He looked back at Romulus with a small, proud smile and nodded. He lifted his hand and an archer hidden on the balcony stepped out of the shadows to light a fire arrow from a brazier beside the doors, then shot the arrow high into the air where it arched out towards the main gate of the city.

Almost immediately, from a cliff a few miles north of the city another arrow appeared in the distance and another, barely visible, further along as the signal moved down the coast away from the city. It was done.

Priam moved back into the room in silence to find both men staring at him, one in cold shock, the other in something akin to awe. He embraced both warmly, and tears ran down the face of Romulus. Stepping back, he said, "There is new armour for you and your men down in the armoury. I will need yours for this plan to work. Now, it's time you left. Agamemnon should be well on his way by now."

Remus turned and walked towards the door, while Romulus was dragged behind by the two guards. The great doors closed, drowning his continued protest, and Priam went on gazing at them for some time.

Chapter Seventeen

A golden streak appeared on the horizon; beautiful in the night, it rose from the darkness arching like a shooting star before disappearing, almost on the edge of vision. Another followed, nearer but half a league away and the next, nearer still, could actually be heard plopping into the water in the distance as it disappeared beneath the calm black sea.

It was a calm clear night, the sky full of a myriad stars, and there were only those streaks of light and the soft lapping of water against the hull to disturb it. There was little but the forest of masts to suggest that Eudoros was anywhere but on a fishing trip with his sons at home.

The first arrow would have been sufficient as a signal, but Agamemnon had been taking no chance that they might face a foggy night which would have obscured the signal and had arranged accordingly that the last arrow should land less than fifty yards from the ships. Any closer would have put a wooden ship at unnecessary risk.

As Eudoros watched, sails were being raised up that forest of masts in silence except for the creak of the ropes tightening as they went up. Every man of the fleet had his orders to keep as quiet as possible until they were in Troy. At this distance, they could have screamed their heads off and no one in Troy would have been any the wiser, but Agamemnon had issued the order so that, by the time they arrived, the habit would be instilled.

Extra stars were appearing low down, as each ship lit a

lantern hung to the bow and stern of their ship. Sailing at night was always risky, and with nearly a thousand ships sailing together the risk was increased exponentially. Sails cracked as the wind caught them, pulling them tight, and Eudoros saw the tiny stars moving slowly away from him across the water as the armada pulled out from behind Bozcaada Island. The sounds of drums began low in the deck of the ships and oars dipped in time with the beat of the drums.

Slow minutes passed while Eudoros held his breath as lights bobbed all around him, each light representing a potential disaster if it ran too close to him. As the last of the lights went past Eudoros watched longingly, wanting nothing so much as to rush to Achilles' side. Since the boy had been twelve and his father had ordered Eudoros to be his shield-bearer, he had rarely left the boy's side and had been proud of Achilles as he'd grown into manhood.

Eudoros had long since left the service of Achilles' father; during the battle against the Northern Thracian horsemen, where Eudoros had lost his eye, the king had declared that he had little need of a one-eyed swordsman, as he would be a liability in battle.

Achilles had found out later that evening, when he'd sought Eudoros among the celebrating soldiers. He had been so furious that he took every man who would follow him from his father's barracks and formed the Myrmidons, making Eudoros his second-in-command, and left his father's household to live the life of a mercenary.

Eudoros reluctantly dropped the shutters on his lamps, to make his ship disappear, and watched as the other Myrmidon ships followed suit. When the last of the armada had twinkled and disappeared from view around the island on their headlong dash for Troy before first light, Eudoros leaned on the heavy steering oar to point his bow for home and signalled the oars master to begin the ominous beat that would pull him away from his lord and his best friend.

Chapter Eighteen

Pedasus woke with a pounding headache, and immediately reached for the amphora beside his bed; anything to wash away the taste from his mouth. He wished he could wash away the memory of everything he had lost, everything he hadn't been able to protect: his wife, his daughter and his little brother. At least with his dying words his brother had given him some hope, when he had asked him to look after his son for him; it had given Pedasus some purpose in life. He couldn't even do that right, though; poor Diomedes was now slave to that animal Achilles, and he had nothing left.

Finding the amphora empty, he threw it at the wall in a rage; he couldn't even drink things away, it would seem. The only thing that ever seemed to go away was the spirit he was drinking, but at least it put him into a dreamless sleep for a little while and gave him some relief. When he woke, all he wanted was to put himself back to sleep. Well, it was time to get up and find another amphora.

As his senses began to reassert themselves, the noise of the outside world began to intrude on his groggy mind and confusion and pain began to push its way into his head as he realised what must have awoken him. The banging and battering from outside was intense, as if the whole city was being destroyed around him. Shocked into coherent thought, he immediately concluded that the city was under attack, that the Greeks had somehow managed to force their way inside.

He was half-clad in the armour hanging in the corner of his room when the lack of clangs of bronze or screams of pain struck him, indicating that a battle was unlikely, and he stopped with just his cuirass strapped on over his chiton. Through a fog he tried to think back to the previous evening, to account for what was happening; although most of it was a blank, nothing he could remember would explain the building noises going on outside.

Without warning, the sheaf of straw roofing his little room was pulled aside, flooding the place in the blinding light of torches and reigniting the burning pain of his hangover, like knives going through his fragile brain. Shouting at whoever was pulling his roof asunder, Pedasus stormed to the door and dragged it open, to see what in Hades was going on. Though the banging continued, laughter permeated the sound as Pedasus opened the door to find Arimnestos and Heraclitus laughing at his outrage.

"What's going on?" he demanded, causing a fresh bout of laughter from the two friends. Turning back to his barracks room, he shouted up at the man removing his roof, "Get down from there and leave my damn roof alone, or I'll have you whipped!"

Red-faced and obviously discomfited, the soldier stopped and looked to Arimnestos for support but made no move to get down from the roof. Pedasus moved towards the ladder to carry out his threat, but Arimnestos grabbed him by the arm and stopped his ascent by the second rung on the ladder.

"What do you remember of last night?" asked Arimnestos.

The question caught Pedasus by surprise. "Not a lot," he admitted

Arimnestos gave a slow, sad shake of his head, "Pedasus, friend, you must pull yourself together. We need you. Diomedes needs you." Seeing the confusion on his friend's face, he carried on. "Diomedes is back, Pedasus; Achilles brought him in the horse last night. We're preparing for the biggest Greek attack yet."

"Diomedes is back?" that seemed to be all Pedasus had grasped.

"Yes, Pedasus; he is up at the palace with Achilles and Hector," Heraclitus put in.

"Diomedes is back?" he repeated, stunned. "But you said Hector - Hector's dead; I saw him die."

"Keep your damn voices down," said Arimnestos. "Hector is alive, Pedasus. The death – well, it wasn't exactly staged; he was poisoned during the fight, but Achilles gave us the antidote. If news of that gets out, Achilles' homeland will pay the price. He and Odysseus have been working with us."

Stunned silence met this information. Pedasus began to walk towards the road leading to the palace. Not even seeming to notice that he was still half dressed in his shock "I have to see him," he mumbled as Heraclitus intercepted him.

"Pedasus, I'm sorry, but I'm afraid that will have to wait." Glancing at Arimnestos for support, he continued. "We've been ordered to construct a second wall within the gates to hold the Greeks when they arrive, and we have only two hours left to finish it. Then we are expected in the palace for final orders before they arrive, and you'll see Diomedes there. Just now, old friend, the best you can do for the lad is to help with the wall."

Pedasus looked from Arimnestos to Heraclitus; the struggle visible on his face before the truth of the situation sank in, and he nodded. "Where do you need me?"

Chapter Nineteen

Agamemnon's heart soared at the sight of dawn rising over the mighty Trojan walls. Left and right, as far as his eyes could see, boats swarmed over the sea; his boats, and soon his city too. Achilles had been as good as his word; even from this distance, Agamemnon could just make out the glint of light poking through where Troy's massive gates had always stood impassable.

It was a great pity that Achilles had to die, but there was no way to work with the man. He had never learned to accept Agamemnon as his rightful king, and letting him live would invite similar rebellious behaviour from the other lords Agamemnon commanded. After twenty-five years building his kingdom and uniting the fractious Greek people, he didn't intend to spend the next twenty-five fighting rebellions to keep it together.

But now, entering the city, let him be the hero of the army. No one would be cheering till they were inside the city walls, around the time when Achilles should be dying; he would never hear them cheer his name, and then Agamemnon would mourn his loss with everyone else.

He could just make out the tiny dark shape of a man on the battlements silhouetted against the sun rising in the east, then the sound of the ram grating on small rocks and sand brought him back to the task at hand, and he gripped the side rail, as the ship ground to a halt, vaulting over the railing into six inches of water.

As he began the walk up the beach, thousands of men

splashed down around him following his lead and moved into silent ranks in their given phalanx. He stopped halfway up to give them all time to get into position. They seemed to swarm everywhere, covering the entire beach; even after ten years of watching them on the sands, it still amazed him to see them all drawn up together.

By the time they were ready, and the commanders had gathered around Agamemnon for their final instructions, so that there would be no need for speech when they grew closer, the sun was still only halfway above the horizon; with a half-hour march ahead, however, there was no time to waste. He issued the final orders, giving Ajax the Locrian the honour of taking the van in the assault as a reward for his loyalty; he would be first inside the city.

Two hundred thousand men in a quick march was never going to be a quiet affair, with armour and weapons jingling as they jogged half a mile up the Trojan road across the vast plains, but every jingle set Agamemnon's nerves on edge. He jogged alongside Ajax at the head of the column, keeping his eyes on Troy as he went.

As he got closer, he could make out the figure atop the wall; it could only be Achilles himself, holding a torch aloft. This close to the mountains, the sun was cresting the hills at a much steeper angle and the gloom of night was just beginning to lift over the city of Troy as dawn arrived just a few minutes later, but those moments were precious to Agamemnon right now.

A man as big as Achilles was hard to mistake, but his jet-black armour in particular gave him away, and Agamemnon thought he could see the smaller, bulkier figure of Ajax Telamon to his back. It was exactly where Agamemnon would have expected to find Ajax, so that he would be in a position to send Achilles on his voyage across the river Styx as soon as they were inside the city and battle was joined.

His men prided themselves on their fitness, but a half-mile jog would leave most in a light sweat and slightly out of breath, so Agamemnon had intended to slow them to a march shortly, to catch their breath and arrive in the city fresh for the battle to come.

All his plans were thrown into chaos, however, when at two hundred yards from the gate a shout was heard from inside; his worst fears were being realised. To be this close to his prize and be thwarted was unthinkable; he couldn't have it, he wouldn't have it. Glancing to where Achilles stood, thinking his men could hold on till the reinforcements arrived, he saw numerous thin feathered sticks suddenly sprout from him as arrows slammed into his body and he disappeared from the wall.

Ajax Telamon was nowhere in sight as they kept jogging towards the sounds of clashes of steel and screams of pain. Suddenly men began appearing at the gates. Agamemnon's hope that they were his were dashed when they began pushing vainly against the huge gates, trying to shut them. Their efforts began to bear slow fruit as more men arrived to help them while Agamemnon was still a hundred yards away.

The decision was taken from his hands in that moment, and he stopped running for the second it took him to make his decision and throw the die. "CHARGE!" he screamed at Ajax Locrian and the Greek line streamed past him at a full sprint for the last hundred paces to stop the gates being closed and barred against them.

Agamemnon stood there watching as company after company sprinted past him. He hadn't expected the battle to begin until they were inside the walls, but he didn't intend to die in the initial charge, since the defenders appeared to be awake and alert.

He estimated that some ten thousand men had passed him by

the time Ajax and his Locrians crashed against the gate like a hammer. The defenders had scattered from the partially closed gate when they were about ten yards away, throwing their spears with devastating effect at such close range. One of the heavy gates was closed completely, and there was a gap of about a foot between it and the other one; it still required considerable effort to push it open, but as a constant stream of Greeks arrived, it seemed to open as easily as any house door before their rush and suddenly, for the first time in ten years, Greeks were inside Troy.

Three full companies were already inside the gates, with thousands more pushing in from behind, everyone wanting some of the spoils of the fabled city, and Agamemnon could feel the knot of stress ease in his chest when the screaming began inside the walls. A satisfied smile spread over his face.

Chapter Twenty

The doors opened before Priam, as he strode the halls of his palace. Most things of beauty and value having already been stripped back to pay for the war, even the once opulent reception rooms now looked austere; and here, deep in the castle, it was downright dreary, with blank, cold stone walls. Agamemnon would find no riches to warrant this war, no hidden chest of gems to pay his troops and buy his boats. All that was left to him was the glory of being the only army ever to have breached the fabled walls of Troy.

This war would destroy him as surely as it would destroy Troy. He had fed his men stories of the riches of Troy in order to keep them here, had told them that they would return home dripping with gold and gems. When they left empty-handed after ten long years of fighting, none would follow him into battle again. But he would not walk away and admit that he couldn't conquer Troy as he had the numerous other states of Greece, showing that he was not invincible; to him, that was unthinkable. Well, whatever happened today, Agamemnon's dream of holding Greece together under one banner was over.

Priam thought of the glories of his youth, the villages he had drawn together through war and through trade, bringing peace and safety to Troy. He was an old man now, and he knew that most of what he had done as a young warrior, whatever atrocities he had committed as a young king, he had been building Troy for his sons. He had built a legacy which he hoped would carry on after his time and keep his family safe.

Only one son left now, he thought, as he stopped and placed a hand, gnarled with age but still strong, against the cold stone walls of the hallway. This is no longer home, he thought, but merely stone. He could sacrifice it and everything he had built up during his life to buy his last son time to get away to safety.

A hand on his shoulder brought him back to himself, and he flinched slightly as the captain of his personal palace guard leaned forward to ask him if he was all right; he shrugged off the hand and mumbled a vague affirmation, barely hearing what the man said through his fog of thought, and continued towards the doors to the stableyards.

In his palace, even these were large double doors, leading to a yard with the dimensions of a sizeable field, to accommodate the hundreds of horses and soldiers which had once made up the Trojan cavalry, the pride of their army. This had been reduced to barely a score of horses, held by Hector to use on raids. The rest had been eaten by his dwindling army in a starving, besieged city. The horses had saved the men's lives one last time, if only through sustenance.

Two of his bodyguard increased their pace in order to pass him and open the doors, so that he could sweep directly into the yard. Mostly, this suited him, adding a sense of prestige and grandeur to his entry on almost any occasion, but now, with a gesture, he stalled their progress. Grandeur was fine for balls and visiting dignitaries, but the officers of his army were waiting beyond the doors, and those gestures wouldn't impress men who had risen through the ranks to their positions. These men had mostly grown up with his legend, in his shadow; while he was still building Troy, they had been mere boys. Now, more than ever, he had to show strength: the strength that had built Troy.

Putting a hand on each huge oak door, with a strength he

didn't feel he pushed and they swung wide. With darkness still upon the city, he was glad that his eyes didn't need time to adjust to the light as he swept through, blood-red cloak streaming behind in his wake, and his eyes scanning the assembled officers. With his bodyguard fanning out behind him in identical armour and cloaks, it was an intimidating sight, even for battle-hardened commanders. Each member of his personal bodyguard had been chosen from the ranks and had distinguished themselves; they were the best.

The waiting commanders, illuminated with torchlight, did not move. They knew this man, and had been waiting for him. He scanned their faces, most of which belonged to men with whom he had worked personally, before handing over leadership of the army to Hector years before, and his eye fell on a dark corner, where a singularly unmistakable figure stood quietly. Priam stopped so abruptly that one of his bodyguards almost walked into his back.

As if everyone else in the yard had disappeared, Priam walked slowly to the shadows and put a hand on the man's shoulder. "I heard, Achenia," he said in a barely audible voice, and genuine sorrow was evident in his features. "I'm sorry." Achenia nodded slowly, lowering his head, obviously trying to hide his red-rimmed eyes in the shadows, as they welled up with fresh tears at the thought of his loss. "You don't need to stay here, old friend, you have given enough to the city; take the ship with Hector."

Now Achenia did raise his head again, tears still in his eyes but his jaw clamped in grim determination. "No, lord, I would prefer to stay. He died defending this city and I will stay where he remains. Besides, what is left for me? Should I start a family? Become a farmer somewhere?" An angry smile creased his face. "I am almost your age, so what are the odds?"

Staring into his eyes, Priam saw that he wouldn't be dissuaded. His hand still on Achenia's shoulder, Priam nodded and said, "Then come, stand beside me; and let us die glorious deaths." He led them back to the front, where the collected host awaited their orders.

Standing before the gathered officers, Priam suddenly felt uncomfortable. "Don't look at me as if you're expecting a speech, full of fine polished words," he called across the yard in the same strong voice he had carried into battle so often. "This isn't a ball." He looked at the stone beneath his feet. "Most of you have fought and bled beside me in the past; you knew me then as I am now. The Greeks, as you know, are on their way back. You know my intentions. Most of you have been working on the defences half the night." Here he looked at Arimnestos and Heraclitus who nodded as he spoke. "Is the wall ready?"

"It is, lord," replied Arimnestos.

"The lords of this city have run out of time," continued Priam. "By tonight Troy will have fallen and most of us will be dead." Feet shuffled at this and men looked around at those near them. "If we must die, let us take this Greek horde with us. Many of us gathered here have family whom we have sent to the ships in the Hellespont; let us give them a chance to escape."

No one cheered his words. No faces brightened. Even Pedasus, who had sent Diomedes with Hector and Achilles, merely nodded and set his jaw in grim determination.

"Agamemnon means to conquer Troy," Priam told them. "More than that, he intends to enslave everyone he finds on this side of the Aegean, to use the conquest of Troy as a rally cry to bind all of Greece to him." Stony silence answered him.

"He can't afford to walk away from Troy, so he won't leave. He will keep coming back." This was the hard part for him, and he thought about how to say it to men who had followed him their whole life. "Alas, Troy *will* fall. But if we make the cost too high, we can still destroy Agamemnon. We can make sure he cannot hold Greece together, cannot hold this side of the ocean. That means we can still win in a fashion, as long as taking Troy destroys him."

It was more grumbling than cheering that met his words, but there was anger there; he could hear it. Anger would take these men further than anything else. He had to be honest with them, and hope would be a false friend. Knowing what to expect would help them stand, if only to take down one last man before they themselves fell rather than trying to run when they saw hope disappear on the battlefield. They had to accept the truth now, before the battle.

Patience was wearing thin, but he allowed them a few minutes to quieten and accept what he had told them before raising a hand to regain their attention. "You all know the plan," he said, "from setting the horse alight just as they arrive to the new inner wall. I know that any wood left in the city is too dry for arrows, and there's no point in wishing for more. We can only use what we have: swords, spears, rocks to drop from the walls. Now I would like some ideas from you. Of what do we have a large quantity?"

"Sand!" called Heraclitus, and a dozen men bawled laughter back at him. Even knowing he was going to his death, Heraclitus would always find time for a joke. Priam and Achenia looked at one another with a small smile and Achenia nodded.

"I'll get started right away," said Achenia, turning to march away.

Chapter Twenty-One

Ajax the Locrian sprinted at Agamemnon's shout. He had seen Achilles on the wall, brought down with arrows feathering his chest as he turned. It was a shame; Achilles was arrogant but Ajax had liked the man. Some among Agamemnon's commanders had teased Ajax, calling him a coward and slave to Agamemnon's every whim, but Achilles had always been nice to him, at least to his face.

On the other hand, he would pay good money to see Ajax Telamon die. No matter what he did, Agamemnon always seemed to prefer him; probably because they both preferred those clumsy hammers in battle. No matter how many foot races Ajax Locrian won, or how many honours he got in the spear competitions, the blacksmith was always there, smirking beside Agamemnon's throne.

This time it would be different. Since they had been discovered, and Achilles was dead, there was a good chance that Telamon was gone too, or would be soon enough. Now was *his* time. In this battle, his speed and ability with a spear would not go unnoticed.

"Locrians!" he screamed, and the call was taken up by the men in his wake, as he sprinted ahead.

At fifty yards, he could clearly see the swarm of men around the gates. Drawing up his arm, he braced himself with the first spear at his shoulder. At forty yards, without slowing down, he threw the spear with all the force he could bring to bear at a full-out sprint. It took a Trojan in the neck and carried on, impaling him into the stomach of the man behind him; both men dropped, but were quickly replaced by others.

He released his other two spears with equally devastating effect, but, each time, the men he killed were replaced as quickly as they went down. At least no archers had appeared on the walls; Telamon or the remaining Myrmidons must be holding the stairs. At about twenty yards, light began to grow from inside the gates, and he slowed, to let some of his men catch up with him. Drawing his sword, he slammed into the gap in the gates, hitting two men with the edge of his shield to send them flying, as his sword took the neck of a third.

More men were arriving by his side at this point, and he barely had time to bring his shield back down and tuck his shoulder behind it before he was thumped in the back by the mighty impact of hundreds of men trying to force their way through.

Beyond the little cluster of men trying in vain to close the doors, whom Ajax now realised were only twenty or thirty men in total, and were being cut down quickly, he saw that the gates opened out on to a huge square. At least, he assumed that it was a square. Someone had managed to set fire to the front legs of the wooden horse, probably thinking that more Greeks might be hidden inside, and the fire was now blazing right up the front legs, and lighting the head and chest of the horse, blazing like the sun. Its blinding glare made the shadows even darker, hiding everything outside its arc of light in a darkness so complete that the edges of the square could not be discerned. This gave Ajax pause; he tried to slow down his initial advance, only to be swept along on a tidal wave of armoured Greeks.

Something about all this began to feel wrong to Ajax; this small number of men could not have taken Achilles, let alone

Ajax Telamon, along with him. Arrogant they might be, but they had good reason. It had been a good plan, and he himself had endorsed it. The ground would be littered with corpses if they had been discovered, and it was quiet. The Greeks had been silent until they stormed the gate and even now made little noise; other than the crackle of burning wood from the horse, there was nothing.

By now the wave of bodies had carried Ajax further in, almost alongside the horse, and still the silence held; the crush of bodies, all trying to enter Troy for the first time, pressed together and darkness hugged the edges of the square. Ajax tried to prevent the light from destroying his night vision, but the fire was so big that he could feel his skin burning even at this distance as the men swarmed in and fanned naturally away from the source of incredible heat.

Everything seemed to slow, as the men pushing through the gates realised that there wasn't an army on the other side waiting to destroy them but a deserted square. War cries died in throats as thousands of eyes scanned the silent darkness for any threat.

As men began to spread out, Ajax managed to stop moving for the first time since he'd seen the arrows hit Achilles on the wall. Shield and sword held warily, he looked around in the darkness, seeing a shape nearly as far away again, which had to be the edge of the square. The courtyard was a lot larger than he had been told, but, with no one's having been inside in ten years, a lot could have changed. He looked down at the ground, and, with an uncomfortable feeling in his stomach, he realised that this was no longer the cobbled stone of the courtyard; he was looking down at an almost perfectly square outline of tramped earth which was outlined in cobblestone. Looking around, he realised that ahead of him were more of the same perfect squares; suddenly, he realised what had caused them.

"This was housing," he whispered, and suddenly he realised what had looked wrong about the edges of the square. It was rough but too perfect; straight, no breaks for streets and no pointed roofs, just a singularly rough top. "It's been cleared," he said, a little louder. "Form up!" he shouted at the top of his lungs as men who were ready for battle moments before started to wander around aimlessly like sheep, now that there was nowhere to direct their violence...

"Form up!" he cried again as the men looked at him in confusion.

His cry seemed to rouse them a little but too late, as it seemed to act like a signal and he heard the snap of many bows releasing their load in the darkness.

"Shields up!" he roared. Shields swung around to meet the threat, but without forming a phalanx every shield was a small island in a sea of men, covering only the body from neck to groin. This stopped most fatal hits but the screaming told its own story, as a burning pain scored along the outside of Ajax's thigh.

Men fell, clutching the shafts of arrows protruding from their legs. Those less fortunate, or perhaps more so, in hindsight, died with shafts through their necks, and, in some cases, through the gaps in their helmets. Through a haze of pain, Ajax read the situation as best he could. A quick glance showed him how lucky he had been; the arrow had lightly grazed him but no more. Having spent much of his life in one war or another, and ten years here, mostly fighting in skirmishes, Ajax gauged that the Trojans had loosed roughly a thousand arrows. With the Greek numbers, this was a mild sting, especially when so many had caused nothing but flesh wounds, but the death of a thousand cuts could still finish them if they stood waiting for more.

Light might just have breached the horizon on the beach, but, within the huge walls of Troy, darkness still held sway. Ajax hated rushing headlong in the darkness, since the Trojans had already proven themselves capable of reversing a trap, but, since the alternative was to be turned into a human pincushion, the decision was taken from him.

"Form up!" he shouted again, above the cries of pain and shock. Discipline reasserted itself in those men who were still standing. He had lost only three, who were lying clutching their wounds. As a second wave of arrows split the morning air, their shields locked into place just in time.

A sound like hail rang off the shield wall, and stones, rolling to a stop near his feet, told him that the Trojans had slingshots with them also. He and his men would have to tread carefully. Easily as dangerous as arrows, stones were cheap, readily available, and, more importantly to Ajax right now, faster to reload than arrows.

"Keep your shields locked, and move forward at a quick march," he shouted, and his men began moving forward, the wall of shields rattling with arrows and stones every few yards; this was much more often than he would have liked. Every now and then another scream went up as one of the less disciplined army groups lost another man or two to the deadly hail through gaps in their walls, but by and large they seemed to be moving forward again, for which Ajax was grateful. They needed to get as many men as they could bring to bear attacking this force of archers as soon as they could.

Thirty yards or so after the latest barrage of hail, Ajax dropped his shield a little, to risk a look at what they were up against. He could make out a rough wall of piled rubble, presumably from the houses they had cleared. Taking a second look at the men lining the top, who seemed to be exclusively archers and slingers, he wondered when they had built this. No doubt the main body of their remaining army were waiting behind the second wall, ready to repel them when they'd taken this one.

With his shield back in place, he waited out the next barrage, before he looked to his left and right, catching the eyes of the commanders of each company there. He signalled that they would break formation and charge the wall after another ten yards. Nods came in return, and they began to move forward once more.

Another ten yards and there would be no commander till they cleared the ridge; it would be every man for himself, as they stumbled up the rubble of a makeshift wall. Phalanxes were of no use here; as he approached the point where they would break cover, Ajax felt horribly exposed.

"Once they fire again, we break and charge them," he called along their lines. The reply came more in grunts than anything resembling language but that was enough; they knew what was expected of them.

The barrage came earlier than he had anticipated, about eighteen yards, he estimated. There was really too much distance left to charge, but the order had been given; as the last of the stones and arrows rattled away, shields began peeling away from the wall, and men started their headlong rush to get to grips with the archers. Like all foot soldiers, they saw archers as cowardly assassins, killing from a safe distance.

As the shield wall disintegrated, again Ajax had the sensation of being terribly exposed; the rubble wall formed a huge semicircle, whence an arrow, fired from the side, could easily get around his little shield. He wished he could persuade himself that it was bravery or a sense of honour that kept him moving, but the truth was that what prevented him from running at that moment was only the sure knowledge that the next wave of Greek shield-walled soldiers was right behind him. With nowhere else to go, he gave voice to a berserk cry and sprinted at the wall.

The light from the burning horse was his friend now that he was close to the rubble. Since it was no longer blinding his vision, it was lighting the way ahead for him; as he began moving, he was already picking his path up the rubble. Any of the other men with time enough to think about it must have been confused by the amount of wood that seemed to be poking out from the rocks, but Ajax had seen the remains of the houses which formed this rubble, and so recognised the roofing beams for what they were. This wall had been thrown up in a hurry, and every part of the houses had been used to make it as big as possible as quickly as possible.

Ajax's speed and long strides soon had him once more at the front of the charging wave as he desperately tried to reach the wall, trying to make the archers think twice and flee, before cutting down the Greeks at such close range with another volley of arrows. As he heard the next wave break the shield wall and charge after them, Ajax felt something pierce his foot, almost pinning him to the ground. As his other foot followed, he had a split second to wonder why he hadn't heard the familiar snap of a bowstring before the same thing happened to his other foot.

Stumbling, he sensed rather than saw the same thing happening all around him before his knee struck the ground and was pierced. By now, others from his own group and those behind him had caught up and stumbled over the falling figure of Ajax, knocking him to the ground. Piercing pain followed as men stood on him and over him in their rush to get to the wall, their weight pressing the pain deeper into him. His thighs, stomach, right arm, neck and even his cheek were burning in pain, and he was pressed to the ground by those pounding over him.

He turned his head to the side and saw others in the same

situation all around him as far as the wall, and his eyes suddenly picked out little metal spokes scattered all across the ground in front of the rubble. He had time for one thought, "Fucking caltrops!" before the pressure of men above him drove the air out of his lungs; some had fallen to the caltrops, and more had died in the next wave of arrows. With a speed that would have shocked him, had there been time to feel anything, the world began to darken. The sun never rose on Ajax that morning.

***

From the top of the new wall, Heraclitus watched the Greeks. The horse blocked his view of the gates itself, especially now that the front legs were little more than a pool of flame. The Greeks had overcome the men trying to close the gates easily enough; so far, Priam's plan was working. All those men had volunteered, mostly the old and the injured who knew they wouldn't survive and preferred to die on their feet, fighting. Now the shining polished bronze of the shields spread quickly as men poured through the open gates to overwhelm the resistance they had expected to await them inside.

His moment was approaching fast as he watched the square fill up from his perch on the wall. He had been given the honour of commanding all Troy's remaining archers and slingers for this moment; this would have been their entire force of skirmishers if this had been a pitched battle, but Priam was too canny a fighter to waste Heraclitus like that.

He expected to get one really good volley into the Greeks before their shield wall stopped the arrows, but he knew that the few men he killed were not what mattered; his job was to draw the Greeks into attacking without thinking too much, as had happened with the men at the gates, except that the archers were less vulnerable.

Blinded by the light of the horse, the Greeks did as expected; they had met no resistance, save the few men on the gate, and the darkness surrounding them spread confusion among the ranks. Shields dropped low as men spread out, looking this way and that for an enemy they couldn't see, and assumed was not there. Anyone defending Troy would naturally be running towards the gates to repel the invaders. This was something different.

As the ranks fell apart, Heraclitus silently gave the signal for which they had all been waiting, watching him expectantly from the wall. The distance wasn't great, so he expected good effects from the first volley, for which he was thankful, since the subsequent ones wouldn't be much use. They each had two quivers: one was full of unreliable old arrows which would shoot but not necessarily straight; the wood in these was old and dry, so although they would still kill, they would probably shatter on impact. The second quiver held his good arrows, those he was sure would find their mark. For this shot he took one of only ten arrows from the second quiver.

Drawing the bowstring back to his ear, he took aim. He could hear some of the slings being spun further down the line and grinned viciously. He hated them; they were essentially a child's toy, used to hunt rabbits on some of the islands, but they could kill. It was an added insult to the honour of the Greeks.

Heraclitus knew the time had come when he heard the commanders trying to reassert control over their dispersing men, and released his arrow. Following his lead, all along the line echoed the beautiful, unmistakable twang of a released bowstring. In the three seconds it took his arrow to reach its mark, he had a second one in the air. Two or three others were able to match his pace of shooting, but most were already switching to the other arrows, sure to hit nothing but shields.

As they landed the screams and shouting began, and it was like music to his ears. He watched his two targets drop, one with an arrow in his throat; the other arrow had managed to punch through the soldier's cuirass to sink deep into his chest. He had a quick glance down the back slope of their makeshift wall to Arimnestos, who was leading the hoplites on this section of the wall, and winked. "Be ready, brother; it's almost your time," he called, as he started to draw on his dry arrows to fire at the shield wall.

This wall was now moving towards him at a good pace, providing very little in the way of a target, but the idea was to draw them in quickly, so he kept firing, hoping to find a gap. He quickly realised that the feet were his best chance, and took another two out of the line, but the gaps left by these were quickly filled, before they could take advantage of them.

Suddenly, further away than Heraclitus would have expected, the wall broke apart, and individual soldiers charged towards him. With so many individuals, it was still a veritable wall, but this time there was human flesh to aim for, and not a wall of bronze. He didn't fire, although his heart was pumping as men came at them, screaming for blood. This was only for a few seconds, however; then the shouts changed to screams of pain, and Heraclitus smiled.

Ten yards of caltrops was a lot, and the first wave of Greek bodies broke on it. He watched as the men in the lead went down from the bronze spikes in their feet, and as men tripped over their fallen comrades they landed face first on two inches of pointed bronze. Two inches may not seem like much of a weapon, he thought, but try pushing a point that depth into your head or chest under heavy pressure.

This was the hard part for Heraclitus, watching the soldiers forcing their way towards him and holding fire. Let them waste bodies here, he reminded himself. As men stumbled over each other trying to find a path to the wall, they fell on everyone who had gone before them, pressing them on to the metal spikes, and crushing the life out of anyone still breathing. A few men ran on the bodies and jumped for the wall to get past the trap, but arrows took them in the air, and they collapsed where they landed. However, the gap was filling up fast, and soon there would be a bridge of bodies to walk across.

No sooner had Heraclitus had this thought than men started arriving at the wall, and he drew the arrow back to his ear again. Taking a deep relaxing breath, he released it, and, from this range, the force of the arrow, although weakened and dry, punched the first figure off his feet into the man behind him.

Heraclitus had never felt so alive as when he was in battle, and so it proved now. He drew and released smoothly, almost relaxed, sowing devastation among the ranks coming towards him. Some of the others were unable to keep up with the pace of the approaching Greeks, and began to be pushed back off the summit; eventually, gritting his teeth, Heraclitus had to decide to back away also, or risk being encircled. No one was fast enough to survive that.

He fired one last arrow, turned and jumped the ten feet to the ground below, past Arimnestos and the waiting hoplites who were crouched down on this side of the wall with their shields and spears. Turning quickly as he landed, he could see Arimnestos and the others, faces set in grim determination, as they anxiously bounced on the balls of their feet. Quickly, he pulled an arrow from its quiver, and shot the first head to come over the top.

This was happening all along the wall as they attempted to hold the Greeks to a point where they would build their numbers on the other side of the wall and storm over all at once; once again, Priam's plan seemed to be succeeding as heads ducked back. However, it didn't take long until the entire top of the wall, catching the first rays of the rising sun, seemed to move all at once, and then they came like an avalanche.

Although Heraclitus continued to fire where he found a likely mark, now was the hoplites' time, and, as he watched, Arimnestos rose from where he was crouched against the rubble. Spear in one hand, shield swinging overhead in the other, he brought the tip of the spear under the helmet of the first man to top the rise, and the shield knocked him back off the spearhead.

The wall turned into a strange, sloping phalanx as the man behind leaned into Arimnestos' back to steady him on the uneven ground, help him force his way forward or stop him being pushed back; he would take his place, stepping forward, should Arimnestos fall to the Greeks.

The shields which knocked the dead Greeks off the spears, in a move which ran along the wall, seemed to lock into place against each other; it happened so quickly that even the second row of advancing Greeks had no chance to avoid the spear points, which licked out like serpents' tongues over the shields, punching through eyeholes, necks, anywhere that would bring a man down.

Heraclitus watched in jealous awe as they held, bringing down Greeks too slow to get their shields up as they scrambled up the rubble on the wall; by the time they were forming some semblance of counter, the crush of dead bodies between the two forces was holding them apart, almost to the effective distance of the spears. The fight was now more a battle of wills, as both walls of opposing men tried to push the other back; although the Greeks had far superior numbers, bringing them to bear up a rubble hill while climbing over their own dead was proving almost impossible.

The defensive wall of dead between them, which was

helping them to hold the Greeks in place, also proved their undoing as the bloody leaks from punctured bodies dripped and poured on to the rough rocks on which they stood, making the stone slippery; even as he watched, a few of the men in front began to lose their grip and slide slightly, and, in a battle of this magnitude, the smallest advantage made a huge difference. One man's foot slipped, and he dropped to his knee for a second, which was enough for the Greek facing him to force aside one of the bodies between them and bring his spear to bear against the rising Trojan.

He went down again, and, this time, didn't get up. The big Greek was fast, already forcing his way forward to the gap left by the fallen man, bringing down the Trojan to his left. Heraclitus sent an arrow at him, but it slipped off his shield, impaling the man beside him through the shoulder, and Heraclitus watched in dismay as the Greek took another man, now that he was in the gap.

They didn't need to hold them long, but this could collapse their entire defence, Heraclitus realised as he watched. The big Greek died with a Trojan spear in his gut, but the damage had been done, and more and more Greeks tried to force their way into the gap in the Trojan defence, which he'd given his life to create. Now that gap grew, as they found themselves within effective reach, with their long spears.

Heraclitus gathered more archers to him, and gave quick instructions to concentrate their fire on holding that point, but he saw the line bulging inwards, as the Greeks attempted to press their advantage. Four men down the line from Arimnestos, the line looked likely to break. The archers helped, but only on the direct line, and the Greeks already in began to find it easier to cut diagonally, as the shield wall left the sides of the first two rows exposed. A crest was working its way towards Arimnestos, which

Heraclitus didn't think he could see, focused as he was on holding the men directly in front of him, and blocking the occasional jab of a spear that managed to reach him.

Heraclitus looked up at the burning horse, wondering how much time had actually passed since they had been forced back off the wall. The vague light from the rising sun seemed to say 'none', but it had to be nearly enough. He could hear the strained creaking of wood; the time was now.

Seeing Arimnestos about to be surrounded, he realised that it might not be soon enough. In the light leather armour of an archer who never saw combat, he drew the sword he carried, dropping his bow to the dusty ground, and charged into the back of the Trojan lines, forcing his way between the straining lines to the left of Arimnestos, where the breach seemed intent on swallowing his friend.

As he approached Arimnestos the man second from him fell, slightly easing the pressure against them, and Heraclitus managed to slip his sword past and under a Greek's shield, bringing the man down. In amongst the heavily-armoured hoplites, Heraclitus felt the press of cold bronze all around him, and felt almost naked in comparison, but it gave him more agility to slip past, and he finally reached Arimnestos.

"It's time," he shouted. "You have to pull back now."

Arimnestos gave a quick glance up, and shouted "Not yet; just a few more minutes. We can hold."

"No!" Heraclitus shouted back. "Now! You're almost cut off; they have broken through here already. Fall back."

For the first time Arimnestos seemed to notice the Greek lines swarming to his left, and disappointment filled his face. "Thrust and fall back," he called at the same time as Heraclitus shouted for the archers and slingers to cover their retreat.

The shout was in vain, however, as it was drowned out by a

loud crack like thunder and the panicked screams of men, as the front legs of the huge horse in the middle of the square finally snapped under pressure from the fire. The legs exploded outwards in a shower of burning wood as the massive weight of the burning head and chest of the horse pressed down on them.

As the horse fell over, the burning head dropped forward towards them, and Heraclitus realised it was coming straight towards them as men ran backwards off the wall. He grabbed the back of Arimnestos' armour and, with arms rippled with muscle from hours using a bow, flung his friend off the wall as he turned to jump to safety himself.

A hand gripped his leg as he turned to jump. He looked down to see the grim bloody face of the Greek whose gut he had opened only moments before. He didn't have time to attempt to struggle out of the man's strong grip before the head of the horse came crashing down on top of him in a shower of flames, and the weight of tons of wood.

***

From up above, he watched the entire scene play out. The Greeks had pushed their way inside in their tens of thousands, using sheer numbers to overwhelm any possible defence of Troy. By now about forty thousand had squeezed through the gates, and a glance over the wall saw at least the same number again pressing those forward to try to make their own way inside.

From up above, the crush of men looked chaotic, even as they formed into lines and pushed toward the internal wall. Stamping their own dead and dying into the ground, they closed ranks again on the far side of the burning horse, and charged up the wall, to be blocked by a stubborn losing Trojan army, creating a secondary wall of dead above the one made by the Trojans.

From up above, Achenia watched the horse first lean, then fall, burning over the compressed ranks of Greeks, who were so intent on coming to grips with the Trojans that they didn't realise the risk posed by the horse until it was too late.

From up above, he watched as the wooded roof beams, which they had coated in pitch and placed so carefully along the Greek side of the wall, ignited from the burning head of the horse where it had landed on the wall and slowly spread outwards. Soon it would encompass the whole wall, creating a wall of fire. The small number of Greeks who had made it through before the horse collapsed would soon find themselves on the wrong side of that fire, wholly outnumbered and quickly dispatched by the Trojans.

How he hated it up here; but every man in a battle has his orders, and this was his part to play. Shielded from view by the parapets, small fires burned all along the wall with pots hanging above them. The fires had now been burning for nearly an hour, every large pot in the city having been collected and placed above the flames. The largest pots had been situated directly above the gates themselves, where the huge army barracks pot hung alongside others from the palace kitchens.

Now that the rubble wall was itself on fire, between the flames and the billowing smoke the Greeks were being forced back; those too slow to realise what was happening to the wall had their chitons set alight or were burned alive, cooked inside their own armour, as it were.

With all Priam's tricks, the Greeks were falling in their thousands. To those waiting outside, however, unaware of what was occurring, it would sound like victory; the raping and pillaging of Troy would seem to have begun, making them ever more eager to gain entry, to claim their share of the spoils, for which they had waited ten long years on a beach far from home.

So the press continued, and every Greek who fell was replaced, with nowhere to go, and trapped by their own men, pushing them ever onwards. The burning wall wouldn't last long, maybe an hour, and the heat would stay in the rocks a little longer, but it was a reprieve. Now came Achenia's command. Chaos already reigned below, with men packed tighter than fish in a barrel.

It was a dirty trick even by their standards, and one which he doubted anyone living had seen before, but he had served with Priam years before when they had fought for the Hittites, a favour which had later been repaid when building Troy.

Shields lay along the wall to hide the light of the fires a little; these were quickly removed but, amid the burning horse and wall and with the sun gradually rising, the little extra light went unnoticed.

The stairs up to the walls had been completely blocked off at this point, so they didn't need to worry about the Greeks' overwhelming them, but they were still within an easy arrow or spear's reach, so they moved with quiet stealth to the line of huge pots. Each man carried a large wooden paddle for leverage, and they now inserted them into the great rings on the side of the pots. The other side of the paddle was set on blocks they had placed on the inner parapets earlier that morning for this purpose, and two men moved into position at either side of each pot.

Achenia gave the signal and they began lifting the pots. It was slow at first as they took the weight of the big pots but then for most it grew easier as the pots slid to the wall. It had been decided to use the pots as a secondary weapon; they would get only one chance at this.

Pushing the poles up further, they began emptying the contents over the wall. They didn't have much left in Troy but Heraclitus had been right, what they had plenty of was sand. Pots of it had been slowly heated for the last hour, and now it drifted down with painful slowness. Imagine walking barefoot on a beach on a hot summer day, burning sand beneath your feet; now imagine it so hot that the bottoms of the pots sent clear crystal dripping in shards and solidifying as it fell.

The drops from the first pots passed the sand in mid-air, the pot following soon after. The first tinkling of glass, shattering against bronze armour preceded the almighty crash of glowing hot pots, crashing down among armoured soldiers, crushing helmeted heads and rolling away to burn anyone unlucky enough to be next to it.

Greeks screamed as the pots stuck to their skin and ripped the flesh from unprotected legs in its path, but this was only a prelude to what came next. The sand settled among them and, due to its weight, drifted out much further from the wall, the fine burning grains working its way into gaps in their armour and becoming trapped beneath to burn chitons and skin, and the armour trapping it in place. Exposed flesh, legs and arms all burned and the sand went in through the visors of their helmets, causing screams to rise to the heavens.

He struggled to drag his eyes from the scene being enacted before him, mesmerised, until a spear hitting the parapet beside him forced him to duck back. It was then he noticed the three largest pots in the centre and the six men still struggling to bring them up onto the wall. One was on the wall, but still hadn't gone over.

He shouted to the rest of the men to get over and help, which they did, but the constant crack of spears hitting the walls around them and the hiss of arrows passing overhead kept them ducking back. The first pot went over, and the spears slowed momentarily as the screaming intensified, but they soon started up again, and the men standing unprotected at the walls, trying to get the pots over, were being brought down as fast as they were replaced.

The second pot went over, and only three men remained standing with Achenia; as he turned and ran to the last pot, a spear tore a line of fire along his leg. He kept going even as an arrow glanced off his helmet, but as he slowed to grab the pole on the last and biggest of the pots a second spear caught him, ripping through his cuirass and stopping in his ribs.

Breathing became difficult as he pulled out the head of the spear but it had bent into many sharp bronze edges and he could hear the air hissing from his lung. Still, he seized the pole to push. Another spear tore a line across his neck as it passed, and Achenia knew it had finished him.

He could feel his strength dripping away with his blood. "Save me a place, my son; today I come to join you," he whispered and grabbed the pole. Pushing with the last of his strength Achenia sent the pot tumbling, spraying red-hot sand over all below and following it into the air, as his legs gave way beneath him.

From up above, he watched the struggling Greeks frantically trying to get out of the way of the falling pot and burning sand, in vain, as there was nowhere to move to, let alone run.

From up above, Achenia watched a sea of Greeks rise up towards him to break his fall, but darkness closed his eyes, and he never felt their warm embrace.

***

Outside the walls, Agamemnon sat awaiting news, waiting for his victorious entrance. His temper rose as more and more of his men broke through the city gates, and more and more smoke billowed over the city walls. Hadn't he made it clear he wanted the city taken intact?

It seemed from the screams that were audible even here, two

hundred yards from the gates, that some of his men, at least, had decided that the raping and pillaging of his newly-taken city could start without him. He would have to make examples of a few men to enforce discipline and ensure that his orders were followed more closely in future. That fool, Ajax Locrian, had been first through the gates; he must be involved. By now they should have sent back word for him to follow. What was going on in there?

***

Xenos had been to the right of Arimnestos, holding the line. His side had held with little trouble, but he had chanced a quick glance to his left a few minutes ago, and had seen the line bulge and weaken, a few men to the left of Arimnestos. It was a worry, but he had to trust those on that side to do their job, and close up the gap. He had his hands full right here, and could do nothing for them at the moment. The die had been cast, and they had to hold on until the horse came down.

Heraclitus' arrival wasn't such a surprise, given what he had seen; the shield-bearer opposite, protecting Arimnestos' other side, must be struggling if the lightly-armoured archer had found it necessary to come to his friend's aid. It took Xenos by surprise, however, when Heraclitus grabbed Arimnestos by the backplate of his armour and flung him backwards.

He saw the huge burning head falling towards them, turned in tandem with Heraclitus, and jumped with all the strength he had in his legs. He knew he had more powerful legs than Heraclitus, but because of the archer's light leather armour, he had expected them to land almost simultaneously on the ground; there was no sign of him, however.

His head flicked around just in time to see the big archer still on the wall as the head crushed him under its weight. Xenos threw an arm over his eyes as the head exploded outwards in a hot blast of fire, and showers of burning splinters rained all around.

Though he couldn't understand why Heraclitus had not jumped alongside him, he knew that he had died an honourable death; he had gone up there to save his friend, and had done just that. As shield-bearer to Arimnestos, it had been his and Agbo's duty to protect Arimnestos during the battle, and Agbo was presumably dead by now. Xenos saluted the bravery of Heraclitus, and thought he could not have had a better pyre.

As the fire spread along the wall, any Greeks who had managed to break through the line were now trapped on this side of the fire, surrounded by Trojans. The Greeks who had almost killed Arimnestos on the wall were one such group; they fought like lions, trying to find a way out of the trap.

Xenos caught sight of Arimnestos lying on the ground, and ran over to him. There was a large dent in his helmet, and blood running down his face. Though Xenos could not manage to remove the helmet, he could feel the life in Arimnestos through the rise and fall of his chest. His job today remained the same: keep Arimnestos alive at all costs. Looping an arm around his chest, he began dragging him away from the sounds of battle.

Every hoplite outside the heat of battle knows that to turn from battle means death, and even worse, the dishonour of cowardice. Although Xenos was following orders that day, doing his sworn duty, the spear in his back would stain his family's honour as long as Trojans stood to testify, as he dragged his lord's body towards safety. The stain lasted another five hours.

Any who looked for survivors among the dead and dying could have been forgiven for missing Arimnestos, as he lay there covered in blood, and Xenos, and the Greek who bore the spear that killed him. But he would waken, too weak to free himself from the bodies on top of him. He would waken just in time to die alone, forgotten, from the weight of men and armour that had crushed him.

***

Priam watched from one of the narrow alleys that led to the palace from the inner wall where the battle had raged, a fierce grin twisting his features as the horse finally fell to the wall. The irony of using their own trick against the Greeks was not lost on him. Moments later, agonised screams could be heard from closer to the main gate. The smoke billowing from the horse and the burning wall obscured his view too much to see what was happening, but he knew that Achenia had just succeeded in dropping the sand; he remembered when he had seen the same trick used with the Hittites, and his imagination provided the rest.

With the smile splitting his face he turned, looking around at those who accompanied him. He was surrounded by his armed bodyguard. It was one of those situations where he wanted desperately to nudge Achenia, or one of the generals who had lived through that previous life with him, and point at the screaming Greeks just to say, "Look, I told you it would work!" but the realisation slowly dawned on him that Achenia had been the last.

It was the first time he had truly realised what these last ten years had cost him. He was still king of Troy, for the next few hours at least, but over the past ten years everyone he had known well, everyone he had fought with and been close to, had died or been killed in one or another of the skirmishes of this war.

There had been a time when he could have looked around in any company of Trojan soldiers and recognised almost every face, but he looked around now, and found he knew none. They were all fiercely loyal, and would die for him when asked to do so, and he recognised them from the palace, but all those he had truly known as only a soldier can know another were dead.

Suddenly he felt very weary, and the old adage rang true to his ears: *you never feel so alone as when in a crowded room.* Today the last of his family had sailed away. Today the last of his old friends had died; although he did not know this yet, he could already feel it. Today he was king to a city, and a people where he no longer felt at home, or as if he belonged.

But he gritted his teeth, as the smile fell from his face, to be replaced by a snarl. Today he would make Greece pay for what it had cost him. Today he would bleed them as they had been bleeding him for ten years. Today he would die.

Chapter Twenty-Two

From the flat roof of a house on one of the three roads between the main gate and the palace, Pedasus was able to watch the fires settle before they died out completely. It wouldn't be long now until it was navigable again, and the final battle for Troy would take place.

From where he stood, he could see the milling ranks of Greeks through the clearing smoke. The slingers with whom he had packed the rooftop's outer edge, standing amid the wreckage of the vegetable gardens, were taking occasional pot-shots at any Greek silly enough to drop his shield within their range. It was an annoyance tactic, forcing them to keep their shields up, which would sap their energy while they were waiting, never allowing them to let down their guard for a moment.

If he looked almost directly down from where he stood on the corner of the street, however, he could see that his own men were currently taking their leisure, although they remained in position and ready to form the phalanx at a second's notice. They were eating, sitting down, and some of the veterans were even managing to snore against a wall, the way career soldiers can when a battle is only minutes away. Pedasus let them be; whatever rest and food they could get now was more than the enemy were being offered, and that advantage would pay off very shortly.

The wall had been burning for nearly two hours now, and the Greeks had stopped pushing men inside just to injure themselves;

they seemed eventually to have got the message that they couldn't force any more through the gates against their own retreating men. There was now a reverse line of their injured being carried back to the ships. Those waiting were being given no respite from holding their shields up defensively.

While he was watching, a gap opened up in the enemy ranks so quickly that even the slingers had little chance to react, and a huge wooden battering ram hit the burning wall, sending burning blocks of stone and timber flying and showers of sparks momentarily clouding the air. Before they had cleared, the ram hit the wall again. It quickly became obvious that the Greeks were not prepared to wait for the wall to burn itself out, and a glance showed him that this was happening in another four or five points along the wall.

The air came alive with the terrifying whirl of slingers winding and releasing their slings as fast as their hands would allow, but either they were missing, or more men had poured in to replace the fallen. Through the showers of sparks he couldn't be sure, and he thought the slingers were also shooting blind, but anything would help at this point.

He shouted down for his men to form up, and could hear the other commanders at other laneways doing likewise, as they prepared to battle with the Greek war machine. Luckily, it was unnecessary, as his men were already jumping off the ground into formation to the sound of the ram; then the head finally punched through the wall and men began to pour through towards them.

The three hours that followed were among the hardest of Pedasus' life, as he passed from rooftop to rooftop with the slingers who hurled death down upon the Greeks from above, occasionally avoiding or falling to arrows that came in return. These proved infrequent, since, when an archer fired, thirty slingers concentrated all their fire on that archer; the Greeks seemed afraid to lose many, but still some slingers fell; and three times a man fell off the planks set between the buildings.

What was hardest wasn't running across the beams, it was watching men, his men, die in the streets, while he and the other commanders directed events from above. He had never been so proud of his fellow countrymen. In three hours of watching death dealt on both sides, not a single Trojan had broken ranks. There was nowhere to run, but sometimes men still tried when faced with a spear. Today, every man held his ground, knowing what was at stake. They all had some family on their way to the boats.

Each commander stood on the roof where the two forces met, and the Trojans were being pushed back slowly by the seemingly unstoppable numbers of the Greek army. This gave them their only chance to keep a line split by buildings in some sort of order, so that if any phalanx was pushed back faster, the enemy couldn't flank the others through the adjoining side streets.

Every step they took, however, was through an area littered with corpses. Any plant that grew there in future would grow red, watered with the blood of the thousands dying in the streets right now; and always the Greeks moved on, like a rock rolling down a hill, too big to stop, rolling over a carpet of their own dead mixed with sons of Troy. By that night, the bodies would be so compressed together that they could never be separated.

It wasn't something that worried Pedasus; by that night he was likely to be among them. Diomedes was among those on the boats, and that was all that mattered. By nightfall Pedasus could rejoin his wife and child in the halls of the fallen.

The gap between the last rooftop and the palace walls was only about twenty yards, but this would be the most frightening twenty yards of the survivors' lives. Here the three main streets converged, and it would be the only time since engaging that the Greeks could bring their superior numbers to bear, encircling them on all three sides.

All the archers had been called back to the palace, to cover the retreating Trojan army from the walls and windows of the palace. Calling them walls, however, was like describing the few hundred remaining Trojans as an army. No one had ever expected any army to make it this far, so the walls were only for show, and for keeping revellers out during festivals. The whole building was decorative rather than defensible.

The doors were solid oak, but only an inch thick; a solid kick would almost be enough to break one in, and the windows were set only eight feet off the ground.

In a show of bravery or fatalism - Pedasus couldn't decide which, and didn't have time to ponder the issue - the slingers had volunteered to stay on the house roofs, as what was left of the hoplites broke and ran for the palace, to help cover their retreat. None of them expected to last very long, surrounded by Greeks, but perhaps the same applied to those inside the palace.

Many took spears in the back as they turned and ran, but the majority made the twenty yards to safety, the street turned into a killing ground by the archers inside the palace and the slingers on the roofs. As Pedasus slammed shut the doors of the palace, his last sight was of slingers dropping from spears hurled up from the ground.

Among the dwindling numbers inside the hall all was exhaustion and dejection; all hope was gone. Even after a whole day spent killing everything they could reach with their spears, the roads were still choked with Greeks baying for their blood. They were like hounds who had caught the scent; they wouldn't stop now till their prey was dead.

Skins of water and what little wine they had left were being passed around among the soldiers. Pedasus thought of the phrase 'out of sight, out of mind'. The soldiers seemed to relax when the doors had closed on the thousands of baying Greeks, as if they were now safe. He could understand it to a degree; they were clutching at straws.

Bulos and Brasides, the two Spartans he had promoted since the death of Arimnestos, had a better grip on themselves and began yelling orders and shoving men towards the stairs. That would be the next bottleneck to try to hold. He expected nothing less from them; the Spartans were ever professional.

As if in answer to his thoughts the door shuddered in its frame and those archers already upstairs were rushing down, apparently being driven inside by opposition archers now that they could gain access to the rooftops without being attacked by the slingers. They quickly moved into position along the upper gallery to cover the doorway, and bows were immediately stretched. They all carried swords now as well, their shields and extra spears laid along the balcony, as they relied on their last few arrows to cover the door. After that, they would all fall into the back of the phalanx to offer support.

The door gave on the third thump, as the Trojans had just got into position. There was a split-second delay before Greek helmets began pouring through the door, their shouts answered by the twang of twenty strings as the archers released their arrows. The first Greeks through the door died instantly, though to look at them that wasn't obvious. Their legs stopped moving and their chests were feathered with arrows, but the sheer momentum of other soldiers, charging through the doors carried them to the foot of the stairs before it slowed enough for the bodies to slide to the ground.

Even with the archers slamming arrows into their flanks, the

Greeks didn't even slow as they pushed into the Trojans who were slowly, inextricably pushed up the stairs. Step by step they were pushed back, and step by step they fell among Greeks they'd brought down.

Eight floors later, with Priam behind him and only Brasides and two Trojan hoplites blocking the path, Pedasus backed through the door onto the roof of Troy's legendary palace. The door allowed only two through at a time, and Pedasus pulled Brasides through with him, leaving the two Trojans slowly backing towards it.

Turning quickly, Pedasus just had time to register that the sun was setting, and twilight was falling on Troy. Priam was heaving a huge barrel from the top of the wall. The five-gallon barrel fell, and he moved to the opposite corner to push another over.

"Hand me that torch," he shouted, and Pedasus immediately obeyed. Priam took the torch and tossed it over the wall, and it disappeared below where the barrel had crashed down. Turning to Pedasus with a huge smile on his face, Priam shouted, "I told you no Trojan would be taken by the Greeks!" just as the air heated up with a huge whoosh, and light split the semi-darkness.

As the last two Trojans fell in the doorway, Priam picked up his huge war hammer and shouted "Now fight like a Trojan!" and charged the Greeks coming through the doorway, as flames built from the barrels of naphtha around the palace.

I wish I could tell you of the glories, the heroism, the *deus ex machina* or last-minute saviour turning back the tide of the Greek onslaught; but this is a Trojan story, and for the Trojans, there is no happy ending.

But no Greek who had gained entrance to the palace left alive.

Epilogue

Sails were down to avoid being seen, as oars dipped and rose, and, silently, five ships sailed out of the Hellespont. Aeneas had wanted to swing further north, to avoid any chance of being seen before they were safe, but Romulus had insisted on a more southerly course so that he could see his city one last time. Remus had reluctantly agreed.

So it was that they were standing at the helm of the *Sea Wolf*, looking over the water from nearly two miles away. Rowing slowed, and eventually stopped, as more and more people shipped oars to stand at the railing and look at the swarm of Greeks still moving into their city. Yet more seemed to be milling on the shore near their boats, but the sun setting in the west would blind them to the Trojan ships drifting slowly across the water.

The gates were open, and behind the city, darkness was setting on the longest day any of them had ever spent. In the twilight over the city, flames could be seen leaping up along the palace. It began to burn, as if it were made of old dry timber, and sparks leaped from it into the dim sky, like beacons in the night.

Remus put a hand on Romulus' shoulder in sympathy, knowing what the fire meant, and Romulus' head slumped down as he stared at the wooden boards beneath his feet.

"No," snapped Remus. "He did that for you, for us, so that we might escape and carry Troy with us. The city has fallen, but we have survived to fight the Greeks another day, and make Agamemnon pay for this. That was his gift to you."

Romulus slowly lifted his head with tears in his eyes. As he watched the flames leap from the tower and sparks fly into the air, tiny from this distance but still visible, one, larger than the rest, seemed to float in the air when a shower went up, and all eyes were drawn to it. Glowing in the night sky, burning red, it hovered above the palace.

"That's Father," Romulus said quietly. "He's watching over us still. We will make him proud." Remus' hand tightened momentarily on his shoulder.

***

Sinon was being held in the infirmary, to heal from his wounds. Although it was the hospital, it felt more like a prison cell, with the tiny windows high up on the walls and the locked door. Priam had said that he would be freed if his claims were confirmed, but it seemed that they had forgotten about him with the attack.

The sounds of battle were like music to his ears, knowing that his fellow Greeks were coming to lay waste to this place and that he would be honoured for the part he had played in deceiving the Trojans, for the risk he had taken.

As the battle got nearer, he tried to see out through the windows, but they were just too high up to reach. But it was not long before he could hear it inside the building, and, suddenly, the door to the room he was being held in crashed open, with his countrymen on the other side.

He tried to make his way into the hall, but found the press of Greek bodies just too dense to pass through; so he settled in his seat, waiting for the battle to be over, so that he could celebrate with everyone else.

The battle soon ended, but the first Sinon knew of it was the thick smoke coming in through the little window, followed by a trickle of burning liquid which ran down the inside of the wall into the basement room. Panic soon enveloped him, but the press in the hall was even tighter, as everyone attempted to escape the burning palace at once.

The thick smoke filled the room, choking everyone the fire wasn't burning, and soon Sinon's eyes closed, as he lay on the floor, gasping his last few breaths…

***

As morning broke over the remains of what had once been the greatest city on earth, Agamemnon counted the cost. Of the two hundred thousand men he had brought to these shores ten years ago, only about twenty thousand remained.

He fumed and shouted most of the night. He would probably have lost control over what was left of the army had not half of them been a combination of his own Mycenaeans and his late brother's Spartans, whom he had been holding back for his honour guard at the end of the battle. There were maybe twenty to twenty-five thousand injured, many with severe burns from the sand; most would never fight again if they survived.

And for what? Everything was gone. There might have been something left in the palace, but it had burned all night, and anything valuable would have melted in the heat by the time the tower had eventually collapsed at dawn.

Still, almost every commander had died; if nothing else, it had tied the joint armies of Greece, with only himself and Odysseus left. Odysseus sat quietly in the corner now, as was his way, and let Agamemnon rage around the tent. A soldier entered.

"Sir," he said, coming to attention. "The poet Homer is outside, and wishes to see you."

"Ye gods!" shouted Agamemnon. "Not now! Tell him to go

away."

Odysseus slowly lifted his head. "That might be a mistake. Homer is going to tell the story of this war, Agamemnon, and you can control how it is seen and how you are remembered. Turn this loss into a victory. We are the only people who know what happened."

Agamemnon thought about this and eventually saw the sense in it. A smile grew on his face. "Yes, of course! Send him in."

And so, the legend grew that all his commanders had already left for home, save Achilles himself: Achilles, who had died of blood loss from an arrow through his heel. No glory there! He would be forgotten in a week.

Made in the USA
Columbia, SC
27 October 2020